Other books by Connie Suttle:

Blood Destiny Series

Blood Wager
Blood Passage
Blood Sense
Blood Domination
Blood Royal
Blood Queen
Blood Rebellion
Blood War
Blood Redemption
Blood Reunion

Legend of the Ir'Indicti Series

Bumble
Shadowed
Target
Vendetta
Destroyer

High Demon Series

Demon Lost
Demon Revealed
Demon's King
Demon's Quest

Demon's Revenge
Demon's Dream

The God Wars Series
Blood Double
Blood Trouble
Blood Revolution
Blood Love
Blood Finale

The Saa Thalarr Series
Hope and Vengeance
Wyvern and Company*

First Ordinance Series

Finder
Keeper*

The R-D series

Cloud Dust

*Forthcoming

CHAPTER 1

My voice didn't come until I was nine. With everything I'd heard and witnessed by that time, I knew better than to speak. Orphaned at the age of two and foisted onto the kitchen and housekeeping staff of the palace in Lironis, I mostly kept to myself as I cleaned ashes and soot out of fireplaces every morning. Afterward, I was expected to spend the rest of my day in the kitchen, scrubbing and cleaning.

Early on, they'd called me girl. I have few memories before the age of four, when I was put to work cleaning dishes. I had to stand on a roughly fashioned stool at that age to reach the counter and the wooden tub set upon it, filled with hot, soapy water. Wolter and Irdith hadn't been kind, either, hitting me with long, wooden spoons or ladles if I didn't clean something thoroughly. I learned to do my job quickly and well.

Later, I was set to cleaning hearths, in addition to my other duties. Nine was the age for other things, too—things certainly not pleasant to remember. I began growing what the palace physician called bone spurs on my shoulder blades, and he ordered them cut away using the same nipping tool the smiths used to trim horses' hooves. The procedure is quite painful, leaving my back sore for weeks.

My hair, shaggy as always, was also cut away at the same time, with shears used to cut a horse's mane or tail. My hair is not unmanageably thick, but I did not own a comb at the time. My locks were chopped away each time until I had only three fingers' width of hair left.

What hair remained resembled a wheat field after a storm, with slender stems going in every direction. The unevenness of it never goes unnoticed by the servant boys and the kitchen staff, all of whom tease and ridicule. Each year since I turned nine, the same ritual is performed. My bone spurs (which continue to grow) are cut away every spring, as is my hair.

I can also read and write, although I've never been taught. I've never been given a proper room in the servants' quarters, either. Happily, my ability to read and write coincided directly with my tiny sleeping space. Located inside a nearly forgotten storage room, it was cluttered floor to ceiling, almost, with bits and pieces of things unneeded and long forgotten.

Most of those bits and pieces were books, many of which had empty spaces where pages had been callously ripped away, leaving ragged, gaping holes in my knowledge of history and geography. What was certain, though, was that troubled times had come to Fyris, and few recognized or understood them.

The King, too, had withdrawn any support for the education of Fyris' children, announcing in a decree during my early childhood that Fyrisians could educate their children at home. Grumbling had begun in the kitchen; after all, who would have time to sit with their children and teach them letters after a long day at work?

It didn't matter, eventually. Babies and children began dying a handful of turns later. Physicians were at a loss to explain the deaths—there was no known disease they could readily identify as the underlying cause—the children were either stillborn or sickened and died soon after.

In the midst of Fyris' uncertainty, my miraculous ability to read had not been reported and went unnoticed by those around me, who thought me a mute imbecile much of the time. That ability was also not the one responsible for giving me my name.

My name eventually came from another talent, and once it had been reported, I'd have given anything to take the knowledge of it back.

When I was six, a minor noble's maid swept into the palace kitchen, frantic and wiping tears away. Her lady had lost a brooch, she'd wept. If she failed to find it, the lady would have her right hand cut away for stealing.

She hadn't stolen the jewelry; I could see that plainly enough. The usual, rough stool was beneath my bare soles while my arms were completely submerged in dishwater as I cleaned pots after breakfast that morning. The maidservant continued to weep and pour out her grief to any who would listen. Every servant inside the kitchen stopped what they were doing to watch the drama unfolding before them.

Carefully drying my hands and arms, I hopped down from my stool and went to the distraught maid, tugging on her sleeve. Removing the hands that covered her eyes as she wept, she stared at me. I'd never been so forward with anyone, but the thought of a hand being chopped off revolted my innocent sensibilities. Angrily, she shoved me away.

Unwilling to be deterred from saving a hand, I went back, tugged on her sleeve again and motioned for her to follow me. At first, she said ugly things to me and pointed me back to my place at the dish tub. Refusing to back away from my offer, I beckoned to her again. Eventually she tossed her hands in the air, spouted more insults in my direction (which made the kitchen staff chuckle), and followed me.

Once we'd reached the lady's suite, I pulled the maid, under the watchful eye of her lady and her lady's husband, toward the edge of the bed where we knelt down. Hidden behind the thick, polished wood post at the head of that massive bed lay the missing brooch. It had fallen off the bedside table and rolled behind the leg, where nobody thought to look. The girl squealed with delight and handed it to the lady, who thanked her absently while staring at me. Her husband, taller and standing behind her, stared as well.

I was called Finder after that, and I was visited often by members of the staff and anyone else who couldn't find something, until tragedy struck and Wolter intervened.

Erdin was ten turns old when he was brought to Wolter, who put him to work in the kitchen. A thin child with a clever face, Erdin worked in the kitchen for barely six moon-turns and often made off with hastily stolen bits of food when nobody thought to watch him.

He had no care that I witnessed these thefts. I was mute—whom could I tell? I was twelve at the time, when Erdin's thievery reached its peak and Lord Yevil's coin purse disappeared. I hadn't witnessed this theft—Erdin had been sent to the King's table to serve wine while I cleaned the dishes.

"I had it at the table!" Yevil thundered at a cowering staff. You must understand; Yevil is the King's right hand. If Yevil speaks, it is with King Tamblin's words and authority. In fact, King Tamblin, whom I hadn't seen until that moment, appeared at Yevil's side and glared at the staff as well.

Irdith, then a bit more spry and mobile than she is at present, poked her knobby cane in my back and shoved me forward. Prior to that moment, I'd been hiding behind Wolter's long legs.

"The girl can tell you," Irdith cackled annoyingly. Amazingly, she still has most of her teeth and she gave me a grinning leer as I turned a hurt-filled stare in her direction. Until that moment, the King and his right hand didn't know about me. I preferred to keep it that way.

"Did you steal my pouch?" I was snatched up in Yevil's grip so quickly I almost lost the filthy apron tied loosely about my waist.

"No! But she can find it." Irdith's irritating laugh made me wish her dead. Dread had overcome me the moment Yevil appeared, shouting at all of us about his missing purse. Irdith, with her interference, was making sure that terrible things would come as a result.

I smelled the wine on Yevil's breath and stared into eyes a hazy green, clouded with drink as they were. Dark hair fell over Yevil's forehead, lending an evil look to his angry visage while a thick vein throbbed at his throat.

"Then find it," snapped the King. I was tossed forcefully onto the flagstone floor, where I rolled twice before coming to a stop. My body was (and still is) slight, and the top of my head even now only reaches halfway between Wolter's elbow and shoulder.

Scrambling to my feet, I hurried away, intending to locate the missing purse as quickly as possible before Yevil chose to break bones. Yes, he is the King's right hand, as well as his voice and arm. That arm falls heavy on the unwary, at times. Would I do things differently now, at age seventeen? I do not know. I am still more afraid of the King and his inner circle than of anyone else, and have little to explain that feeling.

The purse was found quickly—among Erdin's belongings. I'd never been inside his quarters, which he shared with two other kitchen boys. He was ten and he'd been afforded proper quarters, whereas I slept in a storage room. Not that I minded; I'd learned that my storage room offered privacy and a chance to read secretly beyond anyone's notice.

Once I'd pointed to Erdin's straw mattress, where he'd hidden Yevil's purse, I knew death was coming. I just didn't realize how violent it would be. Yevil, who'd followed me closely, snatched his purse from beneath the mattress, counted the coins inside carefully and finding one missing, poured out his wrath upon an unfortunate ten-year-old boy who'd thought to steal from a noble.

While we watched, Yevil, who wielded a long sword drawn from a scabbard at his side, severed Erdin's right arm. Blood gushed from the wound as Erdin screamed, the thick, red fluid staining his bedding and the stone floor. Erdin's left arm was then removed by a grinning Yevil and after that, his head.

That execution is still too horrible to consider, and the youngest of us were forced to clean up the blood as the body and its severed parts were removed by stable workers. I have no idea what was done with Erdin's remains.

Irdith sniffed, her nose high as she stalked from Erdin's shared quarters, her bent body stiff and unrelenting. Wolter glared at her retreating back while the King stared at me and Yevil cleaned his blade on Erdin's bloodstained shirt. Never had I wanted to use my voice as badly as I did then. If I had opened my mouth, many things would have poured out of it, including condemnation for Yevil and the King of Fyris.

Wisely, I kept my lips pressed tightly shut and went about gathering rags to clean up blood while others ran to get men from the stable. In my anger, as I wiped up spilled blood and wrung out bloody cloths in buckets of water, I used my talent to search for Irdith's death. I saw it, right down to the day and the hour. Smiling grimly, I finished my task.

After Erdin's death, Wolter refused to allow anyone inside his kitchen who wanted my help to find things. He was forced to allow the nobles access, but servants were sent away while Irdith scowled. Irdith irritated Wolter as much as she did me, I think, but he never said it aloud. He knew the same as I did, I believe—that Irdith was King Tamblin's spy inside the kitchens. Wolter was as mute as I regarding his opinions around her.

The palace kitchen was my life, up to the present. Had I any idea how quickly things might change around me? Sadly, the answer was no.

"Finder, Lord Hirill is here, wondering where his horse's bridle is," Wolter tapped a wooden spoon against his thigh in guarded irritation while the aforementioned Lord stood behind the tall cook.

I looked up from scrubbing the floor beside Wolter's main fireplace—one of the kitchen boys had spilled half a kettle of soup while he shouted at one of his three fellows. Wolter had beaten the boy's shoulders with a heavy ladle for the transgression, sending the miscreant away with yelps of pain. The offending boy didn't have to clean up the mess; Wolter ordered me to do it.

I rose and dumped my cleaning rag into the bucket of water I'd drawn, dipping my head respectfully at Lord Hirill. It didn't matter what they looked like; I always knew immediately which ones were in the King's inner circle. Those were his trusted advisors—cruel and secretive in all things. Lord Hirill was a member in good standing, his riding crop tapping impatiently against a high, polished black boot as he waited.

He was younger than Yevil; I knew that right away, so he was in what I termed the second tier of inner circle members. Some of King Tamblin's first members had died off, triggering a search for replacements. He'd found them easily enough. Times were hard and becoming harder across Fyris, and a position with the King guaranteed money, fine food, wine and comfortable living quarters.

Nodding again to Lord Hirill, I walked out of the kitchen, my back as straight as I could keep it. Did it embarrass me that I was dressed in stained and filthy rags? No. What can possibly be gained by that worthless emotion?

I could never hope to rise above my present station unless I wanted to offer myself to one of the nobles I despised. Therefore, I kept my face dirty during the day and never asked for clothing other than what was handed down from the kitchen boys.

At night I cleaned myself; it troubles me if my skin is dirty for very long, and my patched and tattered blanket and the cover over my bed are washed diligently each week. None saw me before I began cleaning fireplaces early, so they never saw my face as it was. The tattered and stained clothing I wore was offensive and put most people off, so I continued to wear it.

Following Hirill toward the stables, I moved quietly behind him, far enough that his riding crop wouldn't reach me if he chose to turn and wield it. He and I passed over the threshold of the stable, where Garth, the new stablemaster, waited for us.

The stable around me was built of heavy, wooden beams and smelled of dung, urine and horse. Hay and straw dust floated in the midafternoon sunlight, winking brightly once a shaft of light caught the motes as they danced and whirled inside it.

"There it is." The stablemaster heaved a weighted and much-relieved sigh as I pulled the missing bridle from a pile of straw inside an empty stall and offered it to Lord Hirill.

I could have told him that a groom had knocked the bridle off a nearby peg the night before while dallying with one of the King's chambermaids, but as I'd never spoken, it wasn't wise to offer words now.

"Mystery solved," Hirill offered the stablemaster the bridle and a brief smile. "Spoken with Amlis?"

"My Lord," the stablemaster jerked his head in my direction. I was still standing in the middle of his stall, fresh straw nearly to my knees as I watched sunbeams toy with dust motes. Garth had not been stablemaster long—I knew that from gossip. He'd never chopped off my hair or witnessed the removal of bone spurs as his predecessor had.

"She can't speak. Never has, according to my sources," Hirill's smile widened. "Regardless, we'll speak later, shall we?"

Hirill had named the King's second son, Amlis. I'd never seen the younger Prince; after all, he'd only returned recently from spending several turns with his mother's family in Vhrist. Rumor had it that the King had commanded Amlis to be at his side for the twenty-first anniversary of his naming day. Timblor, the eldest son at twenty-five, was at his father's side much of the time if the gossip were true. Many called Timblor a true son to his sire, which, according to the rumors, made the King smile graciously.

"Doesn't speak, eh?" The stablemaster eyed me with interest. I lowered my head and attempted to make myself smaller.

"Not much there," Hirill agreed.

"I can see that." The stablemaster stroked his chin thoughtfully. "Well, there you go. I'll polish this bridle for you and it'll be ready when you need it."

"See that you do." Hirill nodded to the stablemaster and stalked away while I trotted behind, on my way back to the kitchens.

"Find it?" Wolter thought to ask after a while. The soup had still been waiting in the floor for me when I returned to the kitchen, so I'd set to cleaning the rest of it up with a stifled sigh. I nodded at Wolter's question while I dumped a heavy pot in the washtub to soak.

"She always does," Irdith cackled. Had she any idea how I loathed her? If she'd heard what I had that afternoon, she'd have hobbled straight to Tamblin as fast as her arthritic joints would allow. She, no doubt, would have reported that Hirill and the stablemaster had mentioned hearing from Amlis, his second and less-favored son, as if that were a common occurrence.

"Snow coming," Wolter's chief assistant scrubbed his boots on the step before walking onto clean flagstones in the kitchen. Jerking my head up, I stared at him. Using the gift I had, I searched for the information, determining that it was true.

We were in the second moon-turn of the year, in which the weather was often the coldest and most unpredictable. Snow was definitely coming, even this far south. We seldom saw the white powder (in my experience, anyway), and when we did, it was generally a light dusting that melted away with the dawn. This would prove worse.

"You think it has something to do with," Wolter cut his question off quickly, turning his head to see that Irdith was dozing in her chair by the hearth. She truly was asleep; I used my gift to determine it.

Many times, I wondered how Irdith imagined she was fooling anyone—she did little work, was past the age to do any, and still managed to dress better than anyone else inside the kitchen.

"Yes." Chen's reply was soft and accompanied by a nod from Wolter's short, thin assistant. Chen was softer around the edges than Wolter, and had darker hair with deep-brown eyes. He was quite watchful, his eyes never missing anything, including the mischief three kitchen boys often cooked up with their porridge.

Silently I cursed the ability I had that allowed me to know things about people but not about events. Yes, I could find things if I knew what I was looking for. Events, historical and otherwise, evaded me unless I knew *exactly* what to search for. And, since nobody would ever say anything past what Wolter had almost said, I didn't know what *it* was. The other thing I cursed was the inability to see anything in my visions concerning myself. It frustrated me constantly and ruined many a day.

"Finder, finish the dishes and you may go for the day," Wolter snapped, causing Irdith to jerk and wake with a snort. I nodded at the head cook, pleased that he'd made Irdith jump and went to finish washing pots and pans.

"She'd be perfect. You never have to tell her anything twice. I know most of the kitchen help see her as mute, deformed and stupid, but only the mute portion of that statement is true, my Prince."

Chen bowed to Amlis, who'd invited the assistant cook into his chambers late that evening, on the pretext of asking for watered wine to help him sleep. Chen had carried a bottle of his best red and a pitcher of water to the Prince's chambers to serve the King's youngest son himself.

"Garth in the stables suggested it to me this evening, when I went to check on my horse," Amlis sipped from his glass. He favored his mother, with dark-brown hair and blue eyes, whereas Timblor looked much like his father, with black hair and dark eyes.

"It was a wise suggestion, my Prince. She cannot carry tales if she cannot speak or write."

"Agreed. Garth will be rewarded if this is successful." Amlis offered Chen a seat near the fire. Winds were whipping around the castle walls and chilling the inhabitants more than usual during the winter. Snowflakes were flying, but nothing had settled on the ground for longer than a few seconds before sailing off again. Chen accepted the seat—and the warmth—gratefully.

"Her talent for finding things will surely be an asset," Chen acknowledged.

"Why is it that I have had no news of this before, or that she is still in the kitchen when she displays this sort of ability?" Amlis asked.

"Her inability to speak, coupled with Wolter's threats. He wouldn't allow it before, but then a Prince of the Realm has never asked for her services before. Wolter was terrified she'd be taken when Yevil tore a boy apart who stole his purse—she found the purse for Yevil, albeit unwillingly. If Irdith hadn't shoved her forward and announced that Finder could locate the purse, the girl would never have volunteered. It's as if she knew something awful was coming and attempted to hide behind Wolter." Chen accepted the offered glass of wine from Amlis, sipped from the crystal goblet and sighed in satisfaction.

"How old was she, then?"

"Twelve, I think, if Irdith's calculations are correct."

"Where did she come from? I've not heard of that kind of talent before."

"No one knows. She was dumped in the kitchen at the age of two—again according to Irdith—and the staff was informed that her parents were dead."

"Do you have approximate dates?" Amlis suddenly sounded interested.

"No. Neither Wolter nor I were in the kitchen at the time. The only one still here is Irdith, and we don't wish to stir that nest if we can help it."

"Agreed," Amlis drank more wine thoughtfully. "I'll come for her tomorrow, after breakfast."

"Be prepared; she cleans the hearths and her face and clothing will be filthy."

"I'll order a bath and my tailor. She'll be dressed as a page before the day's out."

"Wolter will be furious when I tell him, but I hope Finder will serve you well, my Prince. And remember, Wolter will have her back immediately if you do not find her work satisfactory."

"I understand."

"Finder?" Wolter's voice startled me and I jerked, dropping the small shovel I used to scrape ashes from a fireplace. I knelt upon a minor noble's hearth, my last of the day before carrying slops and tending to other duties. Turning quickly I gaped, not at the head cook but at the one standing behind him.

Without introductions, I knew I was staring (rudely) at Prince Amlis. "Finder," Wolter's voice was tinged with anger, "Prince Amlis has need of a page. As there are few young men available now, it is acceptable for a girl to take that position if requested. Amlis has asked that you serve him."

Blinking, I weighed information and my options. Jumping from the cooking pot into the fire came unbidden to my mind before I nodded. Truly, what else could I have done? The Prince commanded; I was compelled to serve.

"May I have a word with Finder before she leaves, my Prince?" Wolter asked politely. Inside, I knew he was seething, but he would never show that to a member of the royal family.

"Of course. I will be waiting outside," Amlis strode through the chamber door.

"Finder," Wolter knelt next to me and pulled me to his side. "You have no idea of the intrigue, and I have no time to teach you. Watch your back, always. Not everything is as it seems." I nodded mutely at his words as he rose, patting my shoulder awkwardly. "Don't get yourself killed, girl," Wolter growled and let me go.

"Follow me." Amlis' first command was curt. I trotted obediently behind the Prince as he made his way through a warren of hallways that gradually became wider and more richly decorated, until we arrived in the Royal Wing, a place I never thought to set foot.

CHAPTER 2

Hot water and a bathing tub were unknown luxuries to me before that day. Both waited, with a terse "Clean yourself up," from Amlis' cousin Rodrik. I knew from gossip that Rodrik, several turns older than Amlis and a trained master of the sword, had traveled from Vhrist with twelve men-at-arms to keep the Prince safe on the road.

Vhrist lay on the northern edge of Fyris, and I wanted more than anything to ask Amlis what the mountains there looked like. Asking questions could never be an option for me—trouble waited at the end of that road. Amlis handed me to Rodrik the moment we'd stepped inside his suite, then walked into his bedroom, shutting the door behind him.

Rodrik eyed me with a substantial dose of distaste before leading me into a much smaller room that held a narrow bed, a washstand, a fireplace and little else. Rodrik was compact where the Prince was lean and lithe, and I imagined the muscles that rippled beneath his close-fitting shirt had been gained in sword practice. I was seventeen and somewhat naïve, but that didn't make me stupid.

"After you've bathed, there's a shirt on the bed. That'll cover you until the tailor arrives. He'll have something you can wear until clothing is made." Rodrik shut me inside the windowless bedroom, which I assumed was now mine. Shivering for the first time since the ordeal began, I wondered how this would affect my future.

Stepping into hot water and almost moaning my appreciation, I lowered my body into the tub and allowed the heat to soak into my bones for the first time in memory.

Soap smelling faintly of vanilla had been provided, along with a cloth that bore no holes or stains. I washed—both my body and my hair—several times; making sure every bit of grime was removed. Rodrik, I figured, would send me right back to the tub if I failed to pass his inspection.

Only when the water cooled did I leave the tub, hurriedly toweling off and dressing in the crisply ironed shirt that lay across the small bed. It hung to my knees, covering me well enough as I walked to the door and opened it quietly.

"Ah, here's our new page." I'd kept Amlis waiting. A slight flush stained my cheeks—I hadn't expected him to leave his bedroom to wait outside until I made my appearance. Why hadn't Rodrik pounded on my door like any good man-at-arms, and threatened bodily harm if I didn't hurry? Wolter would have.

"Come out so we can get measurements," Rodrik snapped. Opening the door fully, I stepped into Amlis' reception area, to see three men gaping at me. After several moments, Rodrik shut his mouth with an audible snap. "Get Denis. Quickly," he barked at a servant who stood near the door.

Was something wrong with me? I learned from my gift that Denis cut hair, trimmed nails and did other small things for the nobles. My hair, which had grown nearly to my shoulders, was about to be cut. *Again.*

"Hmmm," Nirok the tailor walked around me as we waited for Denis, studying my small frame. More ancient than Irdith would ever be, Nirok was stooped but refused a cane. His head was nearly bald but his eyesight had somehow remained sharp and his hands steady.

A girl, slightly younger than I who bore the same nose as the tailor, had come with him. She carried his measure-tape, pins and other sewing needs inside a large, quilted bag. "Want standard uniforms?" Nirok asked.

"Three, and two dress uniforms," Amlis replied. "The bootmaker is coming after you're done. He can measure while Denis cuts hair."

"The haircut will help," Nirok nodded as he began to measure my arms, waist and legs. "When I put my hands here, it means nothing, young woman." He set the tape near my crotch, making me jump. He measured quickly down past my ankle and relayed the measurements to the girl.

"Have something brought to eat," Rodrik instructed a servant. "No meat for Finder, she doesn't eat it, according to Chen and Wolter." His eyes sought mine; I nodded briefly, still trying to calm the quivering that threatened after Nirok touched me so intimately. "They'll know what to send for her," Rodrik nodded the servant out the door.

I couldn't eat meat, actually. It made me ill. Irdith had slipped meat or broth into my food at times, and every time I became nauseous. Wolter warned her the last time she'd done it, three turns before. The illness had kept me from my duties for more than a day. I was never sick, otherwise, and Wolter guessed immediately what had happened.

"You like that?" Amlis eyed my lentils with distaste while cutting into roasted chicken with a jeweled knife. Shrugging at his words, I lowered my eyes and ate.

Denis had come earlier, cutting my hair away until it was barely two finger-widths in length, the shortest it had ever been.

"We must make you look as much like the boys as possible, you understand," Rodrik had stood before me, fists on hips as Denis snipped away, my hair falling all around me. Had I looked pitiful as he cut? I certainly felt that way and had, every time the stablemaster had come before and chopped it away. The physician had sent him every time, after he'd cut away the bone spurs.

"I've never seen this before," Denis held out a clump of my hair. Once clean, it was gold in color, streaked with strands of silver and copper. Shaking his head in confusion, he let the hank drop to the floor. At least he didn't do the cut over Amlis' expensive rugs; hair was nearly impossible to get out of a rug.

"Better," Rodrik tousled what was left of my hair, making me shrink away from him. None touched me as he and Nirok had. Since I was small, the only contact others had made with me was to strike me after I made a mistake. I had no idea what to do when someone touched me in any other way, or how to interpret it.

⁂

"You'll run errands for me, and we'll devise a system of hand signals," Amlis informed me later, as we sat inside his private study. I'd never seen anything so fascinating before and could only imagine what the King's study and library looked like.

Shelves of books lined the wall behind a beautifully carved, cherry wood desk. Amlis was seated behind the desk while Rodrik sat off to the side, near a window framed with heavy, blue velvet drapes.

I could see wedges of snow against corners of real glass panes, fit so tightly and so well within the window that not a single draft found its way inside. A thick rug in the royal colors of red and blue lay beneath the desk and chairs. The fireplace covered the wall at my back and it filled the room with warmth. Perhaps being of the royal family did have its advantages.

"Finder, this means you have a message for me," Amlis tapped his mouth with an index finger. "This," he touched his left earlobe, "means I must come immediately. This," he pulled his right earlobe, "means we are in danger. Do you understand?" I nodded. I was tested. He asked me to give the signal for each and I complied.

"Good. I think we're ready to start. Carry a message to my brother, asking him to join me for wine tonight," he said, pulling a piece of parchment from a desk drawer and dipping a feather quill into an ink-bottle that resembled a ram's head. The quill scratched across parchment as he wrote, his letters even and shapely upon the pale surface.

"Wait for a reply, I've asked him to send one back with you," Amlis folded and sealed the message with wax. I watched in fascination as he pressed a heavy, gold ring he wore into the softened substance, leaving a royal imprint in the blue wax. Red was reserved for the royal heir, blue for any remaining siblings. Blinking at Amlis, I handled the message carefully and left his study to deliver it. Using my gift, I found my way to Timblor's suite with no trouble.

Rodrik's sigh almost exploded after Finder left him and Amlis behind to deliver the message to Timblor. "By Liron's testicles, man, I never expected that," Rodrik breathed.

"Neither of us did. How did she keep that from those louts in the kitchen? I have never seen anything that lovely. Thank goodness cutting the hair helped, and her knees and ankles are now covered."

"I hope the fact that she's mute helps instead of hurts. If I hear of anyone touching her," Rodrik clenched his fists.

"No one will dare unless it is my brother or my father; she wears my livery, after all," Amlis rose to pace the length of his study, staring blindly at the books behind his desk. "And if either of those dare, there's not a damned thing we can do."

"She's as skittish as a newborn foal, too. Did you notice?" Rodrik lifted from his chair and gazed out the window. Snow had fallen off and on all day. "Have you read anything about a snowfall this heavy so far south? Have you, cousin?"

"Fyris is being poisoned again, Rod," Amlis raked fingers through his hair, pronouncing a slight curl in the thick brown wealth. "Father has never seen it, until now."

"Every fifteen turns, according to the records," Rodrik agreed. "We have the only remaining written records in Vhrist, and those are hidden. If your father learns we still have them," Rodrik didn't finish.

Every written record had been torn away and burned after Tandelis died, leaving the throne of Fyris to Tamblin. Most of Fyris' population thought Tandelis had been taken by illness. Amlis had been barely five years of age at the time, his brother Timblor, nine. Timblor had witnessed Tandelis' death, as had his and Amlis' mother, Queen

Omina. She'd explained to Amlis the events leading to his father's ascension carefully when he was fourteen, and she refused to come again to Lironis. Tamblin didn't force the issue with his estranged wife—they'd come to an agreement. She wouldn't be forced to return in exchange for her silence.

"What will we do if the land fails?" Rodrik turned his gaze on Amlis.

"I will go north—and beg," Amlis replied softly.

"Ah, my brother's new page," Timblor accepted the message I held out. His fingers cracked the delicate seal and half the blue wax dropped onto Timblor's bed cover. Surreptitiously I watched it travel a short distance and fall into a wrinkle of expensive fabric as Timblor, dark haired and eyed, squirmed into a more comfortable position before unfolding the note to read.

"Brin," Timblor snapped his fingers. Brin, Timblor's page and personal servant, brought parchment, ink and a quill immediately. Brin was past the age to be serving as a page, but as there was a shortage of boys of the proper age, it made sense that he stay with Timblor.

He was nearly of an age with the Prince, but his square face was utilitarian at best, with a thin line of a mouth, heavy black brows and thick, black hair. A few freckles dusted pale skin, most of them littered across the nose.

I had the idea that Brin didn't smile often, but neither did I. Perhaps he thought, as I did, that there wasn't much to smile about. He was also a hand shorter than Timblor, and more sturdily built. Timblor was wide across the shoulders from much sword practice, narrow at the waist and hips, his thighs strong from riding horseback.

These things I knew, not just because I was finally seeing the reality, but from firsthand accounts from many maids who'd dallied with the Prince. I was now in the presence of the one who regularly seduced chambermaids.

Inside King Tamblin's castle, gossip among servants was as common as potatoes in the soup. I learned much from that gossip, half of which was rumor or outright lies, but I was always able to tell the difference. Gossip concerning Timblor's dalliances with chambermaids was almost always true.

I held myself stiffly at the end of the Crown Prince's bed and watched while he wrote. His letters were not as carefully formed or thought out as his brother's were; Timblor carelessly dragged the quill through words as if they held no meaning.

When I wrote (and I did at times), I wrote as carefully as I could. The stones beneath my old mattress held a sheaf of parchment, upon which I'd written many things, much of it notes or recreations of paragraphs from the books surrounding my straw pallet. I felt those notes were safe enough where they were—nobody ever visited the old storage room where I slept—too many ghosts dwelt inside it.

My ability to read and write had come as a wondrous accident—at age seven I'd dragged crates of books around my bed, hoping to keep freezing drafts away while I slept on a winter's night.

I'd seen an illustration on the leather cover of a book carelessly tossed on top of others inside a crate, and using what little light was afforded by a pilfered tallow candle, I touched the drawing reverently. Knowledge of the words printed on the cover traveled through my fingers and lodged inside my brain. I'd held in my hand *The Complete Geographical Works of Siriaa.*

Sadly, it was no longer complete, with numerous pages ripped away from its binding. With enthusiastic amazement, I'd turned fragile parchment pages, absorbing eagerly every drop of information until a ripped out page would halt my progress abruptly. Siriaa, as it turns out, was the planet and Fyris only one (and the smallest) of several continents, surrounded by many seas.

Parchment crackled, drawing me away from my memories. Timblor folded the note he'd written without placing a wax seal on it, then handed it to me, forcing me away from my thoughts and reminding me to tend to my duties. I bowed respectfully to the heir and took my leave.

Where did you find the girl, brother? Timblor's first sentence compelled Amlis to crush the note in his hand. He'd sent the note to his brother as a test. How had he ever imagined that his womanizing brother wouldn't notice, or at least dismiss Finder casually as more boy than girl?

A clean face worked wonders for the hapless kitchen girl, who'd escaped notice until he'd conscripted her services and forced her before dozens of male eyes. Nevertheless, Timblor wouldn't do anything if he felt it would aggravate Amlis. At least not yet. Only time would tell if that would change.

"Boots fit well enough?" Amlis asked me as we strode toward the stables. I nodded. Nirok had dressed me in a young man's clothing, but it hung loosely at the waist and the shoulders were too wide. He promised the new clothing would fit properly before he'd left Amlis' suite the day before. The bootmaker had also brought several pairs of boots, the smallest of which he'd left with me. They were still a bit large and I had no socks so my feet slipped inside them.

I wasn't complaining; the boots kept my feet warm as Amlis, Rodrik and I walked a snowy path toward the stable door, which was closed against the unusual cold. One of Amlis' old cloaks (from when he was a boy) draped my shoulders and I wrapped it closer about me as the wind whipped around castle walls, viciously blowing loose snow into unsuspecting eyes.

"Ever been on a horse?" Amlis asked as Rodrik pushed back the heavy stable door far enough that we could enter. I shook my head at Amlis' query. The stablemaster, who'd seen me barely two days earlier, stared openmouthed now as Amlis wandered toward a large, reddish-brown horse with a white, uneven stripe down his face and white stockings above each hoof.

The horse liked Amlis very much, nosing the Prince's chest in affection. Amlis offered something to the horse from a pocket, which the animal accepted gratefully and crunched with relish, shaking his head in approval as he chewed.

"Runner loves carrots," Rodrik whispered at my ear and I realized I'd been gaping rudely. Runner, having finished his treat, was now staring at me as well. Pawing the straw-strewn floor inside his stall, he whickered softly at me, nodding his head a second time and offering an invitation.

I dared not go. What would the Prince and the others do if they learned that any animal would come to my hand if I beckoned? Visions of wild deer or boar or any other thing they'd failed to capture came to mind, all coming to me so waiting men could deliver their deaths. No. I would not betray that trust.

Not now, I whispered mentally into Runner's mind and he turned away, agreeing to keep my secret.

"We'll need something slow and plodding for my new page," Amlis offered a grin to Garth, the stablemaster. They were allies; I could see it now, although I'd already guessed it.

"I have just the thing," Garth nodded respectfully. He was treating Amlis as a Prince today, since three stable boys were busy mucking out stalls farther down. "Old Broom will not like leaving his warm stall this morning, but he'll only grumble instead of tossing his rider into the street and trotting right back." Rodrik held back a snicker at Garth's words.

That's how it was decided; I would ride Old Broom. Old Broom turned out to be a fat, shaggy brown gelding that had never held hopes of reaching Runner's height. Rodrik saddled his horse—a black stallion that blinked a question at Rodrik when the saddle dropped onto his back.

Yes, I thought the same as Rodrik's Midnight—why were we going out in such terrible weather? What could be so important that it couldn't wait? Neither Midnight nor I could voice that question, so it went unanswered.

I was shown how to saddle Old Broom by a groom, whose eyes kept wandering across my face until the stablemaster whacked him with a riding crop. The boy turned back to his lesson quickly, showing me how to adjust the girth. Had he known it, Old Broom would have stood all day for me, until I'd gotten it right. He wouldn't have for anyone else, however. Maliciously, he swatted the boy with his tail when the boy thought to repeat his lesson.

Rodrik hefted me into Old Broom's saddle shortly after, adjusting the stirrups to a comfortable length. The stablemaster bade the boy open the door for us and Old Broom clopped away from the stable and into cruel, biting winds, obediently following Midnight, Runner and their riders.

My face was frozen by the time we reached our destination—an inn on the eastern edge of Lironis. Both times I'd been outside the palace walls, it hadn't been far beyond the thick stone barrier that stood three times the height of a tall man. I'd never traveled this far in my life. At least not in memory.

It made me wonder (again) about dead parents. Had they loved me? Were they farmers, perhaps? Or poor residents of Lironis? Whoever they were, they had no relatives willing to take in a small child, so I'd been handed off to the first place where a child could be put to work. That, as it turned out, was the palace kitchen.

The others who worked in the kitchen drew a wage, as poor as it was for some of them. Orphans were never offered money for their efforts; they were supposed to be grateful that someone took them in at all, and then expected to work for their upkeep and a small space to sleep. In all my life, I'd never had a coin to spend—nobody had ever given one to me.

A groom took our horses once we arrived at the inn's stable, and he bowed properly to Amlis, taking Runner's reins first. Amlis straightened the gloves on his hands and I watched in envy. I had no gloves and on our journey, I'd let Old Broom have his head, dropping the reins in favor of using my frozen fingers to wrap the cloak tightly around my body while we rode.

My horse knew to follow the others, and he wouldn't have hurt me anyway. None of them would. I slid from the saddle before Rodrik was forced to lift me off Old Broom's back, and we huddled farther into our cloaks as the wind bit into any flesh bared to it on our walk toward the inn's front door.

"I almost expected you to cancel," the innkeeper accepted Amlis' cloak. Rodrik jerked his head and coming to myself, lifted his from his shoulders and took Amlis' heavy blue wool from the innkeeper, moving toward pegs lining a board on the wall. Two cloaks already hung there, nearly as fine as the Prince's. Dutifully I hung both cloaks I held before shedding mine and hanging it away from the others—it had no business being anywhere near them.

The innkeeper was elderly and balding; I focused on the back of his head as he led us toward a room in the back. White hair dipped in a horseshoe shape at the back of his head and wisped over his ears, stopping there to leave his forehead and the top of his skull completely bare. Washed-out blue eyes studied me as he stood aside to allow us inside the room, after which he promised to bring food and drink before shutting the door.

"Amlis, it's good to see you again," one of two men rose and greeted the Prince. I'd never seen this one before, in or out of the Palace. The other I recognized easily enough. Hirill stood and dipped his head to Amlis. Was I surprised? No. Worried? Most certainly.

"Good to see you as well, Uncle Rath," Amlis embraced the first man, thumping him on the back affectionately.

"Father," Rodrik's embrace was more subdued than Amlis', but then he was older and had likely seen Rath of Vhoorth more regularly than the Prince.

Rath was Queen Omina's elder brother; everyone in Fyris knew that. Rath's fault lay in his inability to get along with the King. Also a well-known fact. If King Tamblin knew Rath was in Lironis, he would likely show his brother-in-law to the gates himself, with an invitation never to return.

In my dreams, I could never have envisioned this meeting—Hirill, a member of Tamblin's inner circle, sitting beside Rath as if they were the best of friends. Perhaps Amlis believed that they were. I had my doubts, and my talent supported them in every way. I had no way to pass this information to Amlis, however, or Rodrik, even, so I stood back and waited for the innkeeper to bring food and wine, prepared to serve it if it were required of me.

Rath looked to be an older version of Rodrik, and much like Amlis, since he favored his mother, Rath's sister. Vhoorth was two days' ride south of Vhrist, where she lived.

In my geography and history books, not much was given on the population of either city, or what their holdings were or how they were governed. All I knew was dry information, garnered from a book with many pages ripped away, which said Ridik, Rath and Omina's father, had once ruled both principalities before dividing them between his two children. Then Omina had married Tamblin, followed by many more missing pages.

"Have you any idea how to draft the message?" Hirill hefted a satchel onto the polished, oak plank table. It had seen much use, that table, bearing dents and rings from countless tankards of ale slapped onto its surface. I watched as Hirill withdrew a sealed inkpot and parchment from the satchel, leaning over to search for quills at the bottom.

Hirill would have been handsome to me—if I trusted him. I didn't. The chambermaids discussed him nearly as much as they did Timblor, and with good reason. Hirill had close-cropped blond hair, blue eyes and an easy smile, but to me that smile held a cruel twist at the corners.

"No records exist on how to address the king, or even if there is a king, since we've had no communication with them since," Rath began. He didn't finish the sentence. I'd held my breath for a moment, hoping that he would. What king? Where? Again, I was left adrift, like a rudderless boat upon the sea.

The sea had come to my mind, unbidden. I'd heard tales that one might view the shores of the Southern Sea if one climbed to the topmost turret in Tamblin's palace on a clear day, but I hadn't had any opportunity to go there and rumor had it that it was closed off and locked anyway.

"So, girl, you're the mute one?" Rath pulled me away from my thoughts as a sheet of parchment was handed to him. He accepted the offered quill and inkpot from Hirill as he asked the question. His dark-blue eyes searched my face while I surveyed the many strands of gray in his dark-brown hair. I nodded my answer.

"Are you stupid as well?" I offered a noncommittal shrug.

"Good enough. Let's begin the message this way, then," he scraped quill across parchment with practiced ease. "My Lord," he wrote and spoke aloud, "we are in dire need of your assistance."

CHAPTER 3

By the end of the evening, I was left with a larger mystery than when it had begun. Somewhere past the northern shores of Fyris, a Lord dwelt that might offer assistance with a poison slowly consuming Fyris. Somehow, I had the feeling that the Lord might not cooperate, even with Lord Rath's abasement and carefully chosen words.

No mention was made as to what the poison might be, and the letter made it sound as if this mysterious Lord would have complete knowledge of it, anyway. Why was there need to hide this from King Tamblin? After all, if there were a way to save Fyris and its people as the letter implied, why wouldn't he be writing the thing himself and swiftly?

Dead and dying children came to mind and I wanted to shake my head over the entire thing, but I was kept busy filling wine cups and fashioning sandwiches from slices of thick, fresh bread supplied by the innkeeper—Amlis and the others were quite hungry. After a while, Amlis allowed me to take bread, cheese and a cup of wine to a corner and consume it there.

Leaning back against shaved and sanded logs that made up the walls of the inn, I listened while the debate went on over what to include in the letter. That Lord Rath debased himself so much told me something—the one for whom the letter was intended must be powerful indeed.

None of the history accounts I'd read, nor the geographical treatises, indicated a country or island to the north inhabited by a powerful

Lord. In the maps I'd seen, there was only one continent to the north, filled with barbarians. According to the book, anyway.

Was this Lord a barbarian? If so, could he even read the letter and understand it? A third continent, far to the east of Fyris, was essentially unpopulated, according to the books, and a fourth to the west had never been explored. But the books I'd read were quite old. Who knows how things now stood, or if the missing pages might explain things more clearly?

I had much to ponder as I listened on that snowy evening, devoting half my mind to the ongoing debate while the unanswered questions aggravated the other.

"This is the best we can do," Rath sighed eventually, folding the final draft carefully and sealing it much the same way that Amlis had sealed the message to his brother, with wax and an imprint from a heavy ring he wore.

The wax in this case was green—the color of the major nobles. Yellow was for minor nobles, but I'd only had the opportunity to see that once before, when a message had come to Wolter in the kitchens.

"I will carry this with me and find someone to take it past our northern shore," Rath said. "Beginning tomorrow. Son, shall you and the Prince stay as my guests this evening? The inn has comfortable rooms."

"We must return to the palace, Uncle," Amlis answered in Rodrik's stead. "My brother thinks we're at the brothel."

"Celebrating your majority a few moon-turns early?" Rath grinned mischievously.

"Of course, Uncle. How else would it be?" Amlis grinned back. The discarded drafts of the letter were taken up by Rodrik, who tossed them into the fire. I watched the edges curl and then burn. Rodrik watched, too, until all were consumed.

I helped the innkeeper clear away plates and cups while Amlis and Rodrik made small conversation with Rath and Hirill. Afterward,

I pulled cloaks from pegs and assisted Amlis and Rodrik as they dressed for the cold.

Wrapping myself in Amlis' castoff, I followed my two into the bitter cold, with Hirill not far behind. The Prince's party was served first, our horses saddled and brought out as was proper, and we were away while Hirill searched for hat and gloves in his saddlebag.

The night had not improved the weather's disposition, the bitter winds howling around shuttered homes and businesses as we made our way toward the castle. There was little light, but the road was easy enough to see in the snow. Our horses had their heads down; the return trip was forcing us into the wind instead of away from it, as it had on our journey to the inn.

When the vision hit, I knew Amlis and Rodrik would be cut to pieces if we kept our current pace. I shouted into Runner and Midnight's minds to run as fast as they could to save their lives and the lives of the men they carried.

"Something spooked their horses, my Lord." Yevil stood before the King's massive desk. Carved of walnut, it was stained as black as Yevil's soul.

No books graced the shelves in King Tamblin's library—they'd been emptied when he took it for his own. Most of the tomes had been burned in the fireplace opposite his desk, as he'd had no use for them.

"My men did not pursue; that many horses racing through the streets on such a wintry night would arouse suspicion."

"You did right, of course," the King toyed with the ring he wore on his smallest finger. Tandelis had worn it on the proper finger, but then his hands had been smaller than Tamblin's. *Weak,* Tamblin thought as he twisted the ring. Tamblin snorted—Yevil had failed to kill Rodrik and the boy.

How many times had he suspected that Amlis was not his son, though he'd tortured Omina's maid, attempting to force a confession from her of his wife's dalliance. The woman had breathed her last, professing Omina's continued fidelity. Either way, the boy had too much of his uncle in him for his own good and his death would ensure a smooth transition when Timblor took the throne.

"What about the girl—the page?"

"She was left behind on that plodding old pony. We let her pass—after all, what can she tell any of them?" Yevil replied. A slow smile spread across the King's face.

I will never forget the look of relief that crossed Rodrik's face as Old Broom and I clopped into the stable that night. It was three hours before dawn, an hour after I was normally up and cleaning hearths. Exhausted, I nearly stumbled as I slid from Old Broom's back, offering him a grateful pat that shot chill pains through my fingers and palm.

"I'll make sure he's fed proper. Those other two didn't stop running until they reached the stable," Garth observed. He'd waited with Rodrik, likely hoping that the horse would come back even if I didn't.

As far as Midnight and Runner racing toward the stables—that's what I'd meant for them to do when I'd instructed them to run. They'd followed my command perfectly. Amlis and Rodrik were both experienced riders, and I'm sure they were shocked that their mounts had run away with them, as much as they'd tried to stop the reckless gallop through the streets of Lironis. Ten would-be assassins had been left empty-handed—there would be no terrible news to cry through the streets come daybreak.

As frozen as I was, I went to Runner and Midnight both, stroking foreheads gently before going with Rodrik to the palace. Both horses knew of my gratitude before I left them, and both were willing to do it again if I asked.

Amlis was just as bleary-eyed when he rose as if he'd done what his older brother believed—spent the night in a brothel. Timblor teased him over it, too, at breakfast. Brin poured tea for Timblor and cut his meat, tasting it before serving it to the Heir.

Amlis had to resort to asking a servant to do the same—I would not touch the ham that lay on his plate for anything. I, too, felt the effects of a long night and short sleep, but I forced myself to pay attention as Timblor made his brother the butt of his jokes.

"We were to hunt today, brother. You should be thankful the snow is preventing it. I fear you would have made a poor showing; Runner would have left you behind, I think."

Rodrik grimaced at Timblor's words as he cut into his own breakfast, but as Amlis' man-at-arms, Timblor paid him little mind. In truth, I worried that Timblor's remark was a dig at Amlis for Runner's apparent waywardness the night before, and Amlis' failure to keep the horse in hand.

Was Timblor having his brother watched? I suspected several of being behind the thwarted ambush, but Timblor didn't have the sense to be so devious. Amlis wisely kept his silence and continued to eat.

A knock came on Amlis' door later in the day, while Amlis was sleeping extra hours and Rodrik was at blade practice with some of the twelve men who'd traveled with the Prince from Vhrist. Schooling my face to hide my reluctance to allow Yevil into the Prince's suite, I motioned for him to make himself comfortable and offered wine from a carafe before knocking on the Prince's bedroom door. Yevil refused wine but studied me beneath hooded eyes as I went through the motions.

"What is it, Finder?" Amlis muttered as I peered timidly inside his bedroom door. The window drapes shut out most of the light, leaving the room in near darkness. I pointed behind me, hoping that Amlis would determine that he had a guest. There was no way I'd send Yevil Orklis away; the man held too much power, and I'd seen him kill in the past.

"Ah, Lord Orklis," Amlis didn't pretend that he'd not been sleeping, letting the King's right hand know immediately by politely covering a yawn. "What might I do for you?" Amlis added carelessly, as if Yevil held no importance at all.

"Your father requests your presence at the table tonight," Yevil replied stiffly, the same vein I'd witnessed before throbbing in his neck. He was angry—no doubt about that. I wondered briefly if Yevil thought to have the same importance he now held when Timblor took the throne, but squelched that thought quickly before my talent kicked in and let me know exactly how things could be. A two-edged sword, my talent sometimes was, often revealing things I'd rather not know.

"Of course I will come," Amlis nodded to Yevil, never once taking his eyes away from the King's assassin. I imagined that Yevil had been somewhere in the mix the night before, whether he'd planned the ambush or not.

"I will inform the King." Yevil couldn't get away from Amlis fast enough, leaving the door to the suite open behind him. I closed it quietly after listening for Yevil's fading footsteps down the lengthy hall.

"Have you wondered about the suite across the hall?" Amlis stifled another yawn as he lifted an egg-shaped sculpture from a delicate table just inside his door. The egg looked to be made of green marble, a precious commodity in Fyris. Little of it was found on the small continent—I'd read that in one of my books. I shrugged slightly at Amlis' question.

"You make me want to laugh, your reactions are so neutral," Amlis actually smiled and set the egg down again. "Come. We'll visit my mother's old suite. Nirok will return later today; he has two of your uniforms ready—one regular and one dress, with a few other necessities. In the meantime, we'll explore a little, eh?"

I followed Amlis as he left his suite, crossing to the door directly opposite. "I've not been here since I was five turns old," Amlis mused as he walked toward the back of a massive, darkened suite. Dust was raised as he jerked window coverings back, revealing a huge window. "I'll instruct the maids to clean," he said after his sneezing fit was over.

Light now filled the suite and we found ourselves inside what was once a well-appointed receiving room, with settees and chairs scattered about, along with tables and other necessities required for entertaining. Most of it was sheet-draped, and I might have given anything in my earlier life to have those sheets to lie on at night, instead of patched and worn castoffs. As aged as they were, none bore a hole or stain anywhere.

"My mother used to sit here, and I would crawl onto her lap while she was drinking tea and entertaining her friends," Amlis rambled, his eyes unfocused with memory as he touched the top of a sheet-draped chair. "They're all dead, now, those friends." He sounded troubled over that. "Timblor and I would tussle on her bed, too, but we'll explore that on another day." Amlis was done with his memory trip and heading for the door while I fell in behind him. "I'll have the maids come," he repeated and shut the door once we were both out.

"Serve the wine on the left, and if Amlis desires anything, you will get it promptly, do you hear?" I was getting a lesson from the King's personal servant. I nodded vigorously; Etlund, a tall and exceedingly thin man, seemed to demand that reaction to his instruction. "Otherwise, you will stand at his left elbow and keep your eyes straight ahead, do you hear?" Of course I heard. He spoke loudly, too, as if my mute condition indicated poor hearing as well. Vigorous nodding followed his question.

"Very well. Perform poorly and you will be beaten, do you hear?"

"That mouth has never been kissed, brother," Timblor drew back his bow and let loose the arrow. It thwacked into the target forcefully, very near the center. Timblor, restless after the cancelled hunt, had dragged Amlis to the practice range inside the single-story guards' quarters below the gate.

"Why are you speaking of my page in this manner?" Amlis drew back his own bow, prudently aiming just to the left of Timblor's arrow before releasing the bowstring.

"Is that all she is? A page?" Timblor's voice held disbelief.

"You know Father and Mother have someone selected for me already. I am not the heir and an alliance with Firith will ensure that Lironis never wants for wine or fine cheeses. Father is most enthusiastic over the match, as you recall."

"So, you'd rather ride to a brothel in the freezing cold when you have something readily at hand?"

"Yes. Why is this so hard for you, brother?" Amlis glanced at Timblor. "She is inexperienced—you said so yourself. Why waste time in the teaching, when the well-taught is not far away?"

"I see your point," Timblor said, taking aim again. "Fifty gold pieces says I hit the center this time."

"Done," Amlis nodded. Timblor released the arrow.

Dinner that evening was a sore trial, and placed me in much trouble. Amlis sat at Tamblin's left while Timblor took the Heir's position at the King's right. Yevil sat past that, scowling while his own servant offered wine. Hirill and seven others, all members of Tamblin's inner circle, were scattered down the long table. A few had wives or lovers at their elbow and personal servants cared for both.

Amlis' plate was poisoned, but he was served the same as the King. No suspicion would be cast, once the King's personal servant tasted the veal in an elaborate sauce. Even if there were a cry raised, Wolter and the kitchen staff would bear the blame.

Even though Wolter had beaten me often enough when I was small, I preferred that his head remain on his shoulders. Bumping Amlis' shoulder as I reached in to pour wine (he was about to cut into the meat) I deliberately dropped the wine flagon on the edge of his plate, upending most of its contents in the Prince's lap.

Yes, the blows he delivered to my head and shoulders amid laughs and encouragement from others at the table were expected, but these wounded more than any blows had ever done.

Steeling my heart after cleaning up the plate (which lay face down on the floor) and clearing away the poisoned meat lying on the table, I took it away.

Wolter stared at me in surprise when I carried the Prince's plate into the kitchen, after which he eyed the wrecked meat with a lift to his eyebrow.

"Not fit?" he asked. I shook my head.

"Then it won't go to the dogs," he sighed. I nodded vigorously. I watched as he prepared a second plate and I carried it back to the Prince, who was now dressed in fresh clothing—I'd ruined the formal jacket he'd worn before.

It was a shame; Amlis looked quite good in the blue with red piping. His blows and shouts I felt, still, and refused to look at him, pulling on my right earlobe instead. He failed to notice, Etlund tasted Amlis' second plate, pronounced it fit and the dinner resumed.

Had I thought the evening over? I was very wrong. Meekly following Amlis as he strode angrily toward his suite, I took his jacket and removed his boots when the knock came. Setting the boots aside for the moment, I went to answer the door. Timblor had come, bearing a bottle of wine.

"I just wanted to sit and enjoy the beating," Timblor grinned and held up two delicate wineglasses in one hand, the wine bottle in the other.

I stared at the fragile, blue-tinted wineglasses Timblor carried—glass that thin was nearly unheard of and according to kitchen gossip, there were no artisans remaining in Fyris who could create it. What Timblor held carelessly in his fingers was worth a fortune.

"Rodrik hasn't returned yet," Amlis' expression was sour.

"Ah. Well, we'll drink and wait together." I blinked at Amlis, working to school my face. Had Amlis intended to have me beaten a second time, or was Timblor forcing his hand? Regardless, Rodrik would now deliver blows, and I would learn unwillingly enough how heavy his hand might be.

Quite heavy, as it turned out. Rodrik hadn't been privy to any of the evening's events, so Timblor informed him, ridiculing me and exaggerating my actions, making it sound as if a carnival of performers had left Amlis' jacket ruined and his dinner strewn across the King's dining hall. Rodrik had taken his riding crop to me after that, and several blows had landed on my face and at the back of my neck, leaving red welts and purple bruises behind, which ached. A few of them bled as well.

When he was finished with me, I pulled myself from the floor where I'd fallen and went to put the Prince's boots away while Timblor drank and laughed at my retreating back. Tears would be useless, as they generally evoked more laughter and ridicule, but I wanted to cry them anyway as I finished my duties for the evening.

"I wanted to tell you myself, as the physician has declared it was her heart giving out on her at last," Chen offered the plate of cakes to Amlis the following afternoon. "Wolter set aside the plate of veal you'd been served after Finder brought it back to the kitchen. He was going to dispose of it, since Finder let him know in the way she has that he shouldn't feed it to the dogs. While Wolter's back was turned, Irdith ate a portion of the meat—you know kitchen help seldom gets to taste veal. Two candles later, Irdith was dead in her chair beside the fire. Wolter left her there and went about his business."

"The plate was poisoned," Amlis rubbed his forehead in frustration. "And then Timblor came last night, forcing me to have Rodrik beat the girl nearly senseless. And this after I'd already hit her in the dining hall. She's in my mother's suite this morning, helping the maids dust and clean as part of her punishment."

"I don't know what else you could do, my Prince. Had you held back, they might suspect that she is a bargaining chip and bring their own harm against her to get to you."

"You think I don't realize that?" Amlis rose from the seat behind his desk and walked to the window. At least the weather was relenting and snow was melting on the ground two floors below, making a muddy mess of the courtyard.

"It's this way, always," Chen sighed. "She won't meet your eyes from here on out, so don't expect it unless it's ordered. Wolter didn't notice it for the longest time, and now he harbors regrets."

"Did he know how beautiful she is?" Amlis turned away from the window to ask.

"No. And honestly, neither did I. She kept herself covered in ash and soot. We never looked past that."

"Rodrik hasn't spoken to me since," Amlis muttered, staring out the window again. "It's as if I've had both beaten."

"Life happens as it will, my Prince," Chen whispered. "I must go."

Muscles in my back and arms ached as I rolled up the heavy rug, preparing it for transport to the back garden where it would be hung by menservants and beaten to get the dust out. Maids laughed and gossiped around me, but I was mired in my own misery and ignored most of it.

I did not take comfort in Irdith's death, although it was deserved and long past due. How can I explain that? The answer is simply that I cannot. If I were offered a riding whip and the opportunity to hit both

Amlis and Rodrik, I could not. The whip would be tossed away and I would take my leave.

Rumblings had begun in my head, however, over why I stayed and accepted abuse. Perhaps it was because there was no other place to take me, where I would not be in just as much danger.

"Finder, come." Rodrik was inside Amlis' suite when my day of cleaning the Queen's old quarters was over. I stared deliberately at his chin—he'd beaten me. I would never search his eyes again. I would know everything I needed to know without it. His riding crop was in his hand and truly, I expected a second beating wherever he was taking me. That, as it turns out, was the stables.

Garth waited there, with a tub filled with hot water inside the stablemaster's quarters, located at the rear of the lengthy building. A fresh uniform waited for me as well, draped over a wooden chair, scraped and scarred from many turns' use.

"Clean up," Rodrik commanded. "Garth will put salve on the wounds afterward." Rodrik stalked out, leaving me with a puzzled Garth.

"I'll step outside," Garth offered. Giving him a curt nod, I waited until he was gone before removing my clothing. My neck had ached all day, and when I'd rubbed it, my hand had come away bloodied. Rodrik had broken skin in several places, leaving crusted blood behind.

I'd washed as much of it away as I could that morning, but cleaning the Queen's suite had broken the wounds open again and in places, my clothing had to be painfully peeled away. My back and neck were the worst—I wanted to moan as I forced the fabric away from my body.

Lowering my frame into the tub came next, and it was nearly as painful as removing my uniform. A brush was provided to wash my back, and I was forced to wash the brush, afterward, as the bristles were bloody when I finished with it. The towel was wrapped about me when Garth knocked, and he came in with a pot of salve.

He had no words as he rubbed salve into the back of my neck first, and the medicine stung so badly it brought tears to my eyes. My talent informed me it was the same he used for the horses, but I was a worthless servant after all, and a horse would bring more at market.

Garth pulled the towel lower to get to my back and drew in a gasp. Fingering the bone spurs that reappeared every turn, he rose and walked away. Without a doubt, I knew he was going to Rodrik with the information. I had no choice but to bear the scrutiny of both men as they examined my back. Whimpering would not help me, but I wished to do it anyway.

"Wolter called them bone spurs," Rodrik muttered and I nearly collapsed with relief. "But after seeing them," Rodrik didn't finish and I stiffened again. "Never mind. It's normal for her, or so I understand. Finish up and I'll get her back to the palace." Rodrik stalked out again.

Nirok and his granddaughter were waiting inside Amlis' suite when we returned. My head was down and I watched Rodrik's boots carefully as we'd made our way from the stable to the palace. Futilely, I wished I were back in the kitchen; with Irdith dead, perhaps my life there might ease a bit.

Instead, I was forced to try on two uniforms, both in Amlis' blue. The dress uniform had red piping, patterned after his formal and much more expensive clothing. Mine was fashioned of plain cloth, whereas his was fine velvets or linens.

"These are for you—to wear beneath the uniforms," Nirok's granddaughter had pulled me into my tiny bedroom and offered me underthings. I'd never had any before; they were for better and higher born. Maid's gossip had informed me of the existence of such, and often boasted that this benefactor or that had made a gift of it.

"It will keep your uniforms cleaner and fresher when you wear it," she coaxed, until I relented and pulled off my clothing to try on the delicate chemise and underwear. Six sets had been brought to me, and I was instructed to change every day and have the soiled ones laundered after a single use. Shrugging at the girl, who'd gasped at the wounds across my back when they were revealed, I kept the first set of underthings on and climbed back into my uniform.

"Finder," Amlis tapped a finger on his desk uncomfortably after Nirok and his granddaughter had taken their leave. "I understand now that you were only keeping me from harm." I stared at my feet. Rodrik, too, was inside the Prince's study, watching both of us carefully.

"I want to offer this to you." Amlis pulled a gray leather pouch from a desk drawer and set it before me. It chinked when he settled it on the edge of his desk, and I realized it held coins. Many, if my guess was correct.

Had I chosen to speak at that moment, I'd have told him that no coins could buy his life from those who wished to take it, and no amount of money would ever remove the memory of his or Rodrik's beatings. Risking another beating, I turned angrily and stalked out of his study, slamming the door behind me.

"I only tell you this because I am old and it no longer matters whether my death comes today or next turn," the physician's clouded eyes attempted to make out Rodrik's face. Nearly blind, the old physician had to rely on his sense of touch to treat many patients. If the King had allowed it, he would have left Lironis long ago.

"There were two babes inside Tandelis' court that morning, one of which was Lady Rinda's. That is the one the King sent to the kitchens." A coughing fit engulfed the ancient healer, and his manservant quickly brought watered wine for the old man to drink.

"That is the story he believes, at least," the physician croaked. "Have you ever thought to ask yourself why the deaths and deformities plaguing Fyris have not touched Lironis? I ask you to ponder that. And if you value your life and the life of your Prince, you'd best be well away from here before long." Wetness gurgled in the old physician's throat as he accepted another sip of wine.

Without a reply, Rodrik turned on his heel and walked away. He hadn't failed to see the hopeless expression on the manservant's face, however. It begged Rodrik to take him along as well.

"So Father sent Lady Rinda's child to the kitchens. Was that better than killing her outright?" Amlis studied Rodrik's face. Rodrik revealed no emotion, except for the white lines around his lips. Rodrik was furious.

At the time of Tandelis' death, Rinda was a widow—her husband had died in an unfortunate hunting accident according to Yevil, who'd happened upon the body. Savaged by wild boars, he'd reported. Lord Andwil's death had left behind a grieving widow and a child less than two turns of age. Barely six moon-turns later, Rinda was also dead, as was her child, according to official records.

"Amlis, I tell you this because I trust you. The physician says two babes were inside Tandelis' court that morning. Your father *believes* he sent Rinda's daughter to the kitchens." Amlis' eyes widened in shock at Rodrik's words.

"Finder, there is no time to instruct you in the matters of politics, and it wouldn't matter much to you anyway. Just stand still, don't fidget and whatever you do, don't spill my wine," Amlis muttered as I struggled to keep up with his angry walk. His legs were much longer than mine, although he was still three fingers shorter than Wolter.

We were on our way to a council meeting with the King and his inner circle, who acted as his advisors. Everyone in the palace knew that Tamblin and Yevil had their way in all things; the others merely nodded and agreed, heaping praise upon the King for making such wise and timely judgments.

Even Timblor, usually not at a loss for words, kept silent while his father and the King's right hand spoke. I'd determined that deaths might occur if anyone thought to disagree with Yevil or the King.

"Has our Finder committed any other transgressions? I wouldn't mind a glass of wine and a bit of amusement, brother," Timblor and Brin caught up with us just outside the King's council chambers. Timblor was dressed rakishly in a well-fitted red velvet tunic over blue trousers, his black boots polished until they shone. Brin was good at his job; there was no doubt of that. I turned my face away from the Heir while Amlis slapped his chuckling brother halfheartedly on the back and walked into the council chamber behind him.

The room was built in an oval, with glass windows along the outside wall. The glass itself would have built a city from its worth, and just like the window in Amlis' study, each pane was tightly fitted into the frame and sealed against the weather.

A fireplace large enough for six tall men to stand inside roared against the inside wall and three rugs lay on the floor, one of which supported a long, heavy oak table. Taking my position at the left of Amlis' chair, I prepared myself for a long and trying session of standing still. Things often have a way of veering away from any normal plan, however, and that day proved it easily.

The King, his sons and the inner circle were all seated when two large men bore a sheep into the room and dumped it on the table. Gasps and whispers began immediately, and I could see plain enough that the sheep had two heads and five legs.

CHAPTER 4

"This is happening throughout Fyris," Yevil stood to speak. The King settled for glaring malevolently at the dead sheep instead, as if his will could force the carcass into a normal shape. "At first I dismissed the reports, as a misshapen animal or babe here and there is to be expected. That is no longer true. Six in the same herd were born deformed. This one is the most palatable to look upon." Yevil had been drinking before this meeting; his eyes, normally a clearer green, were clouded, just as they'd been the first time I'd seen him.

Amlis' fingers gripped the arms of his chair tightly, while his brother dismissed the sheep's carcass altogether, preferring to sip his wine and stare out the large windows. "What is this to us?" Timblor sniffed.

"This, coupled with the fact that the herds are not producing lambs, calves or piglets as they should. Hens have ceased laying. We must find a cause for this and rid our land of its taint," Yevil snarled at Timblor. Timblor ignored Yevil's anger—wasn't wise enough to recognize it. Amlis judiciously said nothing.

"What could possible cause that?" Hirill asked. I did not turn in his direction but wondered why he would ask—after all, it was only a few days since he'd sat at an inn with Rodrik's father and Prince Amlis, writing a letter to someone who might consent to control whatever was poisoning Fyris.

"It has to be the barbarians. There's no other explanation," Tamblin growled his first words of the meeting. "They have wizards or conjurers or some such, who are attempting to kill us and take over our land. I want each of you to ride out today and prepare the cities in your principalities for conscription and war. Bring all able-bodied men to Lironis for training. Then we will set forth and attack."

"What about ships?" another of Tamblin's circle asked. "We'll need them to sail northward."

"Ah, that's where my youngest will help," Tamblin turned a nasty grin toward Amlis.

⁂

"There are no wizards or conjurers, and no threat of attack from the barbarians," Amlis angrily shoved personal items into a trunk that Finder had carefully filled with folded clothing. "Father is looking to preserve his own life as long as possible. He knows Fyris is dying, so he looks to take healthy land away from the barbarians in the north."

"I know this as well as you, cousin," Rodrik muttered. "At least we will be back in Vhrist, even if we are forced to oversee construction of Tamblin's fleet."

⁂

Nirok delivered the last of my uniforms, only to see them packed inside a small trunk. Amlis was taking me with him, when he could have left me with Wolter in the kitchens. I did have one last errand to run, however, before I pulled out Amlis' traveling clothes in preparation for our journey in the morning. None saw me as I ghosted through the palace, retrieved my written papers from beneath my old bed and slipped them inside my trunk.

⁂

"Old Broom will never survive the journey. You'll have Stepper instead," Garth led the small mare out of a stall, already saddled and bridled. Rodrik's twelve men were mounted and waiting outside the stable as Amlis set foot in his stirrup and hauled himself into Runner's saddle.

We'll get along fine, I sent to the mare, soothing her with a hand to her nose. She nodded cordially and allowed me to climb awkwardly onto her back. Three men took the lead, four the rear and Rodrik joined the others who rode at Amlis' side, effectively surrounding the Prince as we made our way out of Lironis. *At least I would see what Fyris had for mountains,* I consoled myself as the only life I'd known was left behind.

"They'll do what he tells them," Tamblin informed Yevil. "Forget going after him for the moment. It'll be far easier to bring about his death when we attack the barbarians, eh?" Yevil offered Tamblin a black look and stalked away from the King's study.

The road shifted, rolled and eventually forked after half a day, where our party chose to stop, relieve themselves and get a drink of water before resuming the journey.

"It's shorter this way, as Vhrist is at the northwestern edge of Fyris," Rodrik explained to me after asking if I needed to find a bush somewhere. I shook my head. They didn't know and I had no inclination to tell them that I never needed the slops.

Wolter and the others in the kitchen always assumed I eliminated waste just as they did, but they were wrong. Hoping I could keep it from these, I determined to pretend at times, just to preserve that façade.

No, I have no idea why I have never had to perform this most basic function, and I was grateful that none had ever paid close enough attention to learn of it. My legs and back were suffering from being in the saddle for half a day and I figured I would be very sore come nightfall, when the Prince stopped for the evening at an inn somewhere.

Eventually we would be traveling parallel with the Western Sea—I recalled it from the maps I'd studied. Many towns and villages lay along the western road, most of them thriving on what was netted from the water or from farms and herds situated farther inland.

"We'll see the waters of the Western Sea tomorrow afternoon," Amlis informed me as we rode along. "Have you ever seen the sea, Finder?"

Mutely I shook my head. Surely, he could have worked that out for himself—I'd never been outside Lironis before. Still, I wouldn't meet his eyes and he heaved an agitated sigh.

"It could not be helped," he said. "A beating withheld might give others the idea that they could harm me through you. I hope you come to understand that, one day. Rodrik and I both hope that your skin will not scar as a result. It was more fragile than we guessed." He reined Runner and pulled ahead of Stepper, as if the admission embarrassed him in some way.

"No insult was intended when he offered the money," Rodrik added softly and moved Midnight forward to keep pace with Amlis. What did they think to gain, offering explanations to a lowly servant? I mattered little, after all, and even I knew the beatings were expected. I'd just not thought them to hurt my soul as much as they had.

The inn was a welcome sight after a long day's ride, and none of us had eaten since breakfast. My inner thighs ached so badly when I dismounted I had to hold onto Stepper's saddle until my legs stopped shaking. It surprised me—I could climb up and down palace steps easily every day, but riding impacted my body in other ways, I discovered.

Riding was also not the only thing bringing discomfort—did they all feel it as I did? The wrongness about the land? I hadn't felt it in Lironis, and truly hadn't understood completely when Rodrik's father said that Fyris was being poisoned. Now I fully realized the impact of his statement.

"At least the snow is gone. I was worried," Rodrik hefted his saddlebag from Midnight's back. Struggling to walk and remain upright at the same time, I made my way to Amlis, so I could carry his personal belongings into the inn.

Two grooms and a handful of Rodrik's men stayed to tend the horses; I carried Amlis' saddlebag and worked to keep up with him as we walked into the inn. Rooms were parceled out by a beaming innkeeper and his eldest son, while his wife cooked with the aid of two helpers.

After looking at the innkeeper once, I knew he'd lost a young daughter only two moon-turns earlier. Unable to offer condolences, I settled Amlis' things into the largest room available, then set out soap and the towel the inn had provided next to an ewer of warm water. His jacket I also took, and brushed the dust of the road away from it while Amlis washed his face and hands. While he stood, I wiped his boots—he refused to take them off first, so I knelt at his feet to perform that task. I made myself as presentable as I could afterward before following him to the main room for a meal.

"Finder, how is the food?" Amlis whispered as plates of fowl were set before him and Rodrik, then given to Rodrik's men after that. I would eat last of all as Amlis' servant, and it would be a vegetable stew, since Rodrik informed the innkeeper's wife that I could not consume meat.

I nodded—the food was fine if plain, but Amlis didn't seem to mind. They were all hungry (as was I) and began eating immediately, once the Prince took his first bite.

"They say you can't speak," the innkeeper's wife sat opposite me as I ate my vegetable stew with thick pieces of bread after the others had retired. The bread wasn't as fine as Wolter could turn out, but he likely had better ingredients since he cooked for the King.

"They say you understand things well enough." The wife's face was reddened from working in the kitchen all day; her hair had escaped the bun at the back of her head and clouded about her face in wisps of brown. "They tell me you can find things." Those words had me looking up from my stew, my mouth full of potato, carrots and leeks, to stare at the woman. Who had let that slip?

"My daughter had a necklace, given to her by my mother. Both dead now," the woman sighed and looked away for a moment.

I imagined that in better times, the woman might have carried a bit of plumpness, but the wrongness in Fyris was taking a toll on all its inhabitants. I hadn't seen anyone with excess weight since leaving Lironis. Carefully I laid aside the wooden spoon I'd been handed with my meal and swallowed the bit of food I'd mostly chewed. Standing, I beckoned for the woman to follow.

The necklace was behind a narrow bed covered in a patchwork quilt. A small piece of the rough wood wall had been carefully worked away, leaving a tiny space behind it. The necklace lay there, hidden inside a piece of soft cloth. The woman wept when I handed it to her.

Waving off her thanks, I went back to my stew. Working my way through the rest of it, although it had gone cold and congealed, I handed my bowl back to the woman when I was done and went to prepare Amlis' bed for the evening.

I slept in Amlis' room that night, curled up on a straw mattress provided by the innkeeper. My discomfort at sleeping in the same room with another person may not have gone unnoticed—I slept fitfully and turned often, although my spot beside the fire was comfortable enough.

I had no memory of ever sleeping in the presence of another, and with Amlis being the first one, my uneasiness only increased. What if I spoke in my sleep, as others had? The results of that revelation could be disastrous. Rodrik slept by the door inside Amlis' suite as well, plus, his men switched places regularly to stand guard outside the Prince's room.

Waking at my usual time (which was quite early), I made up the fire and tidied things quietly while Amlis and Rodrik slept. Amlis, I must confess, snored a little, but Rodrik was as silent as a cat.

Both men wanted breakfast in the room when they woke, so I trailed one of Rodrik's men and carried back a pot of hot tea and cups while the man carried the heavy tray. I set out plates of food and fresh bread, but Amlis sighed at the absence of eggs on his plate.

Tamblin had been correct about that, at least—the hens had stopped laying. And with no eggs, there would be no chicks, and likely the poultry living now would sicken and die. Even sleeping on the second floor of an inn, the soil of Fyris had groaned in my dreams.

The leftover bread, butter and a tiny bit of honey were offered to me after Amlis and Rodrik ate, so I nibbled as I packed Amlis' saddlebag while he shaved and dressed. As we were leaving, however, the innkeeper's wife approached me and handed over a small bag. Looking inside, I discovered that she'd gifted me with a small chunk of carefully wrapped cheese and a tiny loaf of bread.

She'd also given me something I greatly needed—a new smallbrush and a tiny pouch of the powder one could use to clean teeth. I nearly wept as I embraced her—none had ever thought to offer a gift to me before. Not like this, anyway. My old brush had few bristles left in it and I worried about finding a replacement. That one had been left behind by a minor noble's wife when I was ten, and I'd taken it before the maids thought to claim it.

"She found this for me," the woman touched the necklace at her throat at Rodrik's questioning glance. It was a pretty necklace, made of small gold links with a blue stone hanging down. I could only imagine that her daughter and her mother before her had treasured the thing.

"I knew when you called her name," the woman said immediately, when Amlis asked how she'd known of my talent. "Someone riding through mentioned a kitchen girl who could find things. It is only fitting that she serve a Prince, with that sort of gift."

"Here." Amlis tossed a gold piece to the woman, who caught it expertly, her eyes wide. "And do not mention Finder to any other, if you please."

"Of course not, my Prince." The woman curtsied deeply to Amlis and backed inside the inn quickly.

The next eleven days went much the same, except I was not called upon to find anything by innkeepers. The weather turned unpredictable, as it usually does in early spring, and at times, we rode through rain or snow. The worst was a brief spate of hail, which the horses did not like at all. I didn't like it either, as a few hailstones bounced off my head. At least the hailstones were small; larger ones might have rendered some of us unconscious.

"Finder, come." Amlis and Rodrik broke away from the road while the guards took a short break. The day was fine, with puffy white clouds floating overhead as I pointed Stepper in the direction Amlis was heading. "I want to show you the best view between Lironis and Vhrist," Amlis explained as I urged Stepper to follow Runner and Midnight.

Half a click away we found ourselves on a high cliff overlooking water that seemed to stretch forever. Early afternoon had arrived and sunlight glittered on the water brighter than thousands of tiny candles. Tall spires of rock stood not far out, while the force of the waves crashed into them, tossing up white spray while birds wheeled and called out around them. It was the most beautiful thing I'd ever seen and I drew in a breath, astonished by the sight of it.

"You like it, don't you?" Amlis chuckled beside me. I nodded in stunned wonder, staring as long as I could without blinking to imprint the vision in my memory. Even the air I breathed was filled with a golden glow as sunlight played across the Western Sea.

Too soon, Amlis reined Runner in and we turned back, all while my imagination ran wild, dreaming of what it might be like to wheel and fly about the spires on the western edge of Fyris.

Wolter was angry, his kitchen staff unruly and out of sorts. Three beatings had been parceled out already, and it wasn't even noon. The palace seemed to be growling with rage for some unknown reason and Wolter was hard-pressed not to walk out of the kitchen in disgust. Chen would come in soon and Wolter wondered for the fifth time if he could leave everything in his assistant's hands and retire to his quarters.

When the maid ran in sobbing, Wolter jerked his mind away from his thoughts and stared. The girl was covered in blood and babbling that two maids had just been beheaded by Yevil Orklis for making too much noise.

Perhaps two clicks from the inn where Amlis planned to spend the night the vision came. A bend in the road was ahead, heralding the beginnings of an evergreen forest. Even I knew the ground was rising—I'd seen the evidence on the cliff overlooking the spires. Moving Stepper up beside Midnight, I jerked frantically on Rodrik's sleeve.

"Finder?" Rodrik pulled Midnight back to see what I wanted. Desperately I gestured that we should avoid the bend ahead. He understood clearly enough, but Amlis had turned Runner around and now he was in the conversation as well.

"Finder, this is the only road in the area," Amlis sounded impatient. Our entire party had stopped by that time and I heard a bit of grumbling around us from men who were looking for supper and bed. Rodrik had said we were still four days out of Vhrist and tempers were running short.

"If we go around, we'll be going through a forest difficult to navigate on horseback, filled with low-hanging firs and scrub. I don't believe the men will like being slapped in the face by resinous limbs."

You, I pointed to Amlis, *danger,* I tugged my right ear.

"We'll take care of it," Rodrik soothed. "Men," he said, "it seems the Prince may be in danger ahead. Be prepared."

They were ignoring me. I wanted to shout at them. Scream my lungs out for the first time ever. They were taking the road, when an ambush lay ahead. Sullenly I reined Stepper in behind Rodrik and the Prince as Rodrik's twelve gathered in a tighter knot around us. None spoke as we trotted toward the blind turn in the road.

"Son," Tamblin sighed as he gazed through the window of his study, "Yevil is getting out of hand. I'd like for you to take care of it. Discreetly, of course."

"I was wondering when you'd ask me to kill the old goat," Timblor stood and raked fingers through thick, black hair. "Father, I don't know why you've kept him at your side all these turns—he hasn't done anything except kill servants and stir up trouble when he drinks. He killed two of my maids only this morning," Timblor added petulantly. "For giggling."

"Son, it is past time that we found a wife for you," Tamblin sighed and sat behind his desk. "No, I'm not saying that you can't dally with the maids," he held up a hand to stop Timblor's words. "Everyone does who has a mind to, and Liron knows we have few enough children." Tamblin's eyes darkened with his thoughts for a moment. "But Yevil performed a service for me once, and I haven't forgotten. Make his death quick, if you wouldn't mind."

"I'll make it quick, Father, but you must give me time to plan."

"Take time to lay plans, son. I'm not in a hurry."

They were hiding in the edge of the forest—the same one that Amlis had refused to ride through—and attacked us as Amlis stared accusingly at me. He thought the danger was fictitious as we traveled nearly the length of the bend and nothing had happened.

Now we were in a fight for our lives as swords were drawn and at least twenty men fought against our fourteen. Frightened out of my senses, I knew not what to do at first—until one of Rodrik's men died as he and the others fought off more attackers. Amlis wielded a sword with the others, leaving me at the center of the maelstrom as Stepper turned and turned in a circle, just as frightened as I.

Dump them! I shouted into twenty horses' minds and the attackers suddenly found themselves on rearing and bucking horses while Rodrik, Amlis and the remaining eleven backed up, confused by the battle between horse and rider taking place around them. Eventually, sixteen riders were unhorsed and on the ground, the remaining four or five galloping off on runaway mounts as riderless horses ran at their sides.

The clang of steel began again as Rodrik and his men dropped onto the ground and advanced on the unhorsed attackers. My eyes kept straying to the dead man on the ground even as others fell, both Rodrik's and their opponents. Still outnumbered, things weren't going well against what appeared to be well-trained and seasoned fighters. That's why I called our horses back and reluctantly ordered them to fight as well.

There was no time for my tears as the first horse fell, screaming in agony as the blade pierced his heart, but Rodrik took down the man as he pulled his blade from the horse's chest. Others, especially Midnight, were having better luck, but the sight of spilled brain after a vicious kick roiled my stomach.

Then it came—what I feared most. The hand drawn back, the dagger flying straight toward Amlis' back as he fought another man. Flinging myself from Stepper's saddle, I knocked Amlis away, only to receive the blow myself. The dagger lodged in my right shoulder and was buried nearly to the hilt. The rest of the battle I failed to see, as I was unconscious on the ground shortly after.

"Child, hold still, we have to get the dagger out." A strange voice woke me, along with excruciating pain in my shoulder. I'd dived in facing the knife-wielder and now the black handle of the dagger protruded from my shoulder, nearly forcing me to heave at the sight of it.

The one who'd spoken had thin, white hair hanging nearly to his shoulder, a lined face and dark-brown eyes. His forehead creased as he stared at me and at the dagger, creating even more lines on an already much-lined face.

"I'll hold her," Rodrik's voice spoke. I lay on a bed, likely at the inn Amlis had been so eager to reach earlier, where a fire was going in the fireplace across the small room. Rodrik came into view, staring down at me with lines also creasing his forehead. Truly, I didn't want anyone touching the dagger. My shoulder was on fire already, and pulling it out seemed a terrible idea.

"We'll have to sit her up," the old man said. That also seemed a terrible idea. It was; I wanted to weep when Rodrik lifted me up on the bed. Clenching my teeth to hold back the scream, I closed my eyes against the pain.

"Baby, don't look," Rodrik said softly against my ear as one arm clamped around my body, holding me still while he used his other hand to cover my eyes. The old man gripped the dagger handle and pulled it out. Darkness thankfully came as the dagger left my body.

"Six men we lost, because I was too stupid to listen."

"We might have lost all of them, and you as well," Rodrik pointed out softly, pouring more ale into Amlis' cup. The two of them were in Amlis' room at the inn, Amlis sitting before the fireplace, Rodrik standing restlessly at his side. "At least we had our guard up."

"I should have been thinking with my head instead of my stomach," Amlis growled. "Scouts should have been sent out before we went anywhere. Yet we blithely walked into that trap, thinking that we were in my mother's lands and safe from this sort of treachery."

"I've no doubt where they came from, though they carried no sigil," Amlis sipped his ale. He was well on his way to drunkenness and didn't seem to care. "We should have paid more attention and asked that woman at the inn days ago—the one who said a rider told her of Finder's gift."

"Makes sense, but I let it pass me as well. We have paid, cousin. Those were good men around us."

"Will Finder be all right?" Amlis turned his gaze to Rodrik.

"The physician says she'll likely heal. I sent two constables to my father to report the ambush. We'll have some of his men here before daybreak. Others I sent out to bring in the dead. We'll examine them more closely once we've had some rest. These were no outlaws, cousin. These were well-trained and not hungry."

"If I fail to listen to Finder again, I want you to beat me," Amlis drained his cup.

"It's willow bark, for the pain," the old man was back and pouring something down my throat. The brew was beyond bitter and I wanted to spit it out, but that would likely be unwise, since he appeared to have plenty of it on hand. Truthfully, I wanted to curl in a ball and moan, I felt so bad.

"There, all done," the man soothed. Belatedly, I realized he was a physician and likely a good one. "Now, we'll clean the wound and replace the bandage. When you travel tomorrow, young woman, we'll tie the right arm to your side—I don't want any movement for several days, do you hear me?" At least he wasn't shouting as Etlund had done, and patted my good hand when he was finished.

"How's the girl?" Rodrik wandered in and looked me over. I wanted to squirm uncomfortably under such close scrutiny.

"I hear we might have lost all in your party if those horses hadn't spooked," the physician stepped toward the door, turning to look at Rodrik before he left.

"That is true, and we still have no reason for that, as ours remained calm. My father is on his way with a cohort of men to help unravel this mystery. Do you recall any strangers in town?" Rodrik asked.

"None, and I've already asked at the other inn. They say the same. No strangers, so these came from the south. I'd stake my reputation on that."

"Thank you, Irvin. Astute as always. Will the girl be able to travel tomorrow?"

"If you'd bother to listen to me, I'd say no. But you never listen, so be careful and don't push too hard. I realize young Amlis wishes to get home where his own men-at-arms wait, but the girl doesn't need to lift and carry for a moon-turn."

"I understand that." Rodrik sighed and turned back to me, raking me with dark-blue eyes. "Rest as much as you can, Finder," he instructed. "We leave tomorrow morning."

"Doing my job for me, now?" Irvin grumbled as he and Rodrik left the room together.

CHAPTER 5

"From the south, there's no doubt. Likely Yevil's principality." Rath examined clothing, tack and even two horses that the local constabulary had managed to capture. Unfortunately, they hadn't found the five men who'd escaped on fleeing mounts, so Rath sent some of his guards out to track them.

The horses told the tale better than clothing or other items—they were bred for speed and endurance in the south. Runner was of that stock, although not a purebred.

"No surprise," Amlis growled. "Yevil would kill me on his own, even without Father's goading."

"He is a dangerous man; Tamblin has no idea how much evil stands at his elbow every day," Rath sighed. "You shouldn't have survived this attack—weren't meant to survive it," Rath eyed Amlis and Rodrik. Rodrik turned away from his father's bald statement. Neither he nor the Prince spoke of Finder's warning. "Six good men lost, too," Rath's voice accused. Rodrik stalked out of Amlis' room.

"Any reply to the message?" Amlis asked quietly after Rodrik's abrupt departure.

"Not yet. But we may not get one."

"You think they'll ignore it completely?"

"It's possible," Rath lifted the wine bottle and poured a cup, sipping from it thoughtfully. "Who knows what might have come after the slaughter? If Tamblin received any message, he never shared it with anyone and truly, not many know who was in Tandelis' chamber that day. Only a few of us are left—the others are dead as you well know."

"Yes. Mother buys many lives with her silence," Amlis agreed, flopping onto the chair before the fire. "But Father still seeks to take mine anyway."

"Your father, boy, is a fool, as is your brother for following at his heel. What can he hope to gain with your death? I cannot see it." Rath drained his wine cup and set it down with a thump. "Your mother won't say it, but you can bet that whatever happened that day, Yevil's arms were bloodied to the armpits with it. They don't die easy, Amlis. At least that's what I've always heard."

"The old physician in Lironis says that Finder may be Lady Rinda's child, and that Father sent her to the kitchens out of spite."

"The child was in Tandelis' chamber?" Rath stared at Amlis.

"Along with a second child, but the physician didn't know who that one belonged to. Likely dead with the others, too."

"Didn't know, or didn't say? Damn, I wish your mother would speak. Anyone else who might know who had babes at the time is dead. Except for that old sawbones. What made you go and ask him?"

"I didn't. Rodrik did."

"So, your page may be royal born, but no way to get Tamblin to admit it. Doesn't matter, the girl is mute and illiterate. No chance of finding a decent match for her, now. She has nothing to offer any prospects."

Except her gifts, which are astounding, Amlis silently added. He wasn't about to inform Rath of Vhoorth that had he listened to Finder, things might have turned out quite differently on the road. And, if she hadn't leapt in front of an assassin's dagger, he might not have lived to regret his actions. "You'll have to give her up, you know, when you wed Mirisa," Rath added thoughtfully.

"I know. I was hoping Mother would keep her." Amlis heaved a regretful sigh.

"If I know Omina, and I do, she'll take the girl in. If for some odd reason she won't have her, I think I can find a place with my cook or housekeeper. The girl's not hard to look at and can't carry tales, after all."

Rath poured another cup of wine while Amlis carefully hid his distaste. Amlis was more than aware of Rodrik's hesitation around his father, and he knew the reasons. Rath's wandering eye upset Rodrik's mother regularly and Rodrik despised his father for it. He'd convince his mother somehow, to take Finder in. After all, the girl was more than useful, and she'd saved his life twice.

Rath of Vhoorth saw us off the following morning, after I'd eaten a little and had my right arm tied securely to my side. Irvin, who'd frowned the whole time he'd explained to Rodrik how to change my dressings if he were forced while on the road, provided extra strips of linen.

The physician also handed over a skin filled with willow bark tea and told Rodrik how much to give and when. Rodrik nodded as if bored by the whole thing, I was tossed in Stepper's saddle and off we rode. That day is a hazy memory, now, as I went in and out of consciousness and Stepper moved drunkenly at times, weaving to keep me in the saddle. The pain of it was terrible and I thought many times of begging Amlis to leave me at the side of the road so I might sleep.

Fever came to call, too, and I blinked away double and triple visions repeatedly. I could not recall later exactly how or when, but when we arrived at the inn that evening, I was wrapped in Rodrik's cloak and sitting before him on Midnight's back, with Stepper tied to the saddle.

Perhaps in another life I might have cared for Rodrik—he was still young as men in Fyris went, and handsome enough, but he'd beaten me quite hard, and he had a wife. I had no desire to become a gossiping maid, waiting until a man found the time to dally with me behind another woman's back.

As a lowly servant, I had no hope of ever finding a man of Rodrik's status—one who might think me more than a page or kitchen drudge who was subject to his every whim. No, I would remain alone, since the options available to me weren't really options at all.

After Rodrik handed me off to one of his men, I was carried into the smallest inn we'd found as yet and put to bed first, with instructions left with a kitchen girl to find suitable food while the local physician was sought. The healer was a woman and fairly young; she frowned at my wound as she pulled linen bandages away that were crusted with blood.

"Men," she growled as she cleaned the wound and gave me warmed willow bark tea to drink. By that time, I was grateful for the relief the bitter brew offered and drank it willingly. "They should have tended to this." I was bandaged again while the woman, who had long, reddish-brown hair and eyes nearly to match, railed against the ignorance of males in general. This was one who might even give the Prince a tongue-lashing, as dangerous and ill-advised as that could prove to be. Amlis might let a slight pass, but Rodrik certainly wouldn't.

The man who'd lifted me down the night before carried me on his horse the following morning. Rodrik must have chosen him—Deeds was his name and he was the eldest of Rodrik's men. He whispered to me when we started out that his youngest daughter was my age. He felt safe to me and I admit I slept most of the time, swaying with him in his saddle. The final two days of our journey to Vhrist went the same, although my fever came down with regular doses of willow bark tea and I was handed over to Queen Omina's personal physician the minute we rode into Castle Vhrist's courtyard.

"This is no ordinary half-breed, as your son and Rodrik believe," the physician wiped his hands after washing them. Omina had come to check on the girl—Amlis had given her the truth of Finder—although he'd warned Rodrik's men to keep her information hidden. She'd saved their lives, so they all agreed readily enough.

"What makes you say that?" Omina, her hair still thick and brown, although strands of gray were finding their way into the wealth that hung nearly to her waist, gazed at Farin Wold, the palace physician. Farin was of an age with the Queen, and they'd known one another growing up. He was going bald, however, his blue eyes faded from long service as a healer.

"The nubs are growing."

"Mother, I've only seen one before, and he was dead. It only appeared to be raised lumps of skin on his back," Amlis paced beside the fire. "What do you think this means?"

"I do not know," Omina sighed, accepting a cup of tea from Rodrik, who stood by, listening to the conversation between his aunt and cousin. "It could be that the poisoning has affected her, as it has so many others. Farin delivered a child just the other day—stillborn, thankfully—that had three eyes and three legs."

"That could explain it," Amlis nodded at his mother's logic.

"Still, I do not wish to touch them, and Farin flatly refuses to cut them away. After all, we may be able to use her to bargain with, if all else fails."

"Mother, you can't mean that," Amlis jerked his head to stare at Omina. Fierce determination glittered in her blue eyes, the same color that Amlis had inherited and the King mistrusted.

"Why not? Fyris is dying, and your father has this fool idea that he can just walk into the barbarian's homes and take what he wants. Do you think for a moment that we have enough ships, or can build enough ships, to carry the troops necessary to destroy them? I've read the histories—they far outnumber us, and the information we have is more than a thousand turns old. Who knows what they are now, or how they've progressed? We are the ones who have failed to evolve, I think. Admit it—we haven't changed much in all that time. We were driving carts and riding horse, and we still are."

"I hold hope that our message will have a reply soon," Amlis said.

"My son, I was there. My brother may hold hope, but I have none at all. We'll watch the girl, and use her if we must."

"Blackmail. That's what Mother suggests. And we'll be sentencing Finder to death, there's no doubt. The moment we turn her over and they learn she's only a half-breed, they'll kill her and we'll never convince them to help." Amlis paced inside his private suite of rooms while Rodrik watched, sipping a cup of wine.

"Face it, cousin," Rodrik sighed, raising his booted feet to a footstool set before the fire, "the girl has no prospects. Yes, I know she's been more than useful, but you have to think of Fyris, first. If we can get what we want before turning her over, then the deed will be done already and they can't take it back. We will sacrifice one, to save all of Fyris."

"But we'll still be faced with Father, Yevil and the madness that consumes both of them," Amlis muttered angrily.

"We will worry about that when the time comes. Fyris first, madness later."

"Don't forget to add mercenaries and attempted assassinations," Amlis said, smiling tightly. "I suppose Yevil is killing survivors. What do you think?"

"Hacking them apart is more like it," Rodrik observed grimly.

"Shall I wed Mirisa early? We could use Firith's aid, should Father decide to march against us."

"Consult with your mother and my father first. We don't want the King's anger earlier than anticipated," Rodrik hid a smile in his wine cup. "Of course, Beatris will arrive tomorrow or the day after. My lady wife might not mind planning a wedding."

"Do you think Northern Fyris will stand against the South and my father, if it comes down to that?" Amlis became serious, suddenly.

"I doubt it. Firith is the only principality we might count on completely, and only because old Mortin wants his daughter on the throne. I hear from Father that Mortin had a fit when Tamblin offered you instead of your brother."

"There's that," Amlis agreed. "Hand over that bottle. I want a drink before you finish it off."

"You will not be Amlis' page here," I was informed by Omina herself. "We have someone here who performed in that capacity before the Prince left for Lironis. You will heal, first, then we will find a position for you among my servants." If Omina had struck me, it might have been a softer blow. I blinked at her, silent as usual and worked not to betray my feelings in the matter.

The Queen wore her age well, and appeared to be at least ten turns younger than she was. I was sitting up in bed, having breakfast when the Queen walked into the tiny room they'd given me, making her announcement without realizing it would kill what little appetite I had. No doubt, I'd end up in her kitchens, just as I had at the palace in Lironis.

"That might have waited, Omina." The physician was back and watching as I carefully set my breakfast aside—there was a table situated beside my narrow bed that held my tray. I wished for the authority to rise and walk out on both of them, but I didn't.

"When would be a good time, Farin?" The Queen swept out, a bit of color in her cheeks. Likely, she would make me pay for that bit of embarrassment, although I'd truly had no hand in it. That seemed to be the way of things; punish the one who could not strike back. I'd seen it often enough at the King's palace.

"You should eat as much as you can," Farin eyed the tray. It mattered not; I was done with it and turned my head away at his words.

"Servants are generally not mistreated here," Farin attempted to make the Queen's statement easier to accept. Perhaps he believed what he'd spoken, but I'd watched silently all my years. Even the best masters mistreated their servants, now and then.

Vhrist, perhaps, was a more interesting city than Lironis, but doubtless it was because the high hills were nearby, and beyond those, the Northern Sea. After three days, Farin allowed me out of my bed and I slipped up many palace steps unnoticed until I came to the upper turret.

Accessed through a door and open to the elements, the turret was built of stones laid in a large circle, with pillars and arches holding up an elegantly domed roof. An inlaid tile design was on the floor, cleverly crafted to depict interlocking crowns. I had no idea what that meant, as I'd never seen a crown—the few times I'd seen Tamblin, he hadn't worn his—it was saved for High Court and special occasions. He'd worn a simple circlet in the Council meeting and at the dinner where I'd been beaten.

The tile depicted two crowns, one smaller than the other, so I had no idea which might belong to the Fyrisian King. One crown's design—the larger one—looked to have been scrubbed away, leaving the image hazy and difficult to make out. Perhaps the smaller one was the Queen's crown, and Omina might have worn it when she was in Lironis. Servants had not cleaned in a while and rain and dust had left swaths of soil across the tiled surface.

I leaned against the balustrade outside the turret and watched the waters to the north of the city. Fishing boats came in with their catch and I imagined that fish were being purchased as soon as the boats docked at the piers. These were no small vessels, after all, but larger ones, carrying up to twenty men who hauled in fish and crustaceans in heavy nets.

Crustaceans such as the Northern Sea could produce were not available in Lironis—there was no way to preserve them on the long journey to the south. Wolter often moaned about how good some of it was and wished he had it to prepare in his kitchen. It mattered not to me; I would not eat fish as well as meat.

"I wondered where you were." Amlis had found me. Why had he bothered to look? I dipped my head respectfully to him and turned back to watching fishing boats in the bay as well as traffic crossing an arched bridge to come into the city.

No wall stood around Vhrist's palace, and I wondered at that. The one surrounding the palace in Lironis was nearly as old as I, according to Wolter. He and Chen complained about it once, claiming that when men their age were younger, they'd run in and out of the Queen's garden, playing hiding games. Now, that was no longer possible—the wall was in the way and guards prevented the unauthorized from coming through.

"My mother plans to put you in the kitchens when you're better," Amlis stood at the balustrade within arm's reach. Why was he telling me this? It was something I'd already guessed. "She'll pay you a little. That's why I want you to take this." He produced the gray leather pouch of coins again. "It was not meant as an offense, or to belittle what you'd done for me, or to mitigate my or Rodrik's actions later. I hoped it would soften the blows." He held the pouch toward me. I turned my face away and kept watching the boats.

"Finder, you have so little. Your comb has half the teeth missing. If the innkeeper's wife had not offered you a new tooth cleaner, you wouldn't have that, either. Mother will have her dressmaker come soon and sew a blouse and skirt or two for you to wear. Use the money to buy something better. I hope you'll forgive me and Rodrik for not informing her and Rodrik's father that you saved our lives on the road."

Amlis set the money pouch on the balustrade at my elbow and turned to leave. "Take the money. Please." And then he was gone. I slipped the pouch into my pocket, but I had no immediate plans to spend it. I'd done without, most of my life. What did it matter, anyway?

On the sixth day, Rodrik's wife Beatris arrived, and Mirisa of Firith traveled with her. Beatris, dark-haired and blue-eyed, was pretty and a good match for Rodrik, I think, but there was a sadness in her. Using my gift, I determined that she'd lost a child two turns earlier and it grieved her still.

Rodrik seemed quite solicitous around her and I watched them with a bit of envy. Mirisa was Amlis' intended, I learned that soon enough, and she was quite high-handed with Omina's servants, ordering them about and demanding even the slightest thing be brought or carried or cleaned away.

She had no desire to do anything for herself, and I despised her immediately. She was pretty enough, with pale hair and brown eyes, but thought herself even more beautiful, and Amlis offered her as much attention as she could wish for. I kept away from Beatris and Mirisa as much as possible, as I was still recovering. My tiny room was exchanged for another in the servants' quarters, where I was fortunate enough to get another corner of a storage room. It seems that none of the other servants wished to have a mute as a roommate, so Omina found alternative quarters for me.

No books were stored in forgotten crates, however, and I missed that greatly. Therefore, it was luck that I found a few things inside what was considered Tamblin's old study—he'd used it on the few occasions he was in residence in Vhrist. Judging by the state of the room, I decided that he would no longer require it, so I slipped inside at times when no one was watching, to pull books from dusty shelves and read.

Just as those in Lironis, these books had pages and pages ripped away, but there were a few things that I hadn't read before, concerning the building of ships, netting of fish and trade between Vhrist, Vhoorth and their surrounding principalities. Yes, it might have been boring at times, but at least I had something to read. A few illustrations were scattered throughout some of the books, and it was fortunate that I was looking at those drawings one day when Omina caught me, frightening me terribly.

"No, you may look at the pictures if you like," she held out a hand. "Liron knows nobody else is going to look at any of this." She held hands on hips as she stared at the dusty shelves surrounding the room. I'd cleaned the dust off the desk; at least it was clean enough as I pored over old books.

"If you feel well enough, go ahead and clean this room and I'll allow you to look at any of the books you like. I warn you, not all of them are illustrated." She walked out then, while I followed her with my eyes. Even then, she thought me too stupid to know anything and nearly too stupid to understand what she'd said.

Two weeks later, I was pronounced fit for duty and the seamstress came to measure for blouses and skirts. Omina was present while the middle-aged woman worked, and informed her to allow the blouses to billow in the back to make room for what she called *nubs*. "Farin says they're growing, and he wants to see what happens if we leave them alone," Omina said.

Farin called them nubs instead of bone spurs? That information came with a bit of shock. I was grateful they wouldn't be cut away—that had always been painful and I didn't mind if my back wasn't perfect, although it would add to everyone's opinion that I was deformed.

What I didn't appreciate were the skirts—it was awkward and uncomfortable to work in the long things. I'd worn trousers as long as I could remember, all of them handed down from kitchen boys. Therefore, after my first week in the kitchens, when I was given a day off, I walked right out of Omina's palace and went into Vhrist, unerringly heading for the street that held tailors' shops. I knew where they were—I could find things, after all.

"You're the girl who came back with the Prince." Obviously tailors gossip just as much as chambermaids and kitchen help. "The one who can't speak. I'm Sofi," the woman held out a hand to me and squeezed my fingers lightly before letting go.

Sofi was still young—perhaps less than thirty, with soft brown hair braided down her back and brown eyes that offered a kind smile. A pincushion was tied to a wrist with ribbon and several pins stuck out of it at every angle.

"What can I do for you?" she asked. I pointed to a pair of trousers that were hanging in the back of her shop. They were of canvas, the fabric used to make trousers for the sailors in the harbor. The same material was used for ship's sails, except this version was dyed a deep black. Omina insisted that the maids wear black skirts, so I was having black trousers made instead.

"You want trousers?" her eyes raked my thin body, staring at the blue trousers I wore from the uniforms Nirok had sewn for me. They were in Amlis' colors, and Omina didn't want me to wear them.

Mirisa, too, glared every time she saw me if I wore Amlis' colors. Jealousy ate at her every moment, and I'd seen her beat a maid only that morning for walking out of Amlis' chamber after cleaning it.

Nodding at Sofi's question, I let her know that I wanted three pairs sewn and then tapped the purse Amlis had given me, silently inquiring about the price.

"Two silvers gets three pairs of trousers," Sofi said right away, and I knew that she wasn't attempting to cheat me—that was her normal price. I nodded and drew out the required coins.

"Auntie, I had a bad dream." A child walked into the room, rubbing her eyes. Sickly, she was, and very thin. Her hair, such as it was, was pale-brown and quite sparse. She was six, my ability informed me. *And dying.* Children and the elderly had little natural defense against whatever poisoned Fyris.

"Yissy, go into the kitchen. I will come soon and give you tea while I cook." Sofi attempted to shoo the girl away, worried that the child would frighten away clientele. I waved a hand in dismissal.

Come, I whispered into Yissy's mind while I beckoned to the weak and sickly child. *We will keep a secret, you and I.*

"You are not obligated," Sofi began, but that was before Yissy cuddled into my arms as if she'd known me forever. What I did then I had only done twice before, and it was for animals.

Whatever it is, it feels as if I touch my spirit to theirs, healing the sickness pervading their body. Yissy was the first child brought within my reach that suffered from what sickened the land itself. I was determined to right what I could. I also sent as much love and caring as I could muster, but never having had that commodity for my own, I had no idea how much it might be.

"I will have the sewing done in six days," Sofi gently pulled Yissy away from my arms, staring at me as she did so. I shrugged and counted off eight days on my fingers—that would be when I would have time to come again. Sofi nodded at my wordless explanation. "Would you like tea?" she asked, pointing toward the back of her shop.

I shook my head, desiring to use what time I had left to explore Vhrist. Sofi held Yissy against her skirts as both watched me walk through the shop door and into the cobbled street beyond.

Many servants were allowed the eighth day of each week off, and used it to their advantage, making purchases for themselves and meeting friends and family as often as not. Most businesses were open on the eighth day, just for the custom of those not graced by noble birth.

As an orphan in the King's kitchens in Lironis, I'd never been allotted a day off before. I wanted to see ships firsthand and not from a distance, and look upon the birds that wheeled and called about the harbor. It smelled worse than I imagined it would when I arrived.

CHAPTER 6

Seabirds have a distinctive call that pierces the salt air, and I could hear them long before arriving at the harbor. The harbor itself smelled of fish guts and sour salt water. Perhaps it was fresher upon the open sea, but I might never discover that for myself, tied as I was to Lady Omina and her palace kitchen.

The water around the heavy, wooden ships was dirty, with bits of debris floating about. Sailors sat on decks, their feet dangling over the tall sides as they drank, laughed or played a musical instrument. Not all of them were talented. The birds fought over any edible bit that had the misfortune of falling overboard or had been tossed into the water as garbage.

Several sailors called out to me, and a few of those were quite vulgar in their language. Not that I hadn't heard such things before; I just hadn't had them shouted in my direction. Walking away from those as quickly as I could, I made my way upward toward the city and the palace. It had taken some time to get down to the harbor, and the climb back would take up even more of my day.

Exhaustion dogged my heels by the time I made my way into the side door that led into the kitchens. Gossip was as thick as the scent of cooking roast from the moment I entered. Mirisa had taken a poker to another chambermaid (presumably for staring too long at Amlis), and injured the girl, breaking a shoulder and a wrist. Now, Lady Omina was short a chambermaid; the injured girl had gone home to her mother after healer Farin had seen to the broken bones.

If Omina and Amlis could not see past the pretty façade that was Mirisa, then I pitied them both. Mirisa would not hold her blows back from anyone, once she had Amlis' vows and a ring on her finger. Perhaps Rodrik would step in and do Amlis' fighting for him, where Mirisa was concerned; the Prince wouldn't lift a finger to prevent her from abusing the staff.

The gossip was ignored after a while as I settled into a corner by the fireplace to eat a bowl of beans—this cook had little regard for one who refused meat. Chunks of carrot had been tossed in as an afterthought and that made me think of Runner and his love of the orange vegetable.

Should I have gone straight to my small space in the storage room? It would only have delayed the inevitable. "Ah, Finder, there you are." Lady Omina stood over me as I looked up at the sound of her voice. "Beginning tomorrow," the Lady had hands on hips as she tapped a shoe impatiently, "you will join the chambermaids and help clean the bedchambers. I have had no luck in finding another girl on such short notice."

Whirling, she walked away from me as I swallowed the bite in my mouth with difficulty, half-chewed as it was. She hadn't said it was temporary. Lady Omina hadn't indicated that she would still be looking for another girl so I might keep my somewhat safe place in the kitchen. No. That was not to be. This was her revenge against me for Farin's words. I would be under Mirisa's scrutiny if I came anywhere near Amlis or his bedchamber.

Sleep evaded me that night and I was wary as a stray cat as I went through my assignments the following day. The other four chambermaids, all having seniority, elected me to clean Amlis' chamber. Therefore, I watched carefully for Mirisa, waiting until she and Beatris walked out with Rodrik for some air before ghosting into Amlis' chamber to clean it and make up his bed. I did not expect to find Amlis at his desk inside his study, and he startled me when I stepped inside it to dust.

"She's out." He dipped a quill into an inkbottle and scratched across parchment. As I already knew that, I didn't even bother to nod, setting about dusting his bookshelves as quickly as possible. I also banked the fire in his fireplace, set out fresh towels beside his pitcher and basin and made up his bed.

He had fresh sheets already and Omina only wanted those changed weekly, so I was spared from spending extra time in his suite. I think his chamber was cleaned in record time and I was out and down the hall in another room before Mirisa returned to the family wing.

Her chamber was between Omina's and Beatris', on the opposite end of a long hall from that of Amlis and Rodrik. At least Beatris cared not that I also cleaned Rodrik's chamber, and he did not appear while I worked, which was much appreciated.

My first week went exactly the same, as I put off Amlis' chamber until Mirisa was absent, then cleaned it as quickly as I could, making sure that all was done and to his and his mother's satisfaction before moving on to Rodrik's and healer Farin's. The trip to Sofi's tailor shop came on my off day and I nearly skipped out of the palace, I was so glad to get away from the worry and burden of it. Sofi had my three pairs of trousers waiting, but there was something else waiting as well.

"You did so well by Yissy," Sofi tossed out a hand as I stared at the three who waited inside her shop. A pregnant woman, a sailor and an elderly man sat on chairs Sofi had scrounged from somewhere. Casting an angry and hurt look at Sofi, who'd obviously broadcast what she thought she knew, I went to the pregnant woman first.

Yissy, looking much better than she had, shuffled in and watched in a curious way as I put my hands on the woman's belly and then on her chest. Her breathing was more shallow than normal and the babe was heavy in her belly. "She has headaches and vomits," Sofi offered helpfully.

"I have pain here, too." The woman, dark haired and brown-eyed, begged me to relieve her suffering as she pointed to her right side, below the ribs. Sighing softly, I set out to do what I could.

The sailor came next—his complaint was, in his words, a cracked ankle. He did not explain what it was exactly that he'd done to crack his ankle, but I repaired it as best I could before moving on to the elderly man. His troubles all dealt with old age, and he knew that. He merely wanted a bit of relief from joint pain, so I gave him that. All three left Sofi's shop easier than they'd arrived, the pregnant woman wiping away tears of relief as she walked away.

After they'd gone, I made a motion to Sofi, telling her no more before snatching up my new trousers and walking out of her shop. I took no walks for pleasure that day, going straight back to the palace carrying my new clothing with me. None of the three had thought to thank me, but they'd thanked Sofi profusely. Had I the propensity, I imagined I'd be muttering angrily as I walked toward the servants' entrance to the palace.

"Today, we dust under beds," the eldest chambermaid announced as I and the other three arrived for our morning chores the following day. My heart thumped heavily in my chest—dusting beneath the beds meant extra time spent within the chambers and increased the risk that Mirisa would catch me inside Amlis' bedroom.

The floor would have to be carefully cleaned afterward, as the dust permeated the stone floor and the rugs scattered throughout the chambers. Diligently I watched, waiting for Mirisa to vacate the family wing. Instead, she chatted with Beatris while they sewed in the receiving room halfway between the men's and women's quarters.

A kitchen servant brought a mid-morning tidbit for both ladies as they tittered and gossiped. I cleaned Rodrik's chamber. I cleaned Farin's after that, and still Mirisa sat and did little while she and Beatris had luncheon together. Two more cleaned chambers later, there was no help for it; Amlis' was the only one left that I hadn't cleaned. Keeping my head down, I walked inside, pulled my rags from the bucket I carried and dived beneath Amlis' bed.

"If she carried a knife or wielded a blade, I'd think her as bad as Yevil," Rodrik huffed as he and Amlis sparred outside the guards' barracks.

"She is our link to Firith's cohorts," Amlis snapped, thwacking his blade against Rodrik's. "I give her as much attention as I possibly can, and still she glares at the maids. They're afraid to come into the same room as it is, and I have certainly stopped looking in their direction, but that does not stay Mirisa's anger. Would that we could protect ourselves without her father's men."

"Parry with the flat of your blade, my Prince," Rodrik instructed as they backed away for a breather.

"I'm just so damned frustrated. What is my life to be like, Rodrik, when I'm married to the sow?"

"Brin, this hinges upon you," Timblor handed the dagger to his personal servant. Brin, his square face expressionless, nodded his understanding and hid the dagger inside his new, red tunic. The tailor had designed the padded jacket with pockets inside at Timblor's request, after Timblor explained that he could not carry everything he required at all times.

Servants were not allowed to carry weapons, and certainly not within the royal palace. Only the guard could carry swords or knives, and never in the presence of the King or his sons. Yevil was the only exception, as he often guarded the King.

Nirok the tailor, thinking Brin might carry flasks of wine or eating utensils for the Prince, sewed the required pockets without question. He never imagined his clothing might be used to conceal a dagger.

That morning, sunlight shone through the clear panes of glass lining a wall of Timblor's study. Like Tamblin's, there were no books, but several ancient swords, shields and daggers graced the walls, amid a tapestry or two depicting centuries-old battles.

Timblor had laid his plan as carefully as he could, but it needed an accomplice—a trusted guard or personal servant. Timblor suspected all the guards of being under Yevil's thumb, so Brin was the final and logical choice.

"I will do as you ask, my Prince," Brin dipped his head as was required.

"Good. Ready?"

Brin nodded silently.

"Good."

⁂

The old physician was dead. Wolter had gone to his quarters in the minor nobles' wing and watched as servants carried the body out. For ninety turns, the physician had tended to the illnesses and broken bones of the palace, and now there was no apprentice to take his place.

The last one died after doing an apprenticeship in the countryside surrounding Lironis. He'd returned to the palace with a wheezing cough that had turned into something more dire, and the physician could not cure it. The man had died before the age of thirty, and the physician at that point had been too old and too blind to take on another trainee.

"What will we do now?" Chen appeared at Wolter's elbow, whispering the question that servant and noble alike, all of them lined up outside the physician's chambers, were asking.

"Without," Wolter snapped and stalked away, striding toward the kitchens and the midday meal his assistants were preparing.

⁂

"Put these away," one of many laundresses for the palace demanded as I, covered in dust, crawled from beneath Amlis' bed. A pile of freshly washed and ironed shirts, trousers and underclothing was thumped onto Amlis' bed by her and a younger girl working as an apprentice in the palace laundry.

The woman, haughty enough for one of her station, huffed away, as anxious to leave the Prince's chamber as I was. Nervously glancing about, her apprentice almost stepped on her mistress' heels in her haste to follow. Now there was another task to accomplish; one that had to be done before I made up the Prince's bed.

Wiping the dust away from my blouse as carefully as I could first, I lifted the pile of shirts and carried it to the Prince's armoire, meticulously stacking the clothing inside on the proper shelves. Amlis' page in Vhrist was quite particular in how everything was done and I knew, although many did not, that he did not prefer women.

Truly, Mirisa should expend some of her jealous rages upon Heeth instead of frightened maids. After all, Heeth was with the Prince more often than most others. It was while I was placing the Prince's underclothes in a designated drawer that Mirisa came, and the beating she delivered I will never forget.

"Amlis, say nothing. We need Firith; that is the only reason I agreed to the match." Omina insisted, glaring at her second-born as they stood inside Omina's private study. The rectangular room was lined with shelves of books, and hidden here and there between other, more innocuous titles, lay complete tomes of history, geography and royal lineages.

Rodrik leaned against an edge of the fireplace, built of massive stones quarried from the hills to the east of Vhrist, watching as Amlis complained to his mother for the first time of his father's selection for his wife.

"She was putting away laundry, for Liron's sake, and Mirisa beats her for touching my underclothes?" Amlis shouted. "Heeth was with me in the courtyard, Mother, and the laundry was left on the bed. What else was she supposed to do?"

"She's a servant. You forget your place," Omina hissed. "What does it matter if a girl gets beaten, Amlis? Answer me that, when Firith's swords hang in the balance."

"Then I suggest you find a boy from somewhere, to clean Amlis' chamber from now on." Farin hadn't joined the conversation until then, settling for watching and listening as Rodrik had.

"But we only have the boys that clean fireplaces," Omina tossed up her hands. "Are you suggesting I put one of them to cleaning Amlis' chambers?"

"That's exactly what I'm suggesting." Farin was angry for the first time in a very long time. "Omina, I tire of treating wounds created by Mortin's bitch whelp. It is difficult enough to treat those that arise from accidents."

"How bad is she?" Rodrik thought to ask.

"A break in the forearm. A knee twisted as she attempted to get away from Mirisa and Mirisa grabbed an ankle to pull the girl back. Many bruises, some broken open and bleeding. I believe we should not leave pokers within easy reach of Mirisa of Firith. I wonder that Mortin has any servants left at all," Farin replied.

"Did you say anything to her?" Omina turned back to Amlis. "To Mirisa, I mean."

"Mother, I came straight to you, as you are still Queen of Fyris, whether you use the title or not. I am a Prince and your son. You rule here at the moment."

"What do you mean by that?" Omina snapped.

"He means exactly what you know already, Omina. Once he takes Mirisa to wife, you will be shunted aside and Amlis and Mirisa will rule here. Your rule lies in Lironis, not Vhrist." Farin walked to a nearby table and poured a glass of wine.

He it was who'd sent for Amlis while treating Finder's wounds. Rodrik and Amlis had come at a near-run, and they'd watched as Farin cleaned blood around a head wound, delivered as a glancing blow by Mirisa who'd been aiming for a shoulder. The entire time Farin worked, Finder had shivered beneath his touch and not a whisper, sigh or whimper had passed her lips.

"How long before the girl is able to resume her duties?" Omina handed Farin a hard look.

"With a broken arm, eight weeks, at least. Likely ten. And that leaves you shorthanded again, Omina. Gossip is spreading and none are willing to work in the palace, no matter the wage offered. You should have left the girl in the kitchen. Mirisa has had nothing but contempt for Finder since she learned the girl acted as Amlis' page. She was merely waiting for the opportunity to strike. Imagine how Vhrist will be, when Mirisa becomes its Lady."

"Amlis will control her then," Omina sniffed.

"Mother, I couldn't control her today. She waited until I was out to do her worst, and there was only Beatris and the other servants, all of whom are less than she. None could stop her. Beatris could only send another girl running for Farin, who came and witnessed the end of the tirade, when Mirisa wore herself out and dumped the poker on Finder's unconscious body."

"Servants die all the time, Amlis." Omina refused to listen to Farin or her son. "And nothing is done about it."

"Is that what we have become, Mother?" Amlis stared at Omina. "You have read the old laws—they're in a book on your shelves. It was wrong, then, to murder anyone, no matter how highly placed the murderer might be. Yet we have come to this. Allowing the innocent to be beaten or killed, all for the sake of our expediency. No," he held up a hand when Omina thought to speak again, "I am just as guilty, and I wish it were not so."

"Beatris and I will be leaving in the morning. What she witnessed sickened her and she wishes to return home," Rodrik announced quietly.

"I will not allow my lady wife to travel to Vhoorth unless I am by her side. Amlis has his guards, here. There is no need for my services." Rodrik nodded to Omina and Amlis before walking swiftly for the door.

⁂

"Rod, I knew she was thoughtless and cruel, and I thought to distract her. That was a foolish notion," Beatris watched as the chambermaid packed her clothing.

"My love, it was a noble attempt. I am sorry you were forced to witness such brutality."

"I cannot wait to get home and away from that bully. She looks and acts fine among her betters, but those lesser than she will always suffer around her."

"She has not mistreated you, has she?" Rodrik's blue eyes examined his wife's face. Beatris turned away.

"Only a little barb, here and there," Beatris muttered. "Nothing that would not be magnified if I were at court in Lironis."

"Then we will be well away tomorrow, and the better for it," Rodrik observed. "Omina counts on Firith, should push come to shove, but I do not trust Mortin or his brat."

"How can we? Your father is the only one who will surely come to Vhrist's aid if the King's hand comes to bear."

"I don't believe Tamblin will make a move until his ships are built. And I worry for the harvests this turn. If the people starve, Tamblin will not have troops to fill the boats Amlis is building."

"You think it is too late already? That nothing might save us now?" Beatris lifted a hand to her throat.

"Beatris, love, do not fret. A letter has been sent and we still await a reply. Let us hope they will honor old oaths and lend assistance."

"Did you ever see them, Rod? Did you? I heard there were drawings and paintings, once, but they have all been destroyed. I have never seen them."

"I saw one, long ago. He came to my father when I was young and they shut themselves inside my father's study. He was gone shortly after, and I learned that Tamblin had assumed the throne when my father sought me out later."

"How old were you, then?"

"Fourteen, and just come back from sword practice. Someday, I will tell you how he arrived and what his appearance was, but that will wait for another day." Rodrik jerked his head toward the chambermaid, who was listening, open-mouthed, at his words.

"Ah. Yes. Girl, pack what lies in the armoire next," Beatris urged the girl to attend to her assigned duties.

Brin stood at Timblor's left, as always. The King had chosen to have lunch with the heir, Yevil Orklis and Hirill Mast, at a round table inside his private chambers. The table overlooked the courtyard and the gate below the palace. Red velvet curtains were swept aside to take advantage of weak spring sunlight filtering through exquisite, diamond-shaped panes of glass set cleverly and seamlessly together.

Timblor had taken the chair to Tamblin's left, garnering the best view from the King's window, as he preferred. Yevil took the next seat, placing him opposite the King, while Hirill settled into the remaining chair, his back to the glass and the view beyond it.

Etlund tasted the food to be served and sipped the wine before setting it before the King. Tamblin gripped a fork in his right hand and lifted the cup of wine to his lips with his left when Brin struck.

I was unconscious when the healer first came, waking halfway through his treatment. Bruises covered my body and a terrible pain was in my arm. The bone was broken, there was no doubt, and I wanted to weep from the intense pain of it. Wordless and without shedding a tear, I watched and shivered as Farin Wold pulled on my hand to set the bone in its proper place, before splinting the injury and wrapping it.

"Let someone know by tapping this," Farin indicated the bandaging, "if it becomes too tight. We do not wish to restrict circulation." My teeth chattering with the onset of shock, I barely nodded at his instruction.

The rest of my treatment went by in a blur, and sometime during the ordeal I noticed that Amlis and Rodrik were watching. Rodrik had gone immediately to Beatris and consoled her, I learned later. Beatris had witnessed my beating, and she was fortunate to receive Rodrik's care as she did—I was not so lucky. None thought to console me. I was merely a servant, after all, and if they believed Mirisa, then I'd been taking liberties with the Prince's underclothes.

What pleasure did she imagine I might have from placing them in a drawer? The logic escaped me, as it so often did with nobles. Willow bark tea was given after my treatment and a litter came to carry me to my storage room.

At first, the same tiny room I'd been given when I first arrived was offered, but as it wasn't far from the family wing, I shook my head in tacit refusal. I wanted to be as far from Mirisa of Firith as I could possibly get.

It was as the two young men who'd carried my litter down two flights of stone steps were setting it down beside my straw-filled pallet that I knew—death had come to Lironis, and it would affect the course of events in Vhrist.

Brin lay on the stone floor of Tamblin's chamber, gasping his last breaths after Yevil had fired an ancient and forbidden weapon at Timblor's servant. Timblor had been carried to the King's bed after a vicious stabbing at the hands of Brin, his own page.

"You didn't think I'd let you live, did you?" Yevil whispered to a dying and terrified Brin. "But you did very well, and I hope you spent the money I gave you earlier, as you will not have the opportunity now. You carry my gratitude, wherever you go from here." Yevil drew a knife across Brin's throat and death came swiftly.

"Did you dispatch that evil?" Tamblin asked as Yevil came to stand at the King's elbow.

"Of course, my King. How is the Prince?"

"I have riders combing the city, searching for healers. That fool physician had the temerity to die only this morning."

"Father?" Timblor moaned as two servants attempted to stanch the flow of blood from Timblor's chest.

"I am here, boy. Yevil, please ask your men to question all of Brin's friends and acquaintances. Find out if this is a conspiracy."

"As you command," Yevil nodded to Tamblin and walked purposely from the room.

"Father, I placed trust unwisely," Timblor coughed up a bit of blood. Tamblin knew what that meant.

"Get away, both of you," Tamblin shoved away one of the servants. "Wait outside until I call for you, do you hear?" Both young men rushed out of the King's bedchamber without a backward glance.

"I asked Brin to do it," Timblor coughed again, bringing up more blood. "Only he turned on me. Father, I think you know." Timblor's eyes unfocused. Three rattling breaths later, Timblor did not draw breath again.

"I will carry word to your lady wife," Hirill offered several hours later. Tamblin had cursed, railed and tossed several pieces of old and priceless furniture through even more fragile and expensive glass panes. The courtyard below his suite was littered with broken and splintered wood and precious fabrics. The red velvet drapery was the last thing to fly out the shattered window. Guards and servants were picking through the remains for anything of value.

"Do it. And bring the bastard back with you. Take men. Twenty at least, and make sure he arrives safely. For the moment, Amlis is my heir. Go." Tamblin waved Hirill out the door. "Wine!" Tamblin shouted as Hirill walked away. "Bring it!" Servants rushed to obey.

I had no desire to inform Amlis that his brother was dead, or that men rode north from Lironis to haul him back to his father. Perhaps Rath or Rodrik might return to oversee the building of ships—the King's goal of building a fleet had not been set aside.

In my dreams, too, I heard Fyris groaning. Trees were dying, their roots poisoned by a virulent toxin I could not name. Warmer weather had arrived, but grasses and seedlings were more stunted than usual. The harvest would be very poor, if it came at all. Farmers plowed and tilled, but gossip had many shaking their heads.

"We cannot live on fish alone, and did you see what came in with the last catch?" Two kitchen girls brought my supper on the third night after Mirisa's beating, handing me the bowl of lentils with a piece of bread and a cup of water.

"Two-headed shrimp? No, thank you," the other girl shivered. "It isn't just the land. It's leaking into the sea."

That worried me and brought up something I'd not thought of before—the poison was spreading past the land itself. Would it eventually sicken and destroy all of Siriaa? That thought motivated me, and during the remaining fifteen days until the King's guards arrived to collect Amlis, I slipped into Tamblin's old study at night, after Mirisa and the others had gone to bed. Old candle stubs made enough light to read by as I pored over books with much missing information.

⁂

The afternoon that the King's guard arrived with Hirill Mast at their head proved to be a stormy one. Men were wet to the skin and cold. Gathering around any available fireplace, they waited patiently while Lady Omina and Amlis were brought to them.

The great hall not far from the kitchens was the place chosen to deliver news, so I stealthily made my way through halls and warrens, determined to listen in. No, that was not something I did as a rule, but I could not deny my curiosity in this matter.

"Hirill, what brings you home?" Lady Omina took his hand the moment she walked into the wide hall. Amlis, walking slightly behind his mother, with Mirisa behind him, stared at the twenty men who'd accompanied Hirill to Vhrist.

"Sad news, I'm afraid, my Lady," Hirill bowed his head to Omina. "Your eldest son's page—Brin, I believe his name was, suddenly went mad and stabbed Timblor in the heart. The heir did not live long from the injury." Hirill bowed his head again to Omina. The cry that came from Omina's throat was strangled, after which she fell to the floor in a dead faint.

⁂

"You must come to Lironis, the King commands it," Hirill informed Amlis over a glass of wine. Omina was receiving care from the healer within her chambers, and Mirisa had been asked as politely as a tight-lipped Amlis could muster to confine herself to quarters and send a servant out if she required anything. "You are now the heir," Hirill added.

"Unless and until he can get another," Amlis huffed, standing to pace. This meeting was held in Tamblin's old study, which someone had bothered to clean, Amlis noticed absently. The last time he'd been inside it, everything was covered in dust.

"There is that, but that opens the door for you, my Prince and royal heir."

"I never thought to hear those words," Amlis raked a hand through thick, brown curls.

"I am happy to be the first to say them to you," Hirill inclined his head.

"I cared for my brother," Amlis stared out a window that had been cleaned recently. Once again, he wondered who had achieved that particular blessing. It allowed late afternoon light into an otherwise dark place.

"Your heart is kind. Your father did everything he could to turn him against you."

"I know that. And he believed Father's poison to the last, I'm sure," Amlis sighed. "I have riders going to Vhoorth. I want Rodrik with me in Lironis. And I want to send Mirisa home. It will take a moon-turn for her father to send someone to fetch her, but I will not waste men or resources to send her back myself."

"Perhaps it will be wise to say that you will send for her from Lironis, once things are settled and your brother's affairs are resolved."

"Yes, that is sound advice," Amlis agreed. "We will string Mortin along; he's had his eye on the Queen's throne for Mirisa anyway. If I have need of him, he'll jump at the opportunity now."

"I knew you'd see reason," Hirill smiled. "And then, when we find an alternate match for you, we will inform her of such."

"Agreed."

"I'd truly like to see her face, when that news is delivered," Hirill chuckled.

"As would I. As it is, I would like to take Finder back with me as my page, but she is recovering from a beating at Mirisa's hands. The sow thought to take slight for Finder placing my clothing in a drawer."

"Jealous?"

"I have never seen it to such a degree."

"Then it is best that we do not cut her off now, and perhaps we should find a suitable replacement when we deliver the news later."

"Good idea." Amlis smiled for the first time all day. "I'll have Finder brought to Lironis as soon as Farin releases her from his care."

"Do so. She has been useful in the past, has she not?"

"Absolutely. I hope Mother has not disposed of her uniforms. She can wear those until red ones can be made."

"Ask that red ones be made here. There is time enough." Hirill rose from his chair.

"Hirill, I will make you first advisor," Amlis laughed.

"Finder, I plan to bring you to Lironis the moment Farin allows you to travel the distance," Amlis knelt next to my pallet inside the storeroom. He'd glanced around at my surroundings upon entering, blinking in confusion at the piles of castoffs and bits of pieces no one ever called for. Shaking it off, he'd settled in a crouch to talk to me. I'd been leaning against the wall while sitting on my straw-stuffed pallet, something he'd never slept upon, I was sure.

"I'm having a tailor brought in to make new uniforms—these with red jackets and blue pants. You'll wear those as my page. Heeth will travel with me in the interim, but you'll take his place and he'll return to my mother when the time comes. You'll look good in red, Finder."

I worked to keep from flinching when Amlis reached out to touch my cheek. Nodding, I let him know I understood—perhaps more than he might have guessed. "I'll have Mother bring the barber before you leave," Amlis stood and stretched. "We'll do this together, Finder. I'll never ignore your warnings again." I watched him walk out of my storeroom, hands in pockets and stepping happily.

CHAPTER 7

Two days later, Amlis rode out. Rodrik would catch up to him somewhere on the road and I imagined that the six who'd survived our trip north would again be following Rodrik. Rath, it was decided, would come to Vhrist and oversee the shipbuilding, at Amlis' request. There was no sense in angering the King just as you'd been named Heir, after all.

I spent many an afternoon wondering how things might work out and what Yevil thought and planned to do. I knew (whether anyone else did), that Yevil had a hand in Timblor's death. Timblor was no innocent, but his betrayal and death left a sour taste in my mouth.

Farin, too, visited every other day or so, to check on my progress. He was also interested in my nubs and examined them regularly. "Fascinating," he muttered, touching them. "Nearly a hand's width long, now."

I had no idea what he meant and was grateful for the gathered backs of blouses. When a tailor came to measure me, Farin made sure to be there and explained what kind of shirts and jackets I would require to accommodate the nubs. Omina was absent most of the time, and Mirisa had done a near about-face, treating everyone in an almost civil manner. Perhaps with Amlis gone her rages quieted, but I was distrustful of her and would always be.

Much of my recovery time was spent in Tamblin's old library, reading books and hoping to find useful information. I found new things, but there was nothing to fill in the gaps of missing pages. I kept a book near my elbow at all times, filled with illustrations in case anyone came looking for me. They did, but not for any reason I ever imagined.

"Girl, there's a woman at the kitchen servants' door, asking to see you." Farin stood in the doorway to Tamblin's old study, giving me a puzzled frown. Looking up from my book, I shut it immediately and stood. "She has a sickly babe and refuses to allow me to look at it," Farin informed me as we wound our way through Omina's palace. I could tell that the woman's refusal to allow the best physician in Vhrist to look at her child annoyed him, but he wasn't saying it.

The woman I recognized immediately upon arriving in the kitchen—someone had allowed her inside so the baby wouldn't be exposed to the light rain outside. She was the one I'd helped in Sofi's shop.

The moment she saw me, she sobbed and held the child out to me while Farin's frown deepened. There was no help for it—she refused to allow Farin near and he likely wouldn't be able to help her anyway. I took the baby from her outstretched hands and began.

The child nursed before leaving the palace and the woman might have continued thanking me if I'd stayed. Instead, I turned on my heel and walked out of the kitchen, leaving Farin behind. Someone offered the mother tea and a little food, so she was eating while the child did. I slipped away as quietly as I could, hoping that Farin knew to keep his mouth shut.

"Do you mind if I take a look?" Farin stood inside Sofi's tailor shop the following afternoon, staring at Yissy, who appeared healthy and smiling. Hair was beginning to grow atop a wispy head and there was color in her cheeks as she grinned mischievously at Farin.

"Not at all," Sofi agreed. "Yissy would have died. Many others have, of the same sickness," she said.

"Are you sure the girl didn't have another ailment? Something she would have recovered from on her own?"

"I'm sure, Master Healer. Two physicians in the city said Yissy had the wasting disease and charged me for looking at her. Then that silent girl walks into my shop, hugs Yissy for a while and Yissy walks away whole. I brought in three others, and they were taken care of when the girl returned for the trousers I'd sewn for her."

"She's scheduled to return to Lironis in two days," Farin mused, forcing a gasp from Sofi. "You have something to say, young woman?" Farin turned back to her.

"I was hoping that she'd stay—there are others who wish to come to her," Sofi held out a hand, her brown eyes pleading.

"I'm afraid Amlis has priority, my dear," Farin rose. "Thank you for speaking with me." He walked out of Sofi's shop, his thoughts turning swiftly in his head.

"We must draft another letter," Farin stepped inside Omina's private study. Her eyes were red from weeping for Timblor, Farin knew, but this was too important to wait.

"Why? They haven't replied to the last one." Omina wiped her eyes with a lace kerchief.

"We didn't have information then that we do now. Rath will arrive tomorrow. The three of us will sit down and write a new one. Amlis may not get the page he desires, Omina, but Fyris might gain new life if we act quickly."

The incident with the baby disturbed me, and there were several inside the palace kitchen who'd witnessed what I'd done. Sneaking inside Tamblin's deserted study to read more, I found myself hoping that news of this growing ability did not follow me to Lironis. At least the child had a chance to live, now. She wouldn't have if a desperate mother hadn't brought her to me. Sighing at the strange course my life had taken, I opened a book and began to read.

Three hours before dawn, I made my way toward my pallet. Perhaps it was fate or exhaustion. Regardless, I was unaware of their presence until a filthy bag was shoved over my head just outside my storage room, and although I kicked as viciously as I could and flailed against large hands that held my arms and legs while another clamped over my bag-covered mouth, it was to no avail. Someone was kidnapping me and I was powerless against them. I might have been frightened, but once I was carried out into night air, there came a blow to the head and I knew nothing for several hours.

My belly roiled when I woke, the bag still tied over my head and my hands and feet bound securely. At first, I thought dizziness made the bench beneath me rise and fall, but that was not the case. I'd been loaded onto a ship after my abduction and now we rode the sea. Had we still been in the harbor, I would have heard the seabirds calling. There were none that I could hear this far out and as I could see nothing from inside the bag, I had no idea where I was being taken.

"The girlie's awake," I heard someone call out. They'd been watching for wakefulness. At least someone had.

"Shet yer eyes, the light'll blind ye elsewise," a voice commanded. I shut my eyes as the bag was jerked off my head. Someone drew in a gasping breath but said nothing as I struggled against the pain of the light. When I could open my eyes without tears blinding me, I discovered why. The sailor whose cracked ankle I'd repaired stared at me in dismay. Behind him were six others, all staring as well. One of them had spoken, while the one I recognized shook his head.

"You will not touch her," he commanded and the others backed away. Had they been planning to take me while I lay bound and helpless? The thought made me want to weep real tears and not those produced by the blindingly bright light all around us. "We'll be there in an hour. See to the rigging."

"I didn't know," the sailor knelt beside me, his head bowed. "Two of the others brought you, and the money was too good. I'm sorry, but we're bound, now. Terribly sorry. I'll see that the Prince knows what happened. The bitch will pay for this." He rose and stalked off.

Mirisa had paid these men to take me. Where, I had no idea, and since my gifts refused to tell me anything of myself, there was no way to tell where I might be taken. Would they drop me overboard, still bound hand and foot? There was no need; I'd never learned to swim. I'd be just as dead either way—there was no land in sight.

Twilight was beginning to fall before someone shouted and the sailor I knew came back to me. "We'll put you ashore—what little there is of it, and I'll ring the bell. Tis now I wish you could speak; they'll likely kill you first and ask questions later. I'll see that the Prince knows, lady. I'll make sure he knows."

Fear gripped me as I sat up straight on the bench, watching as we approached perhaps the strangest sight I'd ever seen. Straight up from the seabed it rose, to impossible heights. Of glass it was made—all of glass—on the outside, at least, in greens, blues and golds.

Glass that color was only found inside the King's palace, and those colors were a pale comparison to these. I wondered at the sight of this huge, glass castle, because that's what it appeared to be, even as my heart hammered against my ribs in fear.

What creatures lived in a glass castle surrounded by waters so deep that none could swim their way to land? I did not see a ship moored anywhere, but then the castle was vast and round—I saw the curving edges of it from my seat on board the ship.

The closer we came, the easier it was to make out terraces in the glass, higher up. Tops of trees peered over glass balustrades, as if growing in the middle of the sea were commonplace and acceptable.

Shortly after, I was placed in a rowboat after being lowered over the side, and the sailor and two others paddled toward the glass castle.

I felt eyes upon us as we made our way slowly to a very narrow shore—a grown man could have lain down at the widest part and had his head against glass, his feet in the sea. Our little boat scraped against sand as we pulled up to the narrow strip, and the sailor cut my bonds away.

"There's a passenger basket just through here," he informed me as I stumbled after him; my feet and hands were numb from being tied for so long. A thin opening allowed us to step past the outer edges of glass, and on any other day I might have placed my hands on thick, opaque glass and marveled at it, but not that day. That day ensured that my life would never be the same, and all of it because Mirisa was a jealous and brutal bitch.

"She gave me a note to send up with you, but I'll read it first," the sailor muttered as we stood inside a cool crevice, surrounded by glass. A thin rope dangled against a wall and the sailor tugged on it while a bell tolled far over our heads. To our left was a hollowed out portion that puzzled me, until a woven basket descended within it, lowered by thick rope. Backing away from it, I bumped into the glass wall on the opposite side.

"Take back this filth that you spawned," the sailor read the letter and then stared at me. "I will not send this with you, I'm afraid," he folded the note and stuffed it into a pocket. "Girl, again I'm sorry for my part in this. I wish there was another way, but if I take you out of here, those in the ship will tear me apart. They only got half their money, you see, and the other half is to be delivered once we make port again."

I turned my head away from him after that statement, and he sighed heavily. By that time, the basket had touched the sand at the bottom of the hollowed out tube. "In you go," he gestured toward the basket.

When I failed to move, he was compelled to lift me over the edge. The ones above who were watching as well as operating the basket, began to pull it up. The sailor turned his eyes up toward me, watching until I was so high up I'd kill myself if I jumped away. I could not see him after he left the crevice, but I knew, with the talent I had, that he'd climbed aboard the small boat and sat while the other two rowed him to the ship.

⁂

Omina glared at Mirisa, who offered a hate-filled stare in return. "What have you done?" Omina hissed. Farin and three of Omina's guards stood by inside Omina's study. Word had gotten out that sailors had carried someone away from the palace, after the night guard at the kitchen door had been bribed. Currently he was resting in Omina's jail, but only after he'd identified Mirisa as the one who'd paid him.

"I sent that filth where it belonged," Mirisa shouted. "None of you were willing to do anything with it."

"That filth, as you call her, had the healing gift," Farin snapped. "Even the ones you sent her to recognize and value that. We were going to use her as a bargaining token, to bring one of the Guardians here to heal Fyris. But you, in a fit of jealousy, throw it away and seal our doom. You stupid, senseless bitch." Farin stalked angrily from Omina's study.

"You sent her to her death, but that's what you planned, wasn't it? We can't get her back and Fyris will die. I could have my guards kill you now, do you know that?" Omina's eyes locked with Mirisa's. "I am Queen of Fyris. I have had greater than you put down. Take her," Omina jerked her head. "I will decide what to do with her before her father's men arrive." For the first time, fear crept into Mirisa's eyes.

⁂

Did I remain standing inside the basket as it was drawn upward? It might have been brave to do so, but I wasn't brave. I huddled on the flimsy floor of woven bark, terrified that my death waited at the top of a glass castle.

I'd seen the look in the sailor's eyes as I was pulled upward—they held no hope—*for me.* The basket reached the top and was pulled inward. I saw above me a well-lit chamber, lined with more glass, and then a face peered over the edge of the basket—a man's face. He frowned down at me, just as the basket was tipped over and I came spilling out, like a glob of thick porridge. When I scrambled to my knees, I gaped at the man who'd frowned at me. Now I knew the secret, and I was likely to die because of it.

Wings. All six of those who waited had wings. Black wings—as black as night. The one who stared down at me rustled the wings at his back in distaste. "Rip her shirt," he ordered and I shrank against the floor as another drew a dagger from a sheath at his belt and cut through the back of my blouse.

"Longer than normal, but that's of no consequence," the man muttered. "Kill her."

CHAPTER 8

Burying my head in my arms, I waited for the inevitable blow, frightened out of my wits. Even through my tightly shut eyes, the blast of light penetrated, and when I lifted my head, all six winged men were against the circular glass wall as a glowing Orb floated between them and me. Astonished, I could only stare as it floated there, all on its own.

"Get the King," the first man ordered and one of his fellows, keeping his eyes on the Orb, inched toward an arched door set in the back of the room. Once reached, he ran down a narrow hall until his footsteps disappeared.

"Captain Ardis, why is it here?" Another winged man whispered. Ardis, the one who'd so callously ordered my death, hushed his subordinate.

"Wait for the King," Ardis hissed, staring at the Orb and then at me. The Orb pulsed with light and the remaining five were afraid of it for some reason. Lifting myself off the floor, I sat cross-legged there, keeping my eyes on the men but straying often to the Orb, just as the others did.

"It cannot be; it hasn't appeared to anyone other than Camryn and Elabeth in nearly two centuries," a new voice floated down the hall. All five bowed to the man entering the circular room, even as I stared at his wings in shock. They were red, these wings. As bright a red as the rare red bird that flitted about in southern Fyris. It was considered good luck to see a red bird and wishes were often made upon its flight.

"Liron be merciful," the red-winged King stared at the pulsing Orb that now floated above my head. "What brought it, do you know?"

"No idea," Captain Ardis replied. "I ordered the half-blood killed and it blasted us with light."

The King was now staring at me, his red wings rustling just as agitatedly as Ardis' black ones had earlier. "A half-blood?" His voice was frosty with contempt as his gaze raked me uncomfortably. "This one must have been made just before—well, if I find the father, he'll have stripes at my own hand. Have you attempted to kill it again?" The King turned back to Ardis.

"No, my King. Do you wish me to do so?"

"Of course. Immediately." I shrank back at the King's demand; he'd tossed up a hand, informing me that my life meant nothing to these. And half-blood? What did they mean by that? Was that why? The wheels turned slowly in my mind and I might have gasped as the truth became clear—*my nubs*—I was half whatever these were, and held in contempt as such, it appeared. So much so that half-bloods were killed if they were unfortunate enough to be sent to them. Mirisa was the worst of the worst, handing me my parentage at the same moment as my death.

Ardis drew his knife and stepped toward me, but I was already backed up as far as I could go unless I wished to plunge down the steep well that served to raise and lower the basket. Two steps away from me, Ardis was thrown backward as the Orb sent out a second blast of light. The captain slid unconscious down the glass wall as I watched in fearful fascination.

"It appears," the red-winged King sighed, "that the Orb does not desire this death. Very well, send her to Gurnil for tonight, and we will consider making a servant of her tomorrow."

"Ride. As fast as you can in that direction, Lady Mirisa," the guard grinned wickedly. "Perhaps you'll get away." He laughed and turned his horse toward the ten others that waited in the distance.

"But my father—he will be angry and bring his men," Mirisa shouted after the guard, causing him to rein in his horse and turn toward the girl.

"Oh, no, Lady. You see—that way lies Lironis. We'll tell him you were so distraught that Amlis did not take you with him that you struck out on your own. Your horse stepped in a hole while you were riding so swiftly and you were thrown. Poor thing, your neck snapped." He laughed again as he rode away. "Ride, Lady," he shouted. "The longer you outride us, the longer you live." Mirisa kicked her horse into a gallop and raced away.

"Master Gurnil, the King sent this to you." I'd been hauled along, a large hand on my upper arm as I was propelled through a maze of glass halls. We moved so quickly and I was so frightened I only noticed that the floors were covered in tiles from which a light shone, illuminating the hallways. Then I was shoved inside what appeared to be a massive Library, with shelf upon shelf filled with books, all lined up in neat rows or along walls. So many shelves of books filled the room that it would take turns to read even a fraction of them. I might have thought it a dream come true if I hadn't been so terrified.

"What have we here?" The one called Master Gurnil looked me over. "Liron's knees, man, is that a half-blood?"

"One the Orb apparently doesn't want dead," the guard muttered. I stared at my arm, which was nearly bared after they'd slit the back of my blouse open. Marks from the guard's fingers were darkening into bruises already.

"The Orb, you say?" Gurnil was quite interested now. He was as tall as Wolter, and nearly as thin, but his hair was brown and his wings blue.

"Yes. We were about to dispatch this one when the Orb appeared and nearly blinded all of us. We sent for the King, who commanded that we try again. It threw Ardis against the wall."

"Did it now?" Gurnil had come forward until he stood before me. "What is your name, girl?" he asked, his dark-blue eyes examining me closely. Staring at the center of his delicately woven tunic, I gave no answer.

"She chooses not to speak, and I suggest that you don't force it." I went light-headed at the sight that stepped around a very tall shelf. Blue-skinned he was, and nearly as tall as the shelf he stood beside. He carried a book in rather large hands and looked me over with eyes so bright a blue they put the sky to shame. His hair, the color of newly-harvested wheat, was close-cropped against his head. The features of his face were even and nice enough, if you were accustomed to blue-skinned giants.

"Sir Larentii," the guard bowed respectfully to the blue man.

"Tell me, Daragar, why the girl won't speak," Gurnil said. Obviously, he was quite familiar with the blue giant.

"You know I cannot explain fully; it would be interfering."

"At least give me her name. That isn't interfering."

"The name they called her is not her name," Daragar the Larentii said, snapping the book shut in his hand. With no effort at all, it floated away from his hand and settled itself on the topmost shelf of the bookcase. I shivered at the sight.

"We have to call her something. Where is that list?" Gurnil muttered, turning away from me and giving me full view of his blue wings. Compared to the blue of Daragar's skin, they seemed almost a dusty blue in color.

Had I ever dreamed of winged people? Never. Would have thought them a child's tale, as outrageous as that might seem to be. I was now surrounded by a child's tale—one that had gone dark quickly when my death had been ordered.

Daragar and I watched as Gurnil lifted a book from a nearby shelf and went through it quickly, coming to a page halfway through. "Here it is," he said. "Quin is the next name. You won't give me your name, I'll give you one." The book snapped shut. "What does Jurris think to do with her?" Gurnil lifted an eyebrow at my guard.

"He wants her to stay with you tonight, then he'll make an assignment tomorrow. Likely the kitchens, unless I miss my guess."

I turned to stare at the guard. I knew, suddenly, that his name was Poulus and he was cousin to Ardis, the captain who'd ordered my death. He, like Ardis, had dark hair and gray eyes. The King—Jurris, was black-haired and green-eyed. Recalling his face now, I realized he reminded me somewhat of Yevil Orklis.

"You must bathe before climbing into bed in one of the Library's guest suites," Gurnil declared as I stared at Poulus, his voice forcing me to turn back to blue-winged Gurnil. He was a librarian. I savored that term in my head. *Chief Librarian,* my senses told me, *and Master Scholar.* What wonderful titles to hold. None in Fyris could claim such, or aspire to it.

"I suppose I'll have to scrounge clothing from somewhere," Gurnil was still appraising me. "A bit small. What do you think, Daragar?" Gurnil swiveled his head to consult the Larentii.

"I think her stature has no bearing upon her character." And just like that, the Larentii disappeared.

"I hate it when he does that," Gurnil muttered, coming back to me. "Never mind," he waved away the disappearance, "it's off to the showers for you. Come."

At first, I had no idea what he'd meant by showers, other than what rain often provided, but I was shown to a cubicle lined with small tiles, and inside that was a metal thing resembling the crooked neck of a goose, poking from the tiled wall. Several hands below that were two more metal handles of a sort, one marked with hot and the other cold.

"Turn them on like this," Gurnil instructed, twisting the handle marked hot first. "The water will heat up, then turn the cold until the water is the proper temperature. The Kondari have supplied the keep with solar panels, so there is hot water and power whenever we require it."

My head swam as I attempted to use my ability to decipher his explanation—there was too much information crowding my brain. I would have to take things slowly, one or two at a time. "I'll look for clothing, but don't count on too much this late in the evening," Gurnil handed a large white towel he'd pulled from a nearby closet to me. "Those nubs are rather long," he examined my back briefly. "Most half-breeds only have bumps of raised skin and it never becomes more than that. Well, off to the storeroom. They won't like it when I knock on the door," he grumbled and walked out of the room.

I admit I played with the handles controlling the heat and cold of the water, almost shrieking at one point when it went icy in an instant—I'd turned the hot water handle too far. Soap was on a small shelf attached to the shower wall, along with bottles labeled *shampoo* and *conditioner*. Eagerly I read the information magically printed on each bottle before washing what little hair I had.

"I was going to suggest to them that she was clairvoyant. That's difficult to prove and might get us what we wanted before they discovered the truth," Farin sipped a glass of wine beside Omina's fire. Omina stared thoughtfully into the flames at Farin's words.

"But she was a healer, and we had no idea. How did that escape those fools in Lironis? Might she have saved my son?" Omina's eyes were red as she turned her gaze to the physician.

"I have heard that miracles might be performed, but according to handwritten records, they had no healer for at least three centuries. The last one tired of his life and left them."

"Why wasn't she there when Timblor needed her?"

"My Lady, I have no explanation."

"Did you examine Mirisa's body?"

"Of course. It is just as your guards explained it; a broken neck and many bruises, all caused by a fall from her horse."

"Good. Mortin will have no complaints concerning the cause of death, then."

"And he will have little recourse against the Queen and the Prince Heir. Mirisa cost us Fyris, My Lady."

"I know."

"This is certainly an improvement. I have no idea what they covered your face in, Quin, but it was certainly filthy, as was your hair." Gurnil shoved a pile of clothing in my direction. I had no desire to inform him of the foul-smelling bag they'd tied over my head or of the headache I still fought from being hit on the head in order to render me unconscious.

I'd wrapped the towel he'd given me around myself after my shower, and now, holding clothing against me, I followed him down a short hall where doors lined each side.

"Kondari scholars come occasionally and read our books," Gurnil explained, opening a door and indicating that I should go inside. "A comb, brush and other necessities should be on the dresser. You can keep this room until another offer is made. If the Master cook does not claim you, perhaps one of the other guilds might. I'll have someone take you to the kitchen in the morning." Gurnil shut the door, leaving me to look about the room reserved for Kondari. Kondar was the continent to the north of Fyris—the one King Tamblin was so eager to attack.

Perhaps Kondari were much like Fyrisians—the bed looked the same as a minor noble's and the comb and brush were certainly adequate. The mirror that hung on a wall above the dresser? That was a King's dream in Fyris. Nearly as wide as I was tall, it hung, unassuming, on walls painted a pale cream.

I stared at my reflection for the first time, I think, and forcibly shut my mouth—I'd been gaping like the fool I was. Blue-gray eyes stared into mine. Short, golden hair adorned my head and there were the streaks of silver and copper that I'd only seen before when my hair was cut away.

Touching my lips, which were full and the color of roses that grew in the Queen's garden behind the palace in Lironis, I felt as if I were meeting myself for the first time. Shaking my head to clear away the tempting vision, I drew away from my image. That mirror could become the trap that others had fallen into and I was determined not to become what they were, Mirisa being chief among them.

Gurnil had supplied two sets of trousers, underclothes for two days and two shirts, all yellow in color, but I was dismayed to find that both shirts were backless, having only a collar and yoke attached, with the back empty with ties beneath the space so wings could move freely.

Going back to the mirror, I turned to the side and caught my first glimpse of the nubs growing there. Sadly, they resembled ugly, plucked chicken's wings and caused me to hang my head in shame. Those nubs would now be exposed to all I encountered, and if tradition continued, they'd be the cause for much ridicule and many a joke.

Putting those thoughts away, I found something more at the bottom of the clothing pile and determined it was clothing to sleep in, consisting of loose, silky trousers and a matching top that tied around my neck and waist, covering only my small breasts and ribs. I'd never had anything so soft against my skin and savored it as I dressed for bed.

"Write a letter for me, I'll pay to have it sent." Orik, captain of the Sea Hawk, stood inside Sofi's tailor shop. Sofi stared at the captain—she hadn't seen him since the girl had repaired his ankle.

"All right. Who is it for?"

"For Prince Amlis," Orik sighed. "Might I sit down? This is a sad tale and worse for the telling of it."

The bump on my head was very sore the next morning, but I was up and dressed long before Gurnil knocked on my door. I'd made up the bed, tidied the room and even scrubbed the tiled shower before his arrival. There was still not much hair on my head to comb through, but I combed it anyway and was as presentable as I could be when the Master Scholar came to my door.

"Much, much better," Gurnil nodded approval and led me down the hall toward the Library door. "Normally I would fly down, but as you can't," he saw no need to finish the sentence and truly I did not require it. I could see easily enough how being without wings in this place was a decided disadvantage.

Likely, the basket I'd ridden inside was the only way in or out on the outside, and once at the bottom, there were no boats in which to sail away from a narrow strip of sand. Because of its location, the glass palace was a sanctuary for those with wings. *Built as the ultimate defense, long ago,* my senses informed me. Stifling a sigh, I followed silently behind Master Gurnil.

The kitchen when we arrived was a noisome place—more so, even, than Wolter's kitchen in Lironis. Pots clattered, voices shouted, laughed or talked and there were no fireplaces anywhere. All of the workers—every single one, had yellow wings. Those wings were either held away from bodies to cool off or clamped tightly against backs as things were stirred or chopped or kneaded. And every Yellow Wing, male and female, eventually stopped talking and stared directly at me.

"What's that doing here?" One large male, brandishing a meat cleaver, pointed the sharp instrument in my direction. An angry frown darkened his face, which was round and normally might have held a sunny smile. Nothing close to that was aimed in my direction. "Send it to the King, for extermination." He chopped furiously at a leg of lamb, venting his obvious displeasure at my presence.

"The King sent her to me last night, after the Orb appeared and prevented her death. Twice." Gurnil's words were clipped and angry.

"She is here, now, by the King's decision. If she does not work out, then bring her back to me and I will search for another post."

"How long?" The words were punctuated by heavy chops into the flesh of a young lamb.

"At least a moon-turn. Mind you, she is to be treated like any other Avii while she is in your kitchen."

"Our laws do not protect that filth."

"Our laws were designed around them. I ask that you recall your history." Gurnil snapped his wings and stalked out of the kitchen, leaving me at the mercy of nearly two dozen angry Yellow Wings. And, since Gurnil had not stayed long enough to give any name for me, I was called girl the rest of the day. But that was not the worst of my troubles.

"You got them killed," a woman hissed in my ear as a tray piled high with filled plates was handed to me and I followed other servers to a wide dining hall, where many Black-Winged men and women waited for breakfast. All were seated on long, communal benches and tea or coffee was offered, in addition to fruit juice, something I'd seen little of during my lifetime.

Counting quickly, I moved past the server before me and began serving past what she held enough plates to feed. When my tray was empty, I returned to the kitchen for another load, then another, until I'd made five trips. Seven others served with me; four of the seven were female, three were male. These were younger than the others in the kitchen, but the eldest of the servers was still older than I.

The entire time I carried heavy trays, I wondered at the woman's words and wondered even more about who *they* might be. In my recollection (at least past the age of three or four), I had never willingly participated in any death, so my curiosity was aroused as to why she would think that of me.

I was set to loading dishes into a dish *machine*, as the woman called it who now supervised my every movement. The moment came while I was heaving rather large pots into the wide maw of this metal monster, the moment I'd expected from the beginning.

"Half-blood naked wing," was sung at my back, accompanied by a thwack from a wooden spoon that landed between my shoulder blades. Ignoring the second blow that landed, I kept loading the dish machine until it was full, added the powder that I understood would make the dishes clean and shut the door, starting the flow of water that sprayed from multitudes of tiny openings inside the machine itself.

"What's the matter, can't talk? Did they cut out your tongue?" The young man backed away when I turned to face him.

"Wouldn't surprise me any," my supervisor said, setting more dishes onto the wide, wood-block table next to the dish machine. "They're barbarians, plain and simple. Probably can't read, either. I hear they're not educating anyone, these days. Doesn't matter, they'll all die in the mud and slop, and good riddance to them when they do." Another pile of plates was thumped onto the table.

I watched the woman carefully as she spoke; she looked young but my senses told me otherwise. Her age surprised me when I searched for it—she was nearing three hundred turns and looked less than one-tenth that amount. It frightened me so badly that I refused to search ages on anyone else for a while.

My day went much the same, with taunts, insults and questions about my breeding coming into play, in addition to several blows while the Master Cook wasn't looking. I was sent away after serving an evening meal—those who came on duty before the midday meal would stay and clean up.

Grateful to get away from the noisy kitchen and those inside it who thought so little of me, I made my way through the halls, intent upon reaching the Library. Unerringly, as was my gift, I made my way, arriving just in time to find Gurnil leaving it.

"I thought I'd have to guide you back," he was quite surprised to find me there. "Have you eaten?" I shook my head. I'd not been offered food or drink the entire day. Punishment for some offense attributed to all Fyrisians, I'd decided. I'd been given an apron, at least, so my clothes were mostly clean although I did smell as if I'd worked inside a kitchen all day, with cooking smells clinging to skin and fabric.

"Well, come with me, then. Your work kitchen is the one that feeds the guard and army. I'll take you to the one that serves the Guild journeymen and artisans." I followed Gurnil down a different path, arriving in a smaller dining hall where I gaped at the different wing colors present.

"I see you haven't been taught, so I will tell you now that the wing colors represent what each one does," Gurnil pointed me to a chair at a table. These tables were not long and had individual chairs instead of benches lining each side. I settled into the seat indicated, while Gurnil sat beside me. Shockingly enough, Daragar the Larentii appeared and somehow, making a chair on the opposite side much larger to fit his size, sat as well.

"He doesn't eat, he just prefers to observe. Occasionally he talks," Gurnil smiled at me. I stared open-mouthed at the Larentii. He didn't eat? How did he live?

He must have read my expression, as he suddenly smiled. The white of his teeth was like sunlight breaking through clouds on a rainy day, it was so dazzling. "I consume sunlight," he informed me gently. "It feeds me. Therefore, I do eat, after a fashion."

"Quin, I've never gotten that much information from him before. Usually he's as silent as a fish twenty fathoms down." Gurnil winked at me before turning to Daragar. "How do you consume sunlight?"

"When Quin speaks, she may ask." Daragar wasn't going to answer Gurnil.

You don't have to answer, I already know, I silently informed him. Daragar blinked at me before smiling again. I did know. As soon as he'd said he consumed sunlight, I realized it soaked through his skin and fed his energy.

"The little one does not consume meat of any kind," Daragar said, causing Gurnil to stare at me. "You should inform the servers accordingly."

"I'll do that," Gurnil rose from his seat and went toward the kitchen door.

"The wings are divided thus," Daragar said after Gurnil disappeared inside the kitchen. "Yellow, the most common wing color, becomes a servant, a cook or a kitchen helper. Black Wings are born to be guards, warriors and officers. Gray Wings are farmers, herders and butchers. Brown Wings are blacksmiths, artists and artisans, including weavers, tailors and such. Green Wings are healers, healer's assistants and chemists. Blue Wings are scholars, librarians and teachers. Red Wings, well, Red Wings are royalty. At this time, there are only five of those, and of those five, only one is female. Jurris wishes to make Halthea Queen, but Justis, his brother and former Captain of the Queen's guard, insists that Queen Elabeth refused to name Halthea heir and so Halthea stews over it. So far, Justis has managed to hold his brother the King off, saying that a Queen will come for the Avii. Jurris grows tired of waiting, little one. If a Red Wing female does not come soon, then Halthea will be placed on the Avii throne."

"They're preparing vegetables for Quin," Gurnil sat beside me again. Too bad he hadn't gotten the information I did from Daragar. The Larentii became quiet when Gurnil returned.

Plates were brought out before long; vegetables for me, tender roast for Gurnil. Staring at the greens on one side of my plate, I carefully avoided them as I ate everything around them.

"What's the matter, don't you like greens? Those are very good, with salt and butter," Gurnil urged me to eat them.

"Then tell your kitchen staff not to spit in them next time," Daragar said and disappeared again. I shoved my plate away at Daragar's verification of what I'd already known.

"I'll blister their ears," Gurnil pushed back his chair. I gripped his arm and shook my head at him.

"It will make it worse next time, won't it?" he settled into his seat. Wordlessly, I nodded. "Did Daragar tell you? I understand he has mind-speech. Camryn and Elabeth had it too, and they spoke to another

Larentii who visited during their time. Well, all that is over, now. We have Jurris, who has no mindspeech. Are you ready? You look weary."

I nodded at his question and meekly followed him away from the dining hall. Most of its occupants had quieted when we walked in and voices were raised the moment we walked out.

Two weeks in the kitchens saw no improvement in my treatment. Insults came every day, food was refused and blows were delivered when no one of import was watching. Mostly they were dealt by a young man named Jadin, who was quite adept at hiding his misdeeds from the others.

Several Black Wings refused to be served by me after a while, so I avoided them. Still, I was shoved by one guard or another as I made my way down the lengthy tables, handing out plates of food. At times, it became a balancing act as I wobbled this way and that after a shove, just to keep from spilling the tray of food onto the floor.

The day came, however, as it surely must, when I did drop my tray, and it wasn't from a shove or an insult or even from a wooden spoon between my shoulder blades. No—on this day, one of the Black Wings decided to pull a nub. Had I known it would be so painful? My vision went black from the hurt of it, the tray went crashing onto the floor and I right behind it, bent double from the agony in my back.

"Do that again," a voice hissed above me, "and I'll have you court-martialed. Do you hear me?" The voice's owner had jerked up the one who'd grabbed my nub and was hissing a threat in his face as I cowered at their feet.

"Yes, Commander Justis." The answer was stuttered—the offender was terrified of Commander Justis. If I hadn't been rocking in pain on the floor, covered in food and broken pottery, I might have recalled that Daragar had mention Commander Justis. Only he'd called him the former Captain of the Queen's guards. With the absencc of a Queen, he'd chosen to command the Palace guards, instead.

"Girl," I was lifted from the floor by a hand on my arm, "Go to the Healer's Wing and ask them to look at the injury. Tell them Justis sent you." I stared into eyes as black as his wings and hair. This was the King's brother, after all, but Justis' face held none of the cruelty belonging to his red-winged sibling.

"She can't speak, Commander. Hasn't, anyway." That, from one of my fellow servers—a female.

"Then go with her. You," he poked the offender in the chest, "You'll clean up this mess and then help serve. Do it now. I'll be watching." Commander Justis stalked away while I waited for the Yellow Wing to come with me. The clatter of broken crockery being piled onto a tray sounded behind us as the girl led me away from the dining hall.

"Master Healer Ordin, this is Quin, a half-blood from the kitchens," the girl introduced me to a robust Green Wing after we climbed many steps to reach the Healer's aerie.

"Dena, how is your mother?" Master Ordin smiled gently at the girl, his brown eyes kind, his brown hair fine and floating about his head in morning sunlight.

"My mother is fine," Dena hung her head, seemingly ashamed.

"Dena, there is no shame in any job well-done," Master Ordin scolded. "And no shame in real love, either. Your mother has three mates and it was a gamble on whether you'd have your mother's Brown or your father's Yellow. Now, what did they do to this one?" He turned me gently to look at my back.

"One of the guards pulled a nub," Dena explained.

"I see that. He should be whipped for this," Ordin muttered. "It doesn't matter if they're half or whole. Nubs this large are tender and fragile. But then you already know that, don't you, child? Hold on, I'll get the salve and bandages."

I jerked my head up at the Healer's words. Salve? Bandages? What had happened?

"They bleed when they're like this," Dena whispered. "As well as being painful if anyone squeezes them. Nine-year-olds here start growing their wings, and everybody tiptoes around them, they're so touchy and the wings so painful. I remember when mine were growing." She didn't finish; Master Ordin had returned.

Gently he cleaned the injured nub, put salve on it and wrapped it carefully. "No work for two days, and the bandage can come off then," he announced. "If it troubles you, come back and I'll have another look."

Dena and I parted after a while so she could go back to the kitchen and I could find my way to Gurnil's Library. He started to ask questions when I appeared, then saw the bandage on my nub and pulled his words back. I walked past him into the Library itself and closing my eyes, searched for what I wanted most. Without fail, my talent answered, so I walked to a shelf three rows back and pulled a book from a shelf almost too high to reach.

The Deaths of Elabeth and Camryn, the title proclaimed. Now I would discover what many talked of when they hurled insults my way. I was determined to know why someone would feel compelled to injure me when they knew from experience how tender the nubs might be. I imagined the pain of it was akin to a kick in the testicles.

"You read?" Gurnil was walking beside me as I opened the book and flipped past the first few pages to get to the actual beginning. What I read that afternoon explained much, and Gurnil kept an eye on me, offering me lunch after a while.

As I read, I learned that there had never been a King in Fyris before Tamblin. Tandelis, his elder brother, had held the throne before Tamblin took it. He and all the previous male rulers of Fyris had borne the title of Prince.

Tamblin, thinking to take the throne by force from his brother and declare himself the first King, killed Tandelis and a group of visitors inside the throne room one summer morning nearly sixteen turns earlier. That group of visitors included King Camryn, Queen Elabeth and Princess Lirin of the Avii.

"All dead," Gurnil read over my shoulder while sipping a cup of tea. "It was most heartbreaking when Lirin's tiny body was delivered with the others. Most heartbreaking, indeed."

"Yevil killed them." My voice cracked from turns of disuse.

"Yevil?" Gurnil hid his shock at my speech as well as he could.

"King Tamblin's right hand. He is evil." I shut the book forcefully and stood.

"Calls himself King, does he? We call him bastard and murderer. If it weren't for the First Ordinance, he would be dead, now."

"None are safe around Yevil Orklis. If you have a word that means worse than bastard or murderer, then that is Yevil Orklis."

"How did you learn to read?" Gurnil trailed after me.

"I have no idea," I told him and became silent once more.

Two days later, I was back in the kitchen, carrying trays of food to waiting officers. Gurnil informed me that Justis' presence inside the dining hall on the day of my attack was a fortuitous accident—he normally ate with the King and other members of the King's Council. Gurnil knew of this because he, as Master of the Scholar's Guild, was a member of the King's Council even as Justis was, being Commander of the Black Wing Guards.

Nevertheless, I was not attacked or shoved again by the guards, but that did not keep Jadin from delivering blows along with his insults, or keep the other kitchen workers from leveling their hatred at me. I wanted to tell them that Tamblin, Yevil and the King's inner circle were only fourteen men out of many people who populated Fyris, and most of those did not deserve the hatred of the Avii. They'd had no hand in the killing of Camryn, Elabeth or their child. Now, all I had to do was find a reference to the First Ordinance that Gurnil had spoken of.

Food was still not offered to me as I worked my shifts in the kitchen, and when I wasn't serving, I was set to peeling or chopping vegetables. I was not allowed near the stove, which fascinated me—it was operated by power instead of burning wood.

Master Cook Barth would frown if I walked anywhere near it, so I quelled my curiosity and stayed away. Every day I went to my small room near the Library, very hungry and increasingly weary. At times, I followed Gurnil to the Guild dining hall, but as I was truly not welcome there, he often brought a plate back to me, after watching the cook dish it up herself.

The first moon-turn was winding down, too—I'd kept count and there were two days left of it as I made my way to the kitchens that morning. The day started like any other, and the normal insults were ignored as I walked to the serving table to pick up a tray. One of the cooks was pregnant and probably two months from delivery. She it was who laid out sliced meats on plates while others dipped porridge or set out cut fruit or eggs.

I was thinking of my own hunger as I pulled a laden tray onto my shoulder. The pregnant one went to her knees with a cry. Jerking my thoughts away from my own misery, I knew immediately that something terrible had happened. If the baby were not delivered quickly, it would die. I also knew that children among the Avii were a rarity, since they lived such long lives.

Shoving the tray onto the table, I ran toward the pregnant cook, who now writhed in the floor, weeping. "Get back, get back!" I shouted at those crowding around her. "Send for Master Ordin. Quickly!" I dropped to my knees beside the distraught mother and using up every bit of energy that I held, pulled the babe from the mother's body so it could breathe.

The cord was still attached and the child was exercising his lungs when Master Ordin and two other healers came through the kitchen at a run. Everyone else had backed away from me the moment I'd taken the child, and a golden haze still surrounded the infant, the mother and me when Ordin knelt at my side.

"He would have died if I hadn't done it," I carefully placed the squalling babe in Ordin's hands. "I should go. I feel light-headed."

I did feel light-headed. Dizzy, too. Three steps I took toward the kitchen door when the blackness came. The last I remembered was the hands that caught me before I fell, and those hands were quite large and blue.

CHAPTER 9

"Mother and child are fine. Perfect. I couldn't have done a better job if I'd been standing over Raina, with a Kondari physician at my back." Ordin accepted a cup of tea from Dena. She'd followed him and the others after a litter had come for Raina and the baby.

"How did she do it?" Gurnil arrived after someone informed him that the Larentii had disappeared with Quin as soon as she'd performed what looked to be a miracle.

"Master Gurnil, I saw it," Dena breathed. "I think she put her hands right through Raina's belly and came out with the child, but Raina didn't have a mark on her afterward, and the cord was coming from the proper place, too, if you understand," Dena's comment was nodded away by Ordin.

"Master Cook Barth says the same, and he didn't want it to be that way. He still wants to find fault with the girl, where there's no fault to be found. Is that correct, Dena?" Ordin turned his eyes toward the girl, who blushed.

"Yes, Master Ordin. She never does anything wrong, but they all insult her anyway, and Jadin hits her when Master Barth isn't looking. Worst of all, Barth never offers her food. I think she doesn't eat until she leaves the kitchen."

"That would explain the fainting," Gurnil stood angrily. "I'll go straight to Master Nina myself. Barth should have a few stripes for that alone."

"My question is this—where is the girl now? That's a powerful healer, and we haven't had one of those in centuries," Ordin snorted. "Where in Liron's countryside do you think the Larentii took her?"

⸎

Disorientation clouded my mind when I awoke, so I blinked several times, trying to bring what I thought to be dream remnants into focus. "It is not a dream, Quin. This is something you should have seen when you arrived. These never think of it, it being commonplace to them," Daragar's voice came.

I was lying in his arms when I awoke and looked out upon a huge glass bowl with meadows, gardens and flocks in the center. Daragar stood upon a glass spire that rose high in the air, and I had no idea how he managed to balance himself and hold me at the same moment.

"This castle is twice as large as Lironis," Daragar informed me as I stared at sheep and cattle grazing below us. The green of the meadows made me want to weep it was so beautiful, with fruit trees growing in neat rows in the distance. This was what Fyris should be, and wasn't. The bowl was so large I couldn't see the far edge of it, and all of it was glass.

"It takes a day to ride across Lironis," I whispered.

"Yes. If you travel by horse, it does. Now, young one, we will find something for you to eat." I looked into Daragar's eyes; they were bright and shining and kind.

"Thank you for catching me," I lowered my eyes, embarrassed.

"I would not have forgiven myself if I hadn't."

⸎

"What have we here?" Daragar and I had disappeared from our high vantage point and reappeared inside a kitchen I did not recognize. A woman with blonde hair piled atop her head stared at me, her fists settled squarely on ample hips.

“The one who saved your daughter and her child,” Daragar put me down. I wavered, but his hands held me up gently. “She has not received a meal from Master Cook Barth since she began working for him a moon-turn ago.”

“This is the half-blood,” the woman sighed as she looked me up and down. “Doubtless a babe when it happened, and blameless in it as well. Barth will know my fury. Soon. After I feed this one, here. Girl, sit before you fall, and I’ll make something for you.”

“She does not eat meat,” Daragar explained for me.

“All the better. I have beans and lentils, and some greens ready.”

I received a bowl of food quickly and set about eating as swiftly as I could without appearing rude. “I am Master Cook Nina, Master of the Cook’s Guild and cook for the Royal family and the Council, most of whom are real asses,” Nina handed a chunk of bread to me. I dipped it immediately in my beans and lentils to soak up some of the broth. It was delicious. Likely, her cooking skills had made Nina Guild Master for the cooks and kitchen helpers.

“Ordin says my grandchild might have died,” Nina settled onto a seat across from me. We both sat at a prep table on high stools while I ate and Nina watched.

“The placenta separated suddenly and the child was deprived of oxygen. If my little one here hadn’t taken the child quickly, he would have died. As it is, the child is perfectly healthy. Ordin is correct on that matter,” Daragar confirmed.

“I’ve never known you or any other Larentii to say more than two words before,” Nina handed Daragar a speculative look.

“I speak when it is necessary,” Daragar said.

“I see that. Well, girl, would you like dessert? I think I have some cobbler left over from lunch.”

My spoon dropped into the bowl and I stared at Master Cook Nina, dumbfounded. None had ever offered dessert to me before—not even Wolter. Leftover pies and cakes were always given to the lesser nobles before any of the servants, and even then, only the highly placed ones could hope for sweets to come their way.

"She's never had any," Daragar said quietly as I continued to stare at Nina.

"You'll have some today," Nina declared and went to get another bowl. Not only did I have peach cobbler for the first time in my life, but a glass of chilled milk to go with it. I could have wept at the taste of both; they were so good together. Every scrap that Nina gave me was eaten quickly and with a great deal of happy satisfaction.

"You could have sent word," Ordin and Gurnil walked into Nina's kitchen together.

"The girl hasn't eaten properly since she arrived. I'll be banging Barth's head with a skillet, rest assured," Nina declared, hands on hips again and a nasty glint in her eyes. I shrunk back the moment Ordin walked in—I feared that he might be angry, since I'd acted as I had. Daragar was correct—I knew the child would die if something weren't done, so I did it. I was prepared to take a beating for it, too.

"Master Ordin is not angry with you, Quin," Daragar placed a hand on my head for just a moment, his blue eyes meeting mine. "I must go." He disappeared, as he always did.

"First the Orb and now a Larentii," Gurnil muttered at my back.

"She's a half-blood and has no wing color. How can we place her in the Healer's Guild?" Justis watched with hooded eyes as Ordin stood before the Red Wing King. He'd argued his case to allow Quin to work with the healers. Jurris was against it and was now voicing his opinion on the matter.

Justis held no doubts as to where that opinion originated—Halthea stood at Jurris' side, just as she often did in Council meetings. Jurris turned to her often, asking her opinion. Simpering always, Halthea never failed to give it.

Jurris' two other wives seldom appeared at Council meetings, although they were welcome as Jurris' mates. Jurris never listened to Green-Winged Wimla or Brown-Winged Vorina as much as he did his Red-Winged princess. Yes, a Red Wing Queen would have as much say as the Red Wing King, and Justis knew that Jurris desired Halthea on the throne at his side. Elabeth had voiced her distaste for the girl many times in Justis' hearing, and flatly refused to name Halthea heir.

Justis thought the matter settled when little Lirin was born, but the child died when Camryn and Elabeth were murdered. Now, Ordin and Gurnil argued for the girl, the others against. He frowned when Nina spoke. No, Nina hadn't said anything against the girl, other than she was half-blood and didn't have wings, but that fell right into Brown Wing Farisa's opinion that no half-blood could be anything other than a lowly servant.

The fact that Farisa had never seen the girl had Justis narrowing his eyes while she argued loudly and gestured wildly. Gray Wing Gordin agreed with Farisa, his voluble dissent likely heard by yellow-winged servants several halls away. Jurris expected his brother to vote his way, but Justis disliked what the detractors were saying.

There were four votes against Quin already, so his would count for nothing. Justis' argument would only anger his brother, who might consider going around him at last and placing Halthea on the Queen's throne against Justis' objections. Jurris and Justis shared the same mother, with different fathers. Justis' father, a Black Wing like himself, had always advised Justis to select his battles with a wise head and a stern heart.

"What say you, Commander?" Jurris had come to him when the other arguments looked to die down somewhat.

"My vote is with my brother," Justis replied, standing and stretching his ebon wings. It was his way of telling all present that the debate had gone on long enough. Enough votes had been cast to keep the girl serving in the kitchens already. She was beautiful, there was no doubt, but she had no feathers and the lengthy, bare nubs were unattractive.

Justis' wingspan was longer than three tall men, standing head to heel. Jurris' Red Wings were six hands shorter than his brother's, but they were *Red.*

Ordin was angry enough as he stalked past Justis, but Gurnil bristled and rustled his wings as he walked past. Justis sighed—he'd have to smooth feathers somehow, and Green and Blue had often been his allies in the past. He'd let them down in order to fight a more personal battle. "Thank you, Justis," Halthea had come up silently as Justis watched Gurnil walk away. Trailing a finger down his chest, Halthea offered a vapid smile.

"Lady," Justis dipped his head respectfully and strode toward the arched doorway, leaving Halthea staring angrily at his back.

"I can't believe Nina would do this. Justis, too. I was counting on both votes, and they abandon us. That girl can likely heal almost anything, and they do this." Ordin paced on Gurnil's private terrace. Outside terraces were reserved for royalty and Guild Masters.

"As it is, if we can't deal with something, we have to carry the patient to Kondar for treatment, and that means another shipment of glass bowls and vases. Farisa should have thought of that before she laid out her sermon. We barely make enough from our imports now to run Avii castle. We can't afford to give our work away to heal anything beyond our abilities, not to mention the problems we're having with any childbirth and the reasons there are no pregnancies to begin with."

"I know," Gurnil held up a hand. "We both know that once Jurris cut off all contact with Fyris after the murders, that our trade with them was cut off as well. Kondar has grown and evolved, Fyris hasn't. Perhaps he should have sought another way around this and backed someone in Fyris who could take the throne and bring the murderers to justice."

"That would have been the prudent thing to do," Ordin agreed. "But Jurris was named heir to Camryn, therefore he rules. Then, just as it was today, the Council majority ruled in his favor."

"And the girl goes back to the kitchens," Gurnil muttered.

"May I join you?" Justis flapped in, landing perfectly beside Ordin who froze in mid-pace. "Here," Justis held out a bottle of wine. "You're not looking at the broader picture here," Justis smiled at Ordin and Gurnil. "Let the girl work the kitchens and send for her if you need her. Barth owes me, anyway. I'll advise him to let the girl go if she's needed."

"So, it's all right to just trample her underfoot until we want something, is that it?" Gurnil stood as Justis' smile faded. "How long do we mistreat a race, Justis, until we become our enemies?" Gurnil nodded to Ordin and walked toward the glass-paned doors leading into Ordin's private suite.

"I have to admit that I have no appetite for it myself. Good night, Commander." Ordin followed the path Gurnil had taken, leaving Justis standing amid Ordin's flower garden on his private terrace.

They'd discussed me during the Council meeting—I knew it without doubt. I also knew how the vote had gone and didn't expect it to be otherwise. It was just as well—why should I have any lofty ambitions? A kitchen drudge had been the extent of my life, a few moon-turns as Amlis' page notwithstanding. He'd been no different, taking what I'd offered him and still treating me as the common servant I was.

Dena, though, I worried for her. She watched the Black Wings covertly, as if she wished for that life. Born as a Yellow Wing in a strict, hierarchical system, she had no hope of attaining that dream. Fyris was the same—if you were born a servant, you died a servant. There was little in the way of bettering oneself. Business owners tended to birth more business owners, while nobles tediously birthed more of the same.

"Quin, we'll have Kondari visitors tomorrow," Gurnil informed me the following evening. "They pay a fee to search our books for ancient history. The money is useful to buy what we can't make ourselves. They'll eat in the Guild dining hall. Two Yellow Wings will come in the morning to clean their assigned quarters and provide fresh linens. Generally they are more respectful than some of ours." I watched Gurnil's eyes carefully as he explained things to me.

"What do they look like?" I asked, curious.

"Much like we do, only without wings or nubs," Gurnil smiled at my question. "Kondari have a different language, but those coming tomorrow speak enough of ours to get by. And Ordin wishes you to come to him sometime in the next week; he noticed that your nubs are thrice as long now as they were when you first arrived."

"They're growing more?" I was dismayed. Jadin still muttered naked wing at my back every day. He still hit me with a wooden spoon, too, when Barth wasn't looking.

"You don't have a hand mirror, do you?" Gurnil frowned. "Let me find one for you. Keep it on your dresser, to see for yourself."

"Glass is a luxury only the wealthy can afford in Fyris," I muttered. Gurnil had walked away a few steps but turned back at my words.

"How are they doing? Those in Fyris, I mean," he asked.

"They're dying. Just like their land," I sighed.

"What is this?" Amlis accepted the tattered message from Rodrik, who'd received it earlier from Garth in the stables.

"A conscript brought it from Vhrist," Rodrik replied. "The brown seal is still intact, no matter how bad it looks."

A brown seal meant the letter had been dictated by one and written by another, who sold their services to do so. If the sender couldn't write or had no wish to write it himself, he often paid someone else to do it and a brown wax seal with a courier's stamp was set afterward.

"Addressed to me?" Amlis accepted the message that looked to have been carried inside a filthy saddlebag.

"To the Prince Heir, Amlis of Lironis," Rodrik said.

"Fine. Open it and read it," Amlis ordered. Rodrik broke the seal and unfolded the paper.

My Prince, the message began. *It is with much sorrow and regret that I deliver this news to you, and had I known who it was we carried, I would never have agreed to accept payment to sail my ship to Aviia. She was brought to me unconscious and bound, her head covered by a bag. The bag was not removed until we had nearly reached the glass fortress. Only then did I learn it was your Finder that the bitch from Firith paid six men to kidnap, and it broke my heart to deliver her to those who would only take her life. I will not sign my name, as I know what my fate will be should I do so. I promised the girl that I would inform you as to what happened to her. My sincerest apologies to you, my Lord, for my mistakes.*

The message was unsigned. Amlis rose and cursed, before flinging much of what sat upon his desk across the study.

"Why do you think Mother would send me this," Amlis rattled the message he'd gotten from Omina a week earlier, "rather than the real one?" Rodrik had gotten Amlis calmed after a while. A good bottle of wine helped.

"I have no idea why she would say that Finder was still under Farin's care, rather than hauled off to the Avii. If I didn't have confirmation on Mirisa's accidental death from one of her father's own men, I'd doubt that, too," Rodrik shook his head. "Something is going on and we have no way to discover what it is," Amlis muttered angrily. "How could she do this? How?"

"Amlis, she was quite overcome with your brother's death. You know this. And she worries that you might fall to an assassin's hand as well. Garth is watching Yevil as well as he can, as is Hirill, but Yevil is playing the solicitous friend to your father right now."

"Father has barely spoken six words to me since I arrived, Rodrik. And he has been approaching Lady Dimita, if my eyes do not deceive."

"Amlis, I have seen few pregnancies lately, and even fewer brought to term. Do not fret about your father replacing you. At this moment, he should worry about what stands at his elbow most days. Besides, he is still married to your mother. To claim a legitimate heir, he must put her away from him, and you know what she might do if he suggests that."

"And that could mean my mother's life is in danger, just as mine is," Amlis sighed and poured another cup of wine. "With her death, he is free to marry again."

"A frightening thought," Rodrik agreed.

"Quin, see me in my aerie when you are finished with your duties tomorrow," Master Healer Ordin had come to me after I'd put off going to him. I nodded to him and lifted another tray to take to the Black Wings waiting in the dining room. Ordin gave me a tight smile, frowned at Master Cook Barth and went on his way.

The Kondari had come, just as Gurnil said they would, and they would go through the stacks in the massive Library until time for bed. For four days, I'd carried trays of food and drink to them as they pored over books well into the night. Gurnil looked at them oddly when they spoke quickly about this or that paragraph in a book, not understanding completely what was being said.

Strangely enough, I understood their language clearly, and could have written it as well, if I'd had the inclination. Another, unexplainable thing that I was left to ponder. They were looking for information on a cure for some terrible disease, and had not the skill to heal it themselves. I guessed, and quickly, that they were physicians. I had no idea what they thought to find in books stuffed in the Avii Library.

"It says here the last talented healer walked through the gate six centuries ago," One of three men pointed to a phrase in his book.

"So, there are no others? High President Charkisul is desperate."

"We know they've asked to bring their severely wounded to us at times; of course there is no other," the third man declared in frustration. "Charkisul is grasping at the moons. There is no cure for this illness, and it is time he faced that fact and made preparations for his son's death."

"We cannot go back and tell him we have not exhausted every option, or read every passage," the second, more levelheaded one pointed out quietly.

"No, we will do our duty as assigned, and give him a complete report upon our return. Come, let us get back to work," the first one chided, and all three went back to sifting through stacks of books.

"Quin, do you know what this is?" Ordin held one of my now lengthy nubs in his hands, fingering a knob at the end of it. We stood before a large mirror, and I turned to look over my shoulder at what he was touching. I shook my head—I had no idea what it was.

"This is the beginning of a hinge," Ordin sighed. "The hinge we have to fold our wings up to keep them from dragging the floor behind us," he added. "You are growing wings, young one. Let us both pray to Liron that they are green."

"But I have no feathers," I pointed out the obvious.

"Quin, I feel the beginnings of pin feathers," Ordin ran a hand down the inside edge of my lengthening nubs. "In two or three weeks, we may have to roll off the pinfeathers so the feathers may grow out. We will know quickly which color they are then."

"Master Ordin, that cannot be a good thing," I quavered. "So many already think me a terrible aberration. What will they do when I grow feathers? I can only imagine the contempt will increase."

"Why are they growing now?" Ordin stroked his chin, muttering his thoughts aloud.

"Every spring, someone from the stables came and cut them away, at the court physician's orders," I hung my head. "Until this turn. The court physician died recently, and there was a new stablemaster."

"Do you mean to tell me those barbarians cut away your wings?" Ordin was furious, pacing away from me in heated anger. "Child, that must have been terrible pain," he hesitated in his muttered cursing to turn back to me.

"It was terrible pain," I nodded. "Master Ordin, I must get back to the Library. The Kondari physicians are searching for a cure to a terrible disease, and they are finding nothing in the books."

"Those are physicians?" Ordin lifted an eyebrow in surprise.

"Yes," I nodded. "They search for a cure for the High President's son. He is dying and they cannot cure him."

"How do you know this? They always speak in their own language when going through the stacks."

"I can understand it," my face went hot with the embarrassing admission.

"And Gurnil has been grumpy for days, because he cannot get them to tell him what they search for," Ordin said. I shrank away when Ordin stalked past me, snatching up a piece of parchment from his massive desk and hastily scribbling a note to Gurnil. "Take this to Gurnil and make sure he reads it immediately. I must go to the King." Ordin shooed me away from his suite, and I nearly ran down narrow, twisting corridors to get back to the Library and Gurnil, who waited there for me.

"The High President's son is ill?" Jurris sat on a comfortable chaise inside his suite, Justis standing nearby, listening but not speaking as Ordin supplied information he'd gleaned from Quin.

"Yes, Lord King," Ordin nodded respectfully. "I believe this is privileged information that the High President does not wish to be broadcast; else they would have asked Gurnil for assistance. They have not."

"I see. And what do you think we will gain from this information?" Jurris asked in a bored voice.

"We could gain much, if we cure the High President's son. We have something they will pay much for, when you think about it. If Quin can heal the boy, what might the High President offer in return?"

"Will he offer money for jewelry? More solar-powered machinery? We can do much with what the High President can offer," Halthea wandered in from Jurris' bedroom dressed in a red silk caftan, a glass of wine in her hand.

"We must pay for their physicians' services," Gurnil pointed out. "Why can we not demand the same?"

"You think the girl can do this? We'll have to cover those ugly nubs," Jurris rose. Ordin knew Jurris was not only considering this suggestion, he was already counting out the credits for his personal treasury. Ordin also knew that Jurris recognized the girl's talents; he was just too stubborn, too prejudiced and too immersed in Halthea's short-sightedness to allow him to take the girl and train her.

Ordin already intended to bring the severely wounded to her anyway, so they wouldn't have to be shipped to Kondari physicians. He hoped, yet again, that the girl would sprout Green Wings. That would make things infinitely better.

"I'll have the tailors make capes," Justis said and strode from Jurris' suite.

"Problem solved," Halthea examined a nail.

I huddled in a corner and trembled as three Kondari physicians by turns shouted and frowned at Gurnil. And this after he explained that I'd healed a mother and child not long ago in halting words, worried over which ones the Kondari might understand.

They were planning to offer my services to the Kondari, for a price. That information lodged in my head as soon as King Jurris had decided it. I had no idea why Ordin wanted to put me through this, but it was obvious that the King (and others) desired much of the technology available from Kondar.

"You and I are going with her, as is Justis," Ordin flapped into the Library, his wide, green robes swaying about him. His wings were ruffled from the flight—he'd flown and landed on the Library's terrace.

I could understand that Ordin and Gurnil might go, but Justis? Unless it was to guard the King's newest asset—me. And just as it had been in Fyris, I'd become a bargaining tool. No, I would reap none of the reward for doing what they asked of me; they would take it for themselves and demand exactly the same the next time. And the times after that. I was used to it, but still it burned.

"The High President will offer nothing until the boy is healed and the healing lasts and is confirmed," the eldest Kondari physician said, arms crossed over his chest.

"Agreed. We expect no less," Ordin nodded. "But once it is confirmed, then we will demand payment. The King waits for you now, to discuss terms."

My next two days were spent proving myself (under Ordin's close supervision) as I healed broken bones, burns and a few rashes. Not much, but that was all Ordin could provide in the way of illness and injury for the physician's approval at the moment. I did not offer that I'd cured a small girl in Vhrist of the wasting disease. The Kondari physicians called it cancer, and a rare form of the disease was what afflicted the High President's son. I worried they would question my talent and beat me, but I did not voice those concerns aloud.

"She seldom speaks," Ordin said when the eldest physician, an old and much wrinkled man, remarked on my silence. He did not elaborate upon my past and I certainly wasn't going to enlighten the man.

Capes were brought on the second day, and I was asked to wear them the entire time I was in Kondar. I didn't mind; I'd gotten a good glimpse of my still naked, lengthening nubs, which hung past my waist. The hinge that Ordin had pointed out to me looked to be growing larger, too, with an extension past the joint. I truly was growing wings, and they looked hideous.

More clothing was provided as well, in a combination of blues, yellows and greens (all backless), to match the capes provided. A Yellow Wing with the talent for hair cutting, makeup and such came to trim my hair so I would be presentable to the High President and his family. Otherwise, I think I might have been sent to Kondar dressed as poorly as I usually was in the stained, yellow outfits I wore in the kitchen.

"We'll fly in their mechanical contraption," Gurnil explained as we made our way onto the grass lying inside the glass bowl, after walking through a door I'd never passed through before. In the distance, I saw a flock of sheep tended by a watchful Gray Wing. Sighing a bit, as there was no time to spend with tiny lambs and mothers who bleated in my direction, I climbed high steps into a contraption that had whirling, blade-like wings attached. In no time, we were fastened into seats, which bore belts with metal ends that clipped together.

"It will take two clicks to arrive," Ordin said beside me, bouncing in his seat when we hit a pocket of unruly winds. Justis sat across the aisle, his eyes hooded and no expression on his features. Gurnil attempted to speak with the physicians, but he stumbled through the Kondari language just as the Kondari stumbled through ours.

The Kondari had communication devices that they employed often, either tapping in written messages or speaking directly with another who was far away. King Tamblin thought to attack these? It would be the same as if a child with a stick threatened a fully-grown man equipped with a sword. There would be no battle and Fyris would be destroyed in a blink.

"Why has Kondar not approached or attacked Fyris?" I turned to Ordin to ask.

"Because of the shield," Ordin replied as quietly as he could. "I will explain it later, young one. In the meantime, do not mention Fyris to any of these." He gripped my arm to drive home the seriousness of his statement. Without his telling me, I already understood that doing so would place Fyris in danger. Somehow, the only ones who seemed to realize the continent of Fyris existed were the winged Avii that dwelt inside a glass bowl in the middle of a very deep ocean.

Huddling into my seat, I spared a glance at Justis, who stared through a window of our flying transport, ignoring all else around him. Perhaps I was the only other there who realized that he wished to be flying himself through the white, misty clouds we encountered on our way to Kondar.

I will never forget my first sight of Kondar, even from the air. Great cities blurred beneath us, and many tall buildings rose high in the air as we flew swiftly by them. With the gift I had, I realized that the population numbered in the millions—a staggering amount to me, who barely had counted anything past hundreds before.

Kondar was large—perhaps seventy times larger than Fyris, and my skin went cold at the thought. Again, I realized how much of a fool Tamblin truly was, and Yevil likely encouraged his erroneous thinking. I also considered what kind of shield would be strong enough to hide a small continent from people as technologically advanced as the Kondari.

Soon enough, our flying machine began to drift downward, until it settled carefully atop a tall building. I'd wondered along the way what one of the structures would look like if one could go inside.

I learned quickly enough. I was herded from the machine and through a doorway on the rooftop upon which we landed, then led toward doors that slid open at the touch of a lighted button at the side.

"I hope this isn't a fool's errand," the eldest Kondari physician spoke as we crowded into the waiting metal cubicle. The doors closed again once we were inside and the cubicle moved downward, giving my stomach a slight jerk before it settled itself.

"You are not required to bow before the High President," another physician instructed as the cubicle jerked slightly and stopped. "As you are foreign, we will observe your protocol instead, and accept a respectful nod."

Ordin had a hand at my back, ushering me from the metal cubicle. We were led down a long hall, tiled in a material unfamiliar to me, and overhead, long, artificial lights illuminated our journey.

Many rooms lined the hallway, some with doors partly open. I saw the sick lying in beds, many of whom were connected by strange tubes to beeping or whirring machines. But these were not the ones I'd been brought to help; like me, they were unimportant. I was here to help the better connected and more fortunate.

"Here." We were led into a room much more spacious than any we'd walked past. A wide bank of windows lined one side, overlooking a lush garden filled with plants and flowers, many of which I had never seen before. Lying in a bed near those windows was a young man, unconscious and oblivious to the garden view he'd been given.

Thin and wasted he was, his cheeks pale and falling in upon themselves. He also was connected to softly beeping devices, and I understood that medicine was slowly being administered. I also understood that it was to keep the pain at bay—the disease was taking the boy, who was just past sixteen.

"Tell me you can help him," a man stood beside the bed, his suffering at the fate of his son aging his features. Here was a man who loved his child. For that alone, I would heal the boy and do it gladly.

"I will do this," I nodded to the man, speaking in his language. Ordin informed me later that when I put my hands on the young man, the golden light was so bright in the room that all present closed their eyes against it. I was unaware, truly, as I was changing the things in the boy's body that had turned against it, reshaping them to follow their natural path.

I also heard from Gurnil that the boy opened his eyes and spoke with his father not long after I finished healing him. I was carried away from the boy's room by Justis; I'd fainted after such a difficult healing, after all.

CHAPTER 10

"We are expected to stay while the tests are run," Ordin informed me when I woke. A tray of fruit and other food was waiting, along with fruit juice and water. Consuming the fruit juice first, I drank thirstily while Ordin watched. He and the others had already eaten; I discovered that as I bit into an apple. So seldom had I gotten fruit, even after coming to the Avii, that I relished every bite, right down to the core.

"Try this," Ordin partially peeled a long, yellow fruit and handed it to me. I almost went into raptures at the taste, it was so good. I was too full to try the rest after that, and wanted to sleep again. Ordin nodded and closed the door of the private suite I'd been given, allowing me the sleep my body demanded.

"How's the boy?" Justis asked when Gurnil entered their assigned apartment.

"So far, all tests indicate the disease has disappeared. Their technicians don't know what to make of this. The President placed guards outside Quin's room, however, and that concerns me. Gurnil is asking to see the President, and they keep putting him off."

"I'm not surprised. My brother asked for an exorbitant amount. Perhaps Charkisul is protecting his investment, until he learns his son is healthy."

"How much did Jurris ask for the healing?" Ordin narrowed his eyes at Justis.

"Four million. Do not say where that information came from. He'll know." Justis rustled his wings. "A parent will pay most any price to save a child. Jurris was counting on that."

"Jurris is still angry that Halthea hasn't conceived," Ordin grunted. "You think he'll ask Quin to fix that, too, then keep her in the kitchens?"

"I'd prefer that didn't happen," Justis turned his back on Ordin to stare out the window in the main room of their shared apartment. "He still has Wimla and Vorina. Either would be happy to provide a child."

"But the odds aren't as good that the children will be Red-Winged," Ordin snorted. "He wants a Red-Winged heir."

"Perhaps there is a good reason Halthea hasn't conceived, then. Few are getting children, even here in Kondar. The President is fortunate to have a child. Doubly fortunate that Quin was able to heal him." Justis shook his head.

"How much of that money will go to Quin?" Ordin asked softly.

Justis snorted his answer.

"Message from my father." Rodrik handed the sealed parchment to Amlis, who sat next to a window in Timblor's old suite, staring at low clouds hanging over the courtyard and walls surrounding the castle.

Amlis accepted the message absently and broke the seal before turning his eyes away from the gray skies outside. "It's as if the rain is poison, as well as the ground it falls upon," Amlis unrolled the message with a sigh. "Three ships built. Father wants six, plus the conscription of all larger vessels. Not much time left, Rod, before we have to devise a plan to curtail this madness."

"Have you seen the recruits coming in? Less than half what your father wants, and half of those look sickly."

"I've seen them. Any news on healers? We sent the conscription notices out ten days ago."

"I have no idea whether there are any to come," Rodrik replied, watching as the first raindrop slid down the window. It was spring, and spring brought rain. "The healers in Vhoorth are too old for conscription, or are women. Perhaps it is the same everywhere."

"Then perhaps it is time to speak to Father about conscripting female healers."

"He won't like that."

"I know. It's time he realized that women are as good as men at many things."

"Better at some," Rodrik muttered. "I worry that the girls aren't being educated, when the boys are."

"True. Rod, so many things need changing."

"And to speak those things aloud could get both of us killed."

"Also true. Where is my father?"

"In his study, with Yevil."

"Then now is not the time to approach him."

"Wise. Very wise."

"Does it ever concern you that this is used instead of coin?" Justis studied the chip embedded in a square, clear substance. It resembled glass but didn't break, as glass would.

"That is only the record of our payment. The actual payment is recorded in a machine at a building. You and your brother have access, through your fingers and your eyes. I fail to understand the machinery required to do the scans, as they're called." Gurnil shook his head.

An envoy from the President had left minutes earlier, after delivering payment for Quin's healing. Quin was still under guard, and the envoy had promised a visit from the President that evening at dinner, before the Avii left for home.

"I think he'll make an offer for Quin," Ordin murmured before rising from his seat and stalking toward the window. "He'll offer to buy her, and your brother will name a price. She is not a slave, to be bought and sold," Ordin whirled to face Justis, an angry scowl on his face.

Justis blinked at Ordin before nodding. Ordin's words made sense. "I owe you," he nodded at Ordin. "I speak for Jurris while we're here. I will refuse, and this will never reach my brother's ears. Should Charkisul have need, he can negotiate with my brother in the future for Quin's services."

"That does nothing to elevate Quin's status," Gurnil rounded on Justis. "He'll leave her in the kitchen until he sells her talents again."

"What do you suggest I do?" Justis snapped. "He is King. The girl's wings are growing. Perhaps she'll have Green Wings, and the problem will be solved."

"I have little faith in that," Ordin said.

"When will the pin feathers require rolling? We should see the beginnings of color soon, don't you think? My black was seen quite early, after all."

"We should see that soon, but there's still no guarantee that the King will bring her out of the kitchen. Quin has little support from the Council, and they will have no idea how much Quin brought to your brother's coffers."

"She is only one half-blood," Justis pointed out. "Are you willing to divide the Council over this?"

"You should ask yourself what is worth dividing the Council, if she is not," Gurnil snapped. "Aviia is no better than Fyris, if we treat the lowliest as they do. I recall the last healer we had, in Elabeth's time. He walked through the gate in disgust."

"I wouldn't mention that around my brother," Justis growled.

"Your brother's Red-Winged father caused it," Ordin snapped. "Or should I not mention that around *you*?"

"Treven is dead—he walked through the gate fifty turns past, need I remind you?" Justis said. "Camryn named Jurris his heir after that. There is no taint on him."

"Treven didn't walk through the gate. He was forced through," Ordin pointed out. "After he'd been caught dallying with Fyrisian women."

"He made no children with them," Justis said. "That has been proven."

"Hmmph," Gurnil sniffed. "That doesn't take into account what else he did that was never proven."

"Please, I've read the records. There's no need to call my brother's parentage into question. Treven was always angry that his brother Camryn was named heir. He made his bitterness known in—shall we say—unusual ways?"

"You're saying that Treven would have been a fit ruler?"

"No. I didn't say that," Justis held up a hand. "I'm saying that Camryn and Elabeth both agreed on Jurris being named Camryn's heir. If they'd been wrong, the Orb would have protested."

"How do we know it didn't?"

Justis blinked at Ordin's words.

"There's more than we suspected," High President Charkisul's chief of security, Melis Norwal, handed the chip recording to the President. "But still nothing regarding what they call Fyris. Nothing useful, anyway."

"We know they're not responsible for the poison waste. They've never had sufficient technology to produce it," Charkisul shook his head. "So where is it coming from?"

"We've only gotten a few mentions of Fyris, and there are no explanations and certainly no information," Chief Norwal said. "It's odd, too, that every time we attempt to place cameras and listening devices in that glass behemoth where they live, they stop working immediately. All we have is what we get after they arrive here."

"We're steered away from certain sections in their library, too," Charkisul agreed. "It's as if they're hiding something important, but what might it be?"

"Have the levels of the poison stabilized?"

"No, the levels continue to rise. It's odd that it should show up like this, when we know there's nothing on Siriaa to cause it. There's some speculation that cancers may become widespread as the toxic levels increase."

"What about the girl? Don't you think it's odd that she hasn't been revealed until now? Why would they come to us—pay our physicians for medical treatment—when that was available to them? You'll hear references that the girl is a half-blood, High President," Melis nodded toward the chip. "As well as discussion on one in their past caught dallying with Fyrisian women. I can only assume that the term *Fyrisian* is connected to Fyris, whatever that means."

"I'll listen, but I'll have my interpreter with me, in case I miss anything," Edden agreed. "I'm surprised the girl can speak our language as fluently as she does. Can you explain that?"

"We know the Avii are special; you only have to see their wings to know that. How many of our children draw pictures of them and wish to fly as they do?"

Edden Charkisul sighed and shook his head. "Perhaps it's no different from any other evolution. Who knows why they grew wings and we didn't? Somewhere, and for some reason, it was necessary for them to do so."

"And we suspect they know where the poison originates, and they aren't telling us."

"The girl is underage; not much older than my Berel. We can't question her, and I don't wish to upset her, anyway. She healed my boy."

"Listen to that," Melis gestured toward the chip again. "They say she won't be paid. The Avii King will keep the funds. If we could ask a few gentle questions, perhaps?"

"What if it places her in danger, or they refuse her services if we ask again? We have a guarantee from the Avii healer that should Berel sicken again, they will bring her back. I have to rely on their word."

"That still brings us no closer to a solution regarding the poison, or where to find it."

"I hope we can contain it when we do find it," the High President nodded.

"If we can't, we're in trouble," Melis agreed.

⁂

"Young one, I am Melis Norwal," he introduced himself as he led me away from the rooms I'd been given. Two others followed us—they'd been standing outside my door for hours while I slept.

"Where are we going?" I replied in his language, although I already knew; dinner waited. He wanted to ask questions so badly he almost burst with the desire of it. He wanted to know what Fyris meant, and a cold, steady terror coursed through me. The poison had already reached Kondar's shores.

"Dinner with the High President," Melis responded. "He wishes to thank you for healing his son. While Berel is still too weak to sit with us, he also extends his gratitude. He says he can't recall feeling as good as he does now."

Melis Norwal was neither as tall as Justis, nor as handsome. Nevertheless, their positions were similar. He had dark hair, cropped close to his head, green eyes that were alert to all about him, a steady hand and a lengthy stride. He was a fit guard for the High President.

"His father loves him. That's why I healed him," I said with a shrug. "I'm glad he feels better."

⁂

Dinner was a trying ordeal. I was served vegetables, finely cooked. The food was not the difficulty. Conversation between the High President, Ordin and Gurnil was stilted at best, while Justis ate determinedly and spoke little. Melis, like Justis, said little, choosing to watch Justis with a wary eye.

He knew Justis was dangerous.

He also knew that Justis was brother to Jurris, King of the Avii.

It was the same political dance I'd seen so many times in Lironis between nobles, the inner circle, the King and his sons. The Kondari were peaceful enough, and had no current thoughts of attacking the Avii. If the poison became worse, and their land sickened as Fyris did, that peaceful notion might slip away in favor of gaining useful information.

King Tamblin had no idea what he would face when his ships sailed away from Fyris' northern shore. He may have held hopes of finding lands better off than his, but his options were dwindling. I felt sure I would feel the poison seeping into Kondar if I were allowed to set foot upon its soil.

As it was, I'd only been allowed in high buildings since my arrival.

"Sir Melis," I said, breaking my silence and surprising those around me. "Might I ask a favor?" He, in turn, looked toward the High President.

"You may ask us for almost anything," the High President responded, as he turned to me and smiled.

"I wish to walk outside," I said, while Justis scowled at me.

"That will be arranged the moment dinner is finished," the High President agreed.

My shoes were off as I stood upon grass that had been treated with its own type of poison—such that weeds would not grow. Still, I felt the beginnings of the wrongness. The High President and Melis Norwal were right to be concerned. Fyris' infection would consume everything if it were not stopped.

"Do you wish to see the gardens?" the High President asked.

"No, thank you," I said. "The grass is enough."

We stood in a courtyard outside the President's palace. His home was a square building, constructed of glass and metal. During the day, sunlight would reflect off every surface. At night, Siriaa's moons and clouds were mirrored in its surface. I watched as clouds moved across the back of it, fascinated that an entire building might be used as a mirror.

"We taught them how to make glass," Gurnil's hand dropped to my shoulder as I blinked at the construction the High President called home. "Long ago."

"Your glass art is still the best—we cannot come close to it," the High President said, coming to stand on my other side. He had no idea that far to the south, Fyrisians had no idea how to make proper glass. What they had was from Aviia, and that door was now closed.

I had questions I dared not ask. First among them was how much had the Avii taught the Kondari before the Kondari surpassed their teachers. "We found the Avii by accident, long ago," the High President chuckled. "We'd gotten adept at sailing, and decided to see how far we might go. On our third attempt, we found Avii castle. We'd never seen anything such as that, and our history books tell us the captain of the vessel stared in wonder as people such as he, equipped with wings, flew to the deck of his ship."

"They discovered Yokaru not long after. That is the continent far to Aviia's west," Gurnil informed me. "While Yokaru is not as advanced as Kondar, there is trade between the two lands."

"Yokaru and Kondar were once a single continent," Melis explained. "They broke apart when the planet was in its infancy. Tests prove that the people there are connected through their ancestry to ours. While many of their customs are strange, we come from the same people. They know this, too, and consider us their family."

How wondrous was that—to find family missing for turns uncounted? I sighed. "How fortunate you are," I mumbled.

"Fortunate, indeed. It improved trade relations immediately, once that fact was recognized," the High President agreed. "They often supply raw materials for our manufacturing concerns, and they in turn purchase finished goods or trade for technology."

"We must leave soon," Justis reminded us.

"Yes. Of course," the High President acknowledged.

"Take tomorrow off and visit Master Ordin in the afternoon," Gurnil said, once we reached the Library. The return trip to Aviia was much like the one that had taken us to Kondar, but it was late and I wanted to sleep. "He says he wishes to examine your pin feathers and decide whether they are ready to roll off."

I nodded, covering a yawn.

"Quin, you did a wondrous thing, and I realize you'll receive little thanks here for it. Never forget that Ordin and I understand the magnitude of it, and we will record it in our personal histories."

"Might I have parchment and pens?" I asked hesitantly. I'd never considered making a personal history, but Gurnil had just sown the seeds of it.

"I will supply them tomorrow. Go to bed, you're exhausted."

"Thank you, Master Gurnil." I turned and headed toward my bedroom.

Dena had come to Master Ordin for a burn to her fingers. I found her inside his workroom when I arrived for my appointment the following afternoon.

"Quin," she smiled, pleased to see me for some odd reason.

"May I?" I held out my hand.

Surprised, she placed her burned fingers in my outstretched hand. It was a simple fix and there was no scar left behind when I released her hand.

"That's—thank you," she breathed. "Burns are always the worst."

"I still say take the rest of the day off and report to Master Barth tomorrow," Ordin nodded at Dena. "Your shift was almost over, anyway."

"You're welcome," I said, giving Dena a nod as well. She almost skipped out of Master Ordin's workroom—the burn had blistered and looked painful to me. No trace of it, or the pain accompanying it, had remained.

"Quin, remove your cape and I'll look at your pin feathers," Ordin made a circle with his fingers, indicating that I should turn around. I removed the cape first, then turned so he could examine my wing nubs.

"Definitely getting longer," he acknowledged. "They're down past your knees, now."

They were—I'd checked in the mirror after my shower. I'd begun washing them, too, although they were tender to the touch.

"Yes," Ordin grunted, touching my left nub with practiced fingers. "This won't be comfortable, but it must be done," he said and rolled off the first pinfeather. I gasped at the pain of it.

Ordin gave me the bitter brew for pain after a while and continued working. Tears came to my eyes several times, and I'm not sure I would have made it through the ordeal had Daragar not arrived.

I blinked at the tall Larentii through a pain-filled haze. "I will remedy this," he said before Ordin could stop him. Touching a long, blue finger to my forehead, I was rendered unconscious while Ordin continued his work.

"I can only see the barest hint, but there is no precedent for it," Ordin accepted a cup of wine from Gurnil.

"What do you mean? What color are they?"

"I saw white. With silver, gold and copper, like the threads in her hair. I don't know what to make of it." Ordin gulped half his wine before shaking his head in confusion. "Daragar transported her to her bed afterward."

"I find it astounding that the Larentii has taken such an interest in her, although you and I find her just as fascinating."

"Certainly something we've never seen. No half-blood has ever had talent."

"We can't say that with absolute conviction—Fyris kills them as soon as they learn what they are, or sends them here, where Jurris does the same."

"Except for Quin," Ordin pointed out. "I wonder that she was allowed to live, even with the physician there calling her nubs bone spurs and cutting them away every turn. How she suffered that abuse in silence, I can never guess."

"The physician saved her life, but at great cost," Gurnil poured more wine for Ordin, who held out his empty cup. "Her wings should have grown eight turns earlier, in my estimation."

"Fyris had no idea what they had, or they'd never have sent her here," Ordin said. "If they had, they'd have asked to ransom her."

"Jurris never sent a reply to the letter they sent."

"They should know better than to expect a reply. They severed ties with Elabeth and Camryn's deaths. No, I'm not saying they're all responsible, or that they should all suffer for it. Tamblin will never be brought to justice, because of the First Ordinance."

"Yet half-bloods don't fall under the First Ordinance. Unfortunate, wouldn't you say?" Gurnil shook his head. "We can kill them as readily as Fyris can."

"Fyris kills whenever it wants," Ordin responded. "Tamblin has proven that repeatedly."

I overheard much of their conversation. Again, the First Ordinance had been mentioned. Ordin and Gurnil were familiar with it, but in all my searching in the Library, I hadn't come across a single book containing that phrase.

No books on Fyris were shelved there, either, which troubled me. The information I held was from the book in my old storeroom inside Tamblin's castle, and many pages had been ripped away from it.

Fyris was a turnip-shaped land south of Kondar, and as there were no other continents listed in the book farther south, I had no idea if any ships, sailing or flying, had ever gone past Fyris' shores and not known of it.

I was reading an accounting written by a glassmaker when Gurnil came looking for me later. I'd propped myself against the headboard of my narrow bed, taking care that my sore wings didn't press against the wood.

"Have you tried to move them? Without your hands?" Gurnil offered a sympathetic smile.

"No, Master Gurnil."

"Perhaps we should work on that. Ordin sent a message to Barth, saying you wouldn't be back to work in the kitchen for two more days. Pinfeather days are sore days. Would you like your evening meal served here, or would you prefer to come with me to the dining hall?"

"Do you have geography books? For Fyris?" I asked.

"There are some in my personal library. Come in the morning, and I'll let you borrow one or two of them."

"Thank you," my words tumbled out in a breathless rush. I'd been terrified that they'd be withheld—if they existed at all. "All the geography books in Fyris have pages torn out."

"Working to rip our existence from their lives?" Gurnil snorted after his question. He already knew the answer, so I didn't reply. I did slide off the bed, however, and followed him to the Guild Masters' dining hall.

I had breakfast with Master Ordin the following morning—he'd joined us for dinner the night before and asked that I come to his study for my morning meal, as he had books on anatomy that he wanted me to read.

Eager to get my hands on anything of that nature, I'd quickly agreed to share a meal with him. Gurnil promised the geography books and writing supplies when I returned from breakfast with Ordin, and my day was happily planned out. Medicine and geography; such diverse and fascinating subjects.

"Follow me," Gurnil said after I'd laid the medical books on my bed and went in search of geography. "I don't allow many inside my personal library," he added.

I trailed him as he walked into his private study, then gasped as he pressed a bar on the wall—another door opened, when I had no idea a door was there. A smaller library waited, and my breath caught as we walked past shelves meant for browsing. These were shorter than those in the main Library, and I could reach the top shelf if I stretched.

We came to the end of the first set of shelves and made a turn. I gasped a second time—a painting hung on a back wall, in full view of anyone who walked this deeply into Gurnil's private library.

A woman with golden hair was portrayed in the painting, her hand outstretched while the Orb pulsed nearby. Her body was what drew my attention, however. It appeared to be encased in the trunk of a tree, the roots serving as long skirts. I had no idea whether she was emerging from the tree or becoming the tree. Either way, the work was breathtaking, and I couldn't stop staring at it.

"Elabeth," Gurnil sighed. "In the Saving."

"I thought she had wings," I mumbled absently as I continued to stare.

"She did, but this was always done during the molting. You can't see the molting wings behind her—the artist chose not to depict them."

"What is the Saving?" I breathed.

"Young one, I cannot explain that. Jurris forbids it. The books you want are this way."

I was led away from the painting, and wondered why it hung here, instead of some other, more important portion of Avii Castle.

Dena brought our lunch. "You should go outside—it's a fine, spring day," she said when she found me sitting on my bed, reading one of the geography books Gurnil lent me. "Gurnil has benches on his terrace."

I blinked at her, feeling stupid—I hadn't been forbidden from going outside to read, and imagined it might be wonderful to do so. Marking my place with a scrap of parchment, I followed Dena as she made her way toward Gurnil's terrace.

"Ordin reports that the feather tips are white, with traces of gold, silver and copper," Justis reported. He didn't tell his brother that Ordin didn't want to reveal that information, but Jurris demanded, therefore it was required.

"That's preposterous," Jurris huffed. "None have wing colors like that. White possibly, as she is an aberration, but the colors of precious metals? Impossible." Jurris rustled red wings in agitation at his brother's description. "Ordin is merely attempting to make her appear better than she is."

"As you say, brother," Justis nodded. "I worry that she will be attacked again in the kitchen, should she go back there. Need I remind you that payment for her services was well-received?"

It had been—Halthea giggled when Justis handed the money chip to her, and immediately made plans to spend it.

"With that sort of income, I'd think you'd look to protect the asset," Justis continued.

"Then where?" Jurris began, before flinging up a hand. "Never mind. Send her to Ordin to fetch and carry for him and the other healers, and let her sleep in Gurnil's quarters if he still wishes to house her."

"I will ask," Justis bowed respectfully to Jurris and turned to leave.

"Will you accept this now?" Justis handed a bottle of wine to Ordin, after landing on Ordin's terrace shortly after twilight.

"Why?" Ordin held out a hand and accepted the offering.

"I managed to convince my brother to protect his asset. Quin will report to you when she is ready to work again. Jurris says she can keep her quarters with Gurnil, or he can move her into something better; I know he has larger suites connected to the Library."

"Is this true?" Ordin blinked at Justis, shocked by the news.

"There is usually a path to get one's way, if one is willing to make a convoluted journey," Justis smiled. "Shall we send word for Gurnil to join us?"

"Most certainly," Ordin laughed.

The last light of day was fading as I closed my book—I'd eaten on the terrace and then read again as long as the light lasted. When I rose to go back inside, they flew past—parents with a child perhaps ten turns of age, who was learning to use his wings.

He laughed as he dipped his wings, taking joy in the flying, as his parents flew to the side and slightly below, to assist if needed. I have no idea why tears came to my eyes, but they did.

I ran inside before I sobbed aloud.

CHAPTER 11

"You're to report to Ordin every morning after breakfast, and on end-days, you'll have breakfast with us." I'd never seen Gurnil smile so much. "Ordin says you may take the last two hours of your workday to study here, in the Library. It only seems fair, since you never received a proper education."

Too astonished to speak at first, I could only nod at Gurnil. "Ordin says he wishes to check your feathers and the length of your wings," Gurnil added. "Go now, then you may use the rest of the day to read or wander outside."

"Thank you, Master Gurnil," I said, stuttering my words. Almost afraid to feel the joy that threatened to burst out of me, I walked swiftly toward the Library entrance, my destination the Healer's quarters, to thank Master Ordin as well.

"You'll see the blood feathers soon," Master Ordin said as he gently examined my wings. "They're growing more quickly, and I can feel the give in the hinge. You'll need it soon; in a week, your wings should be down to your ankles."

"Blood feathers?"

"The body needs a supply of blood to grow the feathers. Once the feathers are fully grown, the blood supply subsides. Before that time, it is wise not to damage the blood feathers. Much bleeding might result, and it could be more than painful."

"What will happen—if my feathers are white?" I asked. Yes, it troubled me that I might have wings in a color that none of the others had.

"Have you ever seen an albino animal—one that is white?" he asked.

"Yes, but only once. It was a deer, dead of course, that was brought for the King's table."

"Quin, don't call him King here," Ordin warned. "He isn't a King. He only believes himself such."

"I know what he is," I muttered, feeling embarrassed.

"What is that?"

"A blight upon his people," I replied. "And Yevil, who stands beside him, is even worse."

"Your wings may be cause for talk," Ordin steered the conversation away from Tamblin and Yevil. "You already have experience with prejudice, so I hope it won't be too difficult for you."

"I know not to expect anything else."

"Life is never easy, even for those who seem to fit the mold," Ordin turned and walked toward his desk. "It can be more than difficult for those who are different."

"I know what deformed and outcast mean," I said, turning away and wandering toward the door to his terrace. "I am beginning to understand what half-blood means."

Ordin sat at his desk with a sigh. "You must stay strong, Quin. You are here, instead of the kitchens. That in itself is something, and we should thank Liron for that."

"Liron? I only know of him as part of a curse Fyrisians utter when angry. I doubt any of his body parts have not been included in a profane oath."

"Gurnil has ancient texts, describing how he once visited us at times. No sightings have been reported for decades."

"I saw a painting yesterday," I began. "In Gurnil's private library."

"Ah. Elabeth and the Orb," Ordin nodded. "Halthea wouldn't have it in the royal chambers when she and Jurris took them. Gurnil kept it from being destroyed."

"It's beautiful," I mumbled. "Gurnil said that her wings were molting, so the artist chose not to include them."

"We molt every five turns. The reason Justis lives is that he was molting during Elabeth and Camryn's last visit to Fyris. He sent his second-in-command instead, as the winds between Aviia and Fyris can be brutal, and not all his primary feathers were regrown. The second-in-command died with Camryn and Elabeth."

"He feels guilty about that," I sighed.

"I know. He refuses to discuss it. He also refuses to stand as Halthea's guard. He commands the palace guards, instead."

"There is nothing he could have done. He would have died with them," I shrugged. "While Tamblin may have issued the order, Yevil was the one to carry it out."

"I keep hearing his name," Ordin blinked at me when I turned toward him. "Yevil. Why do we not have records of his existence?"

"I don't know. Wherever Tamblin is, Yevil is never far away. Any evil attributed to Tamblin involves Yevil. Yevil paid Timblor's page to kill the Prince," I added. I knew that as well as I knew anything.

"Which Prince?" Ordin stood in alarm, his eyes boring into mine.

"Timblor. Why do you ask?"

"Because I helped deliver Amlis," Ordin muttered. "Omina had difficulty, so I was present at his birth."

"He is the heir for now," I said.

"What do you mean, for now?"

"Tamblin has always imagined that Amlis is not his son. He attempted to kill Amlis on one occasion, and Yevil tried more often than that." I didn't add that I'd managed to save Amlis more than once.

"You think he'll get an heir with another woman?"

"There are few births, and many of those die not long after the birthing," I said. "If he gets another heir, it will be most unusual. He is aging and may not survive long enough."

"I will let Gurnil know. He still keeps records, such as he can, with little information coming from Fyris as it does. We were not aware of Timblor's death."

"I wasn't there; I was in Vhrist when word was brought," I said.

"What were you doing in Vhrist?"

"Working in Omina's kitchen, and as a chambermaid," I answered honestly. I decided that listing my work as Amlis' page might prove less than prudent, so I withheld the information.

"Why don't you go out and enjoy the day?" Ordin shook his head as if clearing his thoughts. "Tomorrow, I will begin teaching you anatomy."

The central bowl of Aviia, containing much land where animals grazed and fruit and vegetables were grown, was too large for me to explore in a few hours, so I walked to where I'd boarded the flying vehicle before traveling to Kondar.

I'd seen sheep there before, and hoped to see them again. A boy tended the ones I found when I arrived.

"What are you doing here?" he sounded sullen.

"Looking for your sheep," I said, nodding to the grazing animals nearby.

"You're the half-blood."

"Yes."

He looked to be fifteen or sixteen, with gray wings folded tightly against his back, indicating his unease. Brown hair lifted in the breeze while gray eyes scowled at me. With my gift, I knew his morning lessons were over, so he was watching the sheep while his father ate a noon meal.

"Stay away from our sheep." He turned his back on me and walked toward the animals. Yes, I could have called them, and they would have flocked about me. I didn't. I walked away, too. Perhaps I might find geography books more friendly than the shepherds of Aviia.

"I've moved you to a larger room," Gurnil announced when I walked into the Library half an hour later. "I've placed an order for more suitable clothing. Keep those old things you wore in the kitchen if you want them, but you're no longer required to wear them."

"Thank you," I mumbled. The shepherd boy's words still stung, and that had affected my mood.

"Who did you meet?" Gurnil lifted an eyebrow.

"Only a shepherd boy. I wanted to see his sheep. He wanted me gone."

"You know, I haven't requested a permanent Yellow Wing to clean the Library in a very long time. Perhaps I should consider doing that," Gurnil mused as he motioned for me to follow him. He led me to my new quarters.

"Everything here is yours," he said. I stared. This was a bedroom a minor noble's daughter would be proud to call hers. A bed twice as wide as the one I'd previously had stood against the far wall of a spacious room. A carved headboard graced the bed and a soft, blue cover lay over white sheets and plump pillows.

"Master Gurnil, I," I floundered. Mere thankfulness seemed inadequate for this gift.

"I believe you deserve it," he offered, his words dry and accompanied by a chuckle. "I wish I had a window to offer, but I don't. Those are sparse throughout the castle."

"May I use your terrace?"

"Whenever you want. You don't have to go to the bowl for sunlight if you don't want to. Ordin will allow you to use his, too."

"Thank you. I've never had anything," I said.

"I know how orphans are treated," he shrugged. "I assume you were orphaned—you never spoke of parents."

"I have none," I agreed. "I don't remember having any, either."

"Did others tell you anything?" Gurnil seemed interested, suddenly.

"No. Nobody knew anything. An old woman in the kitchens said I was handed to the cooks when I was two. That was nearly sixteen turns ago."

"Sixteen turns? Which kitchen?"

"The King's—Tamblin's kitchen," I blushed and hung my head. "I was moved to Vhrist shortly before I was brought here."

"You have no memories before your arrival in the palace kitchen?"

"No, Master Gurnil. I wish I did."

"I'll leave you to settle in," Gurnil said, although I could tell he was preoccupied suddenly. Without another word, he left me alone. I heard his footsteps as he walked swiftly toward the terrace, then the door opening and a rush of large wings immediately after.

"The time period matches," Gurnil shook his head.

"If word of this gets out, it will place her in danger—more than she's in already. It matters not that she may have white wings; they're certainly not red. You know some will see her as a threat, anyway, no matter what talents she may have," Ordin responded.

"But what if she is?"

"We can never speak of this, you know it," Ordin said.

"I make this suggestion, then," Gurnil offered. "When we see the Kondari healers again, we ask for their tests. They can tell if she's full or half-blood, I know it."

"We can do this for reference purposes, and slip it past the others in that way, should they ask," Ordin nodded. "We will hold this information between us. There is no need for the others to know. It may lay our curiosity to rest concerning the matter," he added.

"I would certainly prefer to know. After all, we only saw the babe's bloody remains and buried them quickly."

"Perhaps we took the word of murderers and liars too quickly?"

"Perhaps, indeed."

"We'll need something of them, for the physicians to make a comparison, don't you think?"

"I believe we can supply that; Jurris still has the bones of the first half-blood sent to us after the murders."

"How will we get a sample?"

"Let me worry about that," Gurnil smiled.

❧

"Just a fragment? I think I can ask for the entire skull," Justis said. "All I have to tell Jurris is that I desire it for target practice."

"Just a fragment," Gurnil said. "For research."

"Easy enough," Justis said. "It's still laid out on the bench on his terrace."

"While I realize he wants to see it rot, that one wasn't responsible for the murders."

"I know. Somewhere in his mind, he knows it as well. Camryn became his father when Treven died, and was a much better parent than Treven ever was. He can't exact his revenge on those responsible, so he does this, instead."

"I will not comment further, then." Gurnil shook his wings. "Unless I miss my guess, all of them will die before long. The time for the Saving is long past, as you know. Tamblin was never a witness to it, as his brother never wanted him to know. He has no idea what he did to Fyris when he planned those murders."

"Do not say that bastard's name within my presence," Justis hissed. "I will get your fragment, never fear."

❧

"The anniversary approaches," Farin settled his cup on its saucer with a sigh. He and Omina sat inside her study, sharing a cup of tea before the fire.

"For the second time," Omina agreed. "Tamblin thought it some archaic ritual they performed, and a wickedness against Fyris. Tandelis never wanted him to know what sickened Fyris, or that Fyris might be sick at all."

"Your husband never watched or listened with a wise head to anything any other did or spoke. If he'd used any intelligence, he'd have known that the land seemed renewed afterward."

"Every sixteen turns," Omina shook her head. "Tamblin is a fool. Likely, it was he who is responsible in some way for my Timblor's death."

"Yevil will have had a hand in it, too. I hear he has been short-tempered of late."

"Bodies are always left in Yevil's wake."

"I hear from Vhrist's physicians that more are falling ill with the wasting disease."

"Farin, we will all die, just as those who are sick now will die."

"We'll all die, if Yevil doesn't manage to kill us before then," Amlis shook his head while handing the letter to Rodrik. "From Farin. It's a report of the spreading sickness in Vhrist and Vhoorth."

"Will we have healthy troops to load on your father's boats?" Rodrik scanned the letter quickly before handing it back to Amlis. "Have they not cleaned in here?" Rodrik scuffed his boots on the dusty floor of Amlis' study.

"I'm afraid to let anyone in, so I told the maids to stay out of this room. I wish we had Finder back. She would do this for me and I wouldn't worry about my notes and books falling into the wrong hands."

"She's dead. They kill the half-bloods," Rodrik sighed and strode toward Amlis' wide window. "I hope it was a quick death."

"I'm not sure we can count on the mercy of the Guardians," Amlis rose and stretched before joining Rodrik at the window. "Are those the new conscripts?" He watched the training of troops in the courtyard below.

"Yes. Few know the proper grip on a sword."

"I've heard rumors," Amlis said.

"What rumors?"

"The ones concerning the way my brother's page died. Those that say he didn't die solely of a knife or blade wound."

"How else might he have perished? I heard Yevil killed him with his bare hands."

"Not true, according to Garth. He told me there was a gaping hole in Brin's chest. What weapon might cause that?"

"None that I ever heard tales of," Rodrik replied. "Is Garth sure of his information?"

"He saw the body."

"Was it not savaged, somehow, before it reached the stables?"

"He supervised the removal. Unless the savagery occurred immediately after Brin's death, there was no time for such."

"What was done with the body?" Rodrik turned to Amlis in curiosity.

"Likely in the boneyard, where thieves and murderers are buried."

"How difficult would it be," Amlis began.

"I'll have it done tonight." Rodrik turned abruptly and strode out of Amlis' study.

"Information requested by the Master Scholar," Justis set the fat, sealed envelope on Ordin's desk.

"You were right to bring it here; he plans to have tea with me at midmorning," Ordin nodded to Justis. "I thank you for this swift response."

⁂

I was surprised to find Justis in Master Ordin's study when I arrived for my first lesson in anatomy. His black wings shone nearly blue in the early morning light from Ordin's window.

That window was open to the day, while sunlight filtered in with abandon and played about the papers and objects on Ordin's desk.

"Ah, Quin," Ordin greeted me with a smile. "Ready for your lessons to begin?"

"I am, Master Ordin," I nodded.

"I will speak with you later," Justis dipped his head to Ordin and turned to walk away. Something troubled him, I could tell, but I refused to use my gift to determine what it was.

He brushed past me on his way to the door and a tiny, black feather floated in his wake. I waited until he was through the door before reaching out to catch it in my hand.

"That is a down feather," Ordin explained as I cradled the fluff in my hand. "Probably loosened somehow in flight. He's not scheduled to molt again for four turns."

"May I keep it, or should I return it?" I asked, blinking at Ordin.

"You may keep it. Children make a game of collecting colored feathers they find. The black ones are much prized, but red are the rarest, as you might imagine."

"I saw a child learning to fly with his parents," I said.

"Those are good days and usually make good memories," Ordin replied. "Here. I have books for you. While these first two are in the Kondari language, the images are accurate for bones and organs.

"I can read them," I accepted two heavy books from Ordin.

"You can read their language?" Ordin stared at me in shock.

"Yes. I read all the numbers and signs at the hospital when we arrived there," I said.

"And you speak and understand their language. This is unprecedented," Ordin rubbed his forehead. "I have never heard of such."

"I don't know how it is that I know these things. I just do," I shrugged, hoping I wasn't buying trouble for myself by revealing hidden talents.

"Then go through those books as best you can. Make notes in our language from their text and I will review your work. Write down any questions you have, and I will answer as best I can. Understand, Quin, that their technology far exceeds ours."

"I know," I said. "May I read on your terrace?"

"Of course. Tables and benches are there, for that purpose."

"Do we have other texts from them—the Kondari? For learning purposes?"

"Much of their information is on small chips that are displayed through the use of machines. We have none such here. I will ask, however, when I see them next."

"Thank you, Master Ordin. For these, and for teaching me." I indicated the books in my arms.

"It is no trouble, young one."

"I have this," Melis held up a small, transparent bag. "Found in her room."

"That's a pin feather," Hadris Jem, High President Charkisul's Chief of Medical Sciences, said, accepting the sample and examining the contents. "We'll run DNA, and see how it matches with the DNA we have from the others."

"There's something there, and I want to know what it is," Melis agreed. "I know their children grow wings at age nine. By the time they're her age, they have fully-grown wings and know how to fly rings around anything. That girl was only getting hers—they're not long enough for her condition to be an exaggerated molting."

"I examined the images from the security cameras," Hadris agreed. "The wing hinge is not fully realized, so your assumptions are correct. We continue to run tests on Berel, but the disease has been eradicated and the boy is weary of our poking and prodding."

"The Avii royals have already spent half the money," Melis huffed. "On jewelry, furniture and solar-powered machinery. Nothing for the girl, as far as I can tell." Melis hadn't forgotten the slave remarks in the recorded conversations, either.

"I may have a suggestion, then," Hadris offered.

⁂

"Unprecedented, but certainly worth consideration," Charkisul nodded to Hadris. "Naming her a citizen of Kondar will afford her the rights given to any of ours. I listened to that recorded conversation, had it translated into text afterward and then read it, several times. I didn't like what they said concerning the girl."

"I worry that granting her citizenship will create a rift between us," Melis pointed out judiciously. "We may be placing her life in danger, after all."

"They thought we would buy her? Preposterous. Slavery and the selling of sentient beings has been outlawed for hundreds of turns."

"Their customs are not ours, and their laws are certainly not the same," Hadris observed. "Can we not make her an honorary citizen, at least? They will think it an empty gift, when it will be, according to our records, citizenship."

"Perhaps," the High President agreed. "Let me think on it. Meanwhile, are there other illnesses that might need her attention? I realize we'll have to pay, but it will get her here."

"I'll do research," Melis replied.

⁂

When I returned to the Library after reading medical texts from Kondar most of the day and making notes, I found Dena dusting books. I stared. She turned and offered me a brilliant smile.

"Master Gurnil asked for me," she almost danced with excitement. "I get to live in the Library quarters. With you."

I blinked—nobody had ever been excited to be near me before. "I hope this means you get to read if you want," I said.

"Master Gurnil says so, after my cleaning chores are done for the day. I like reading about the Queen's Guard—there are so many stories about them."

I knew she wanted black wings more than anything, but I wisely didn't remark on the subject, choosing to nod my understanding instead. In my mind, it would harm none if she trained with the young Black Wings. The thought made me sigh.

"My bedroom is next to yours," Dena said. "I hope you don't mind."

"Why would I mind? I am more than happy you're here," I said. "You can teach me the everyday things that I can't find in books."

"And we can be friends," she added, a note of hopefulness in her voice.

"Yes. Friends. Most certainly." I didn't tell her that I'd never had any, before. Instead, I helped her finish the dusting, then we went to collect dinner trays for us and Master Gurnil from the guild dining hall.

Garth pulled back the edge of the tarp for Amlis to see. "It's not pretty, my Prince," Garth explained.

"Nor would it be," Amlis replied as he studied Brin's decomposing corpse. As Garth reported, a large, gaping hole lay near the center of Brin's chest. Amlis steeled himself—worms worked their way through exposed, putrid flesh and buried themselves in rotting, exposed organs.

"We've seen enough," Rodrik waved away the stench while Garth flipped the thick, canvas tarp over the body. "Take it back and let no one see you do it."

"It will be done."

"Chen, what have you heard?" Amlis sat before the fire in his suite, sharing a bottle of wine with Wolter's assistant cook and Rodrick.

"The guardsman outside the door reported a sharp noise, such as he hadn't heard before, then Yevil stalked out of the King's suite, telling him to call for the stable master and any healer that might be found."

"A sharp noise?"

"Like a metal pot dropping or such. He had nothing to compare it to. When others rushed in, they found the King kneeling next to Timblor, who was bleeding from a knife wound. Brin was already dead. Timblor didn't live long." Chen shook his head before sipping his wine. "That is all I heard, and that was shortly after. Lately, all seem afraid of Yevil and the King's wrath, so gossip has dwindled."

"At least we have this information," Amlis said. "Is there anything else to report?"

"Just this," Chen said. "One of the recruits coming in from the south recognized Yevil's name. He made the sign of warding upon hearing it."

"He made Liron's ward? Any idea why?"

"I couldn't find him after that, and discreet inquiries have gotten no results."

"Interesting." Rodrick stood, emptied his cup and nodded to the Prince. "I'll make my way to the barracks tomorrow."

"I'll get back to the kitchen—tomorrow's bread will be set to rise, soon." Chen stood and bowed informally to Amlis before walking toward the Prince's door.

"The reports say Yevil is from Meede, here," Amlis tapped the place on his map, indicating a principality south and east of Lironis. "He became Father's man-at-arms a turn before Tandelis was killed."

"Meede is bordered by Warrel and Rondes," Rodrick said. Warrel was always Tandelis' ally, while Rondes seldom supported him. Warrel no longer sends anyone to court, while we are overrun with those from Rondes."

"Do you think the recruit in question may have been from Warrel?"

"Possibly. Perhaps you should ask the field marshal for recruit records. I'd like to speak with anyone from Warrel. Privately, of course."

"Of course."

"Is the dough set out to rise?" Chen asked the moment he walked into the kitchen. He never saw who clamped a hand over his mouth, and once the long blade sliced his throat, he no longer had the ability to shout for help.

Chen's death woke me from a dream. It had been troubling, that dream, but the waking reality was worse. Chen had breathed his last in a bubbling of blood, and I wept for his loss.

"Is Master Ordin in?" Justis landed on Ordin's terrace, not far from where I studied a Kondari anatomy book at a table. The day had started out fine, but became cloudy and I was about to go inside before rain fell.

"He is," I said, closing the book after marking my place.

"I hear you have one of my feathers," he said as he followed me inside.

"I do. Do you want it back?" Ordin said he didn't, but then one can never predict another's decisions where I was concerned.

"No. I just thought it odd that you'd want it."

"Ordin called it a down feather. I find it amazing that something so soft might come from someone so hard."

Justis stopped still for a moment before continuing to follow me toward Ordin's study.

"You find me hard?" he asked, reaching for the handle to Ordin's study door before I could do so myself.

"You seem that way. The High President's guard thinks you're dangerous."

"Does he, now?" Justis smiled for the first time since I'd known him.

"Master Ordin, Commander Justis is here to see you," I said when we walked into Ordin's study. He looked up from the paper he was writing and invited Justis to sit. I turned to leave.

"Stay," Justis held out a hand. "This involves you."

Before the meeting was over, Master Gurnil had been summoned and tea was served. My talents were required a second time in Kondar, for the promise of payment. The issue of no payment coming to me was skirted—skillfully—by Justis, who refused to go against his brother on the issue.

"Do we know what the illness is?" Ordin set his cup down as he asked the question.

"Much like the one before, I believe. Jurris received the message; I only have secondhand information."

"When?" Gurnil asked.

"Two days. They're sending another airchopper."

"Is that what they call them?" I asked.

"Has no one explained that to you?" Justis asked.

"No." I huddled in the chair I'd been given, fearing any reprimand that might come.

"What do you think of that name?" he asked instead.

"It is appropriate, I think, although a bit blunt."

Gurnil laughed. Ordin coughed after swallowing a mouthful of tea. The corner of Justis' mouth threatened an upward turn.

"What does Kondar look like?" Dena asked when I returned to the Library later.

"It has cities filled with tall buildings, some of them made of glass," I replied. "Those are surrounded by fields of crops and trees. Vehicles fly or roll everywhere, without the aid of horses or any other animal."

"I can't imagine how big it is. I've always been here," Dena sighed.

"I thought I would never leave Fyris," I said. "You cannot say where you might be from one day to the next."

"Do you miss it?"

"I cannot miss what has never treated me kindly," I said. "I was an orphan. Orphans are considered less than animals, much of the time. I was never paid for my work, or given a kind word. I was beaten for mistakes, real or imagined, and never treated as one would expect to be treated. At least here, Master Gurnil and Master Ordin treat me kindly and allow me to read and learn."

"I have only heard of Fyris through the cursing of others. I was small when Elabeth and Camryn died, and don't remember them at all."

"Will you help me pack a few things?" I asked. "Master Gurnil said to take enough for three days, although he doesn't expect to stay that long."

I wanted to direct Dena's attention away from Fyris and the happenings there. I felt increasingly concerned, not only about Tamblin's intended attack upon a land he knew nothing of, but of the poison that continued to spread across the planet. Eventually, it would kill everything, including the Avii.

CHAPTER 12

Had I known that Halthea would join us on our journey to Kondar, I would have been more reluctant to go. Two Yellow Wings and an extra black-winged guard accompanied her, while I was escorted by Gurnil, Ordin and Justis, as before.

Halthea monopolized Justis' time, chattering away while he pretended interest. I knew she wanted him; wanted to take him as a lover or a second mate, she cared not which. Justis wanted nothing to do with her, and I imagined that he knew, just as I did, how shallow, empty and cruel she was.

Her yellow-winged maids cowered about her, and I recognized their demeanor—Halthea didn't hold back her blows if she were angry. I felt disgusted by that; those in power should protect the vulnerable, instead of abusing them.

Perhaps my sense of fairness was finally waking—it had remained buried while I lived in Fyris. There, it was even worse. The laws against murder and theft were only created to protect the privileged and not those considered inferior to them.

"Quin, you're frowning," Gurnil said softly beside me. He'd taken the seat next to mine on the flight to Kondar, and allowed me my thoughts until now.

"I was thinking, Master Gurnil. My apologies."

"No need to apologize. You must be concentrating quite hard on your thoughts," he offered a smile.

"I was. Will we request more books while we're there?" I asked, betraying my hope that more might be supplied.

"We will ask. Ordin and I intend to speak with their Master Healer concerning more books on medicine and such, so you might learn from them."

"Thank you, Master Gurnil."

"Master Ordin says your feathers are peeking out, and your wings are longer. Have you attempted to flex them, yet?"

"No. I'm afraid to. Afraid they won't move," I mumbled. I was terrified that they'd never be useful as wings—that they were merely a decoration I'd accidentally received from one of my parents, whoever they were.

"I think they will. Ordin will go into detail about the muscles connected, and how they work. Young ones generally spend hours before a mirror, flapping away and getting used to the exercise."

"How long do you think it will take before they are fully-grown?" I asked.

"Usually it takes the better part of eight moon-turns, but yours are growing quite rapidly."

"I have much time to make up," I said.

"Very true," Gurnil agreed.

Our first destination was the hospital, just as before. High President Charkisul didn't meet us; his Chief of Security, Melis Norwal did. I blinked at him as he greeted Halthea in a solicitous manner—he wasn't expecting her arrival, just as I'd not known that she planned to make the trip with us.

Perhaps I should have made the attempt to read her intentions sooner, but I didn't. She meant to watch the healing, with more nefarious plans in mind for the future.

"This is the price paid for supporting me," Amlis said softly, shaking his head. Chen's body had been loaded onto a wagon brought by his brother, to bury outside Lironis. Rodrik stood beside Amlis outside the stables, where the body had been kept until it could be collected.

Weak sunlight shone in the early afternoon hours as thick canvas was laid over the wrapped corpse. Chen's brother had given Amlis the briefest bow out of duty, reminding Amlis of what he already knew—that Chen's faithfulness had resulted in his death.

Amlis let out a breath as Chen's brother climbed onto the driver's seat and clucked to his horse. The wagon creaked and its wheels crunched on the stones of the courtyard as it was driven away.

"I never thought an assistant cook could become a target," Rodrik agreed. "I will be more watchful from now on."

"Rod, we can't watch everybody; that will raise more suspicion," Amlis muttered. "You know what happened to Finder. This time, it was Chen. Who will be next? Garth? I haven't taken another page for the obvious reasons—my brother's turned against him, and Finder was sent to her death."

"I've located two recruits who came from Warrel," Rodrik said, attempting to turn the conversation away from death. "I will wait a day or two before seeking them out. It is my hope they are willing to tell me what they know, if anything. We need information, my Prince, and there is little to be had while time grows short."

"We must put a stop to these murders. I cannot approach Wolter, to convey my condolences. Whoever killed Chen may target him, next."

"That is also my concern."

"Quin, this is Charlis, of the High Council," Hadris Jem, the High President's medical advisor, informed me as Justis, Ordin, Halthea and I were led into Charlis' hospital room.

"Charlis has," he began.

"I know what she has." I did—the wasting disease had first settled in her lungs, then began to spread to other organs. Charlis was of middle age and still young enough to warrant the healing. At that moment, I wanted several things. I wanted to ask Ordin to protect me. He couldn't. I wanted to ask Justis to take me elsewhere. He wouldn't. I was forced to allow Halthea to watch as I healed Charlis of a disease that would ordinarily take her life in a matter of moon-turns.

⸙

"I will have the tests done in a few days, and send the results to you," Hadris agreed.

Gurnil handed the samples from Quin and the half-blood to Hadris with a nod. "I appreciate this," Gurnil said. "We cannot determine Quin's parentage, as she is an orphan. I hope you will be able to tell something from these samples, as to whether they are connected or not."

"We'll run all tests, never fear," Hadris nodded. "The information will be sent to you directly. When will your party be ready to leave Kondar?"

"I don't know," Gurnil sighed. "Halthea wishes to visit the shops."

"Ah."

⸙

"We can't do this, with the Princess here and glaring at Quin as often as not," Edden Charkisul tossed the chip onto his desk with a troubled sigh.

"We were fools, to think we could gift citizenship, I suppose," Melis shook his head. "They have an archaic government, where the monarchy rules absolutely. Yes, they have a Council, but the King can overrule most anything. I fear for the girl."

"As do I."

⸙

"I heard you were here."

I knew him. Had healed him. His renewed health had added flesh to his frame and color to his cheeks. Berel, the High President's son, had come looking for me.

I'd been placed in a suite with an adjoining walled garden, where I'd gone to sit in the early-morning sunlight the day after Charlis' healing. That's where he'd found me.

"Where are your guards?" I asked.

"Outside your door. I asked them to wait there. My father trusts you, when he doesn't trust many others."

"Your father works to be fair to all. I have not met many like him who were placed so highly."

"Kondar elects High Presidents for ten sun-turns. Presidents in the four principalities are elected for shorter terms—half that, actually, with the option of reelection once. High Presidents can only serve one term. My father's term ends in three sun-turns."

"Kondar should weep when he walks away from his office," I said.

"His opponents on the Council would be happy to disagree."

"Fools are everywhere," I responded with a shrug. He laughed. It was a good sound to hear.

I'd only seen him in a bed before, where he'd been thin and wasted. This Berel had curiosity in his blue eyes, combined with a hint of mischief. His hair was quite short and dark brown—the disease had caused it to fall out before; now it was growing back as it should.

"Tell me about Avii castle," he begged. "I've only seen images of it, and most of those from the outside."

"I haven't seen much of it, either. I didn't grow up there," I hedged. It was truth, and I worried about how much truth to give him.

"That's all right," he said. "Have you seen their library? I heard it's filled with paper and parchment books, instead of vid-files."

"It is. I was hoping to find more books available in your language," I blinked at him. "I'm reading two books on anatomy, now, and making notes for Master Ordin."

"Where did you study? You're smart, if you can make notes on anatomy texts."

"I didn't," I said. "Somehow, I know those things without the teaching. Master Gurnil is much surprised, too."

"You learned how to read and write on your own?"

"Yes. It just happened," I said.

For the first time, I felt it. I'd moved my wings in agitation, much like I'd seen the others do. I stopped still for a moment, savoring the act, as if a miracle had occurred. For me, it felt just the same. Sadly, my feathers weren't present enough to rustle as most others were, but perhaps someday soon, that might transpire.

"I'd like to learn how to read the Avii language. Father says I must finish my required studies first, before moving on to another language."

"Are you behind—because of your illness?" I worked to steer the conversation away from the Avii and me.

"Yes. A half-turn, at least. I must begin again, next week. The physicians say I'll be strong enough, then."

"Do you like your studies?"

"Some of them. Others are tedious."

"What do you find tedious?"

"Science and mathematics. I prefer history and social sciences."

"I like geography and history," I said. "I'd really like to see books on those subjects."

"Paper books?"

"Yes. I don't have any other means to read."

"I might be able to fix that."

"How?"

"Let me speak to my father."

"It recharges in the sun," Berel explained barely two hours later. "It has an entire library of books on it, all you have to do is tap a word into the search line, and it will offer all sorts of choices."

"What is this?" I accepted the thin, metal tablet gingerly, as if I might break such a precious thing in clumsy fingers.

"It's a tab-vid, with the library available to those in the higher learning classes. That means that anything we can use to learn is available to you. There are maps, too, in addition to the texts on geography."

"This is the greatest gift ever," I held the tab-vid against my chest, as if I were afraid someone might take it from me. More than thankful that I'd received it while the others were engaged elsewhere, I contemplated where I might put it so it would remain my secret.

"Most people I know would consider it work and not a gift," Berel grinned. "I'm glad I could do this for you, after what you did for me."

"I was happy to do it, for you and your father." I didn't add that it shamed me that others had demanded so much in return for my services.

"That's all my physicians can talk about—that you healed a disease that would have killed me and they couldn't stop it."

"I can't explain how I can do it," I said. "It just comes."

"Those who know say it's an amazing gift."

I blinked at his words, then using the talent I had, discovered more that he was unwilling to say—that some members of his father's Council might consider my healing gift as something unnatural or evil, and would work to see it banned or destroyed. Therefore, only a few were trusted enough to know of Berel's recovery, and how it was accomplished.

I should not have been surprised. In Fyris, which was much smaller than Kondar, there was always dissent, although those who thought to oppose the King were continually wary. Yevil would kill because of an unguarded frown aimed in Tamblin's direction.

While I had no problem with disagreement, I found it abhorrent if disagreement resulted in unnecessary deaths. As for superstitions, I had no use for them at all. Why would anyone consider the healing gift an evil? It made no sense to me. If something were an evil, then it would have evil intentions. I had none.

"What do you think might happen to me—if word of my ability became public?" I asked.

Berel didn't want to say. For a sixteen-year-old, he was well educated and savvy in the ways of Kondar's politics. Hunching his shoulders, he turned away from me before he answered.

"You could die," he admitted. "Or be used by the wealthy who are striving to cure the illness of old age, and that shouldn't be. Father wants to protect you by offering citizenship, but the arrival of Princess Halthea put a stop to that."

"Did she know?" I began.

"No. Father didn't wish to interfere with you or the Avii form of government, so he withheld the offer."

"I thank him for it, anyway," I sighed. "It was a good thought, as none have sought to protect me like that before." I worried that Gurnil and Ordin's protection might come to an end soon, but didn't explain that to Berel. He was barely recovered from an illness that was taking his life, and had more than enough worries as it was.

"Can we be friends, at least? I wish I had more political power than I do, as I see that something troubles you."

"I wish I had the power and confidence to tell you all those things, but I don't," I responded. "I marvel at your maturity. I've worked with others near your age, and they have displayed mostly juvenile behavior."

"When you grow up in the political system here in Kondar, you grow up fast," Berel shrugged. "A careless word can cost more than most are willing to pay. Foolish words or acts are often blown out of proportion and the vid images are broadcast throughout Kondar."

"I understand that, more than you know," I agreed. For seventeen turns, I'd remained silent for exactly that reason.

"Quin?" Master Gurnil's voice arrived before he did. "Are you ready to go? Halthea wishes to leave immediately."

"I am ready, Master Gurnil," I nodded. Did he know, as I did, that my life would change again, once we arrived at Avii castle?

Probably not.

Berel took my hand in a steady grip before I left him to join Gurnil. I turned to wave as we walked away. He lifted a hand in return, and it pained me to see the concern in his eyes.

"She will serve as one of my maids, and when the Kondari ask for her assistance, those messages will be brought directly to me," Halthea waved imperiously. She'd demanded that our party join her in meeting King Jurris after the trip to Avii castle.

Jurris seemed surprised by Halthea's announcement, but didn't say anything. Gurnil and Ordin, however, were angry immediately. "She needs to learn more about traditional medicine, in order to work better with the Kondari physicians," Ordin sputtered.

"She was allowed to stay in the suites surrounding the Library, and I wish that to continue," Gurnil said. He wanted so badly to point out that neither Jurris nor Halthea wanted anything to do with me before.

All that was before they could command four million Kondari credits for my ability to heal. Between filling the Avii coffers, I would be allowed to serve as one of Halthea's maids. Had I functioning wings at that moment, I would have flown away from Aviia and never looked back.

"She may continue her studies with you, Ordin, and continue to sleep in the bed you've given her—after she has performed her duties for my Halthea," Jurris dropped his hand, ending the matter. "No more than six hour's work from her, my darling," He turned to Halthea. "The messages from Kondar requesting her services will be delivered to you, as you desire."

To placate Halthea, who wanted to monopolize my time, he lifted her hand and kissed it, then offered her a smile. Halthea smiled back, and in that forced expression lay peril for me.

"Say what you're thinking—it will go no further," Justis nodded to Gurnil. He, Ordin and Gurnil had gathered in Gurnil's private study, to have their conversation.

"That bitch," Gurnil hissed. "She intends to ask as much as possible for Quin's services, and offer them to any and every Kondari who has the money to pay. Not all Kondari are well meaning, as the High President is. I heard rumors of dissent among the Council, from Kondari who thought I didn't understand their language."

"Her life could be in danger, and Halthea doesn't care," Ordin snapped. "She has no care or understanding of the politics involved. Do you know how it angers me that Quin is to serve as her maid? This is her way of pinning Quin down and keeping her subservient."

"I know." Justis rustled his wings. "Halthea isn't the kindest person to her maids, and this concerns me."

"Our laws protect any Avii from assault and murder, but those laws don't apply to the half-bloods or Red Wings, do they?" Gurnil's anger increased. "Quin has been mistreated enough, in my opinion, yet Halthea promises more of the same, if not worse, while taking every credit that comes from Quin's talents."

"Let me talk to my brother," Justis shook his head. "I didn't see this coming, but I should have. Halthea is a greedy bitch; she spent half the payment from Quin's healing this time before we ever left Kondar."

"On jewelry, shoes and fabrics," Ordin grumbled. "That money could be better spent elsewhere, yet Halthea uses it for personal gain. You don't see Jurris' other wives getting anything from this, do you?"

"They won't," Justis shook his head. "They're wise enough not to ask."

"All because she has red wings, and is fortunate enough to be the only female with red wings." Gurnil shook his head. "Elabeth was right in refusing to name her heir."

"Elabeth saw her for what she was, instead of the red wings she bears," Justis growled. "My brother only sees red wings."

"Convenient, too, that both her Red-Wing parents are deceased."

"They walked through the gate together," Gurnil nodded at Ordin's words.

"Halthea used that to play on Jurris' sympathy for weeks," Justis said. "And found her way into his bed shortly after."

"All this would be moot if Elabeth and Camryn were alive. Or had Lirin survived," Gurnil said.

"I couldn't stop her from taking the baby," Justis rumbled. "Elabeth seemed concerned about something, but wouldn't say what it was. I didn't press her, as time was short before she and Camryn had to leave for Fyris."

"Perhaps it was an omen, and she misread it," Gurnil suggested.

"Perhaps."

"This is Quin's report. This one is Gurnil's, and this is the third sample," Chief of Medical Sciences, Hadris Jem, handed the information chips to Melis Norwal.

"What did you find?" Melis asked.

"There is some connection between Gurnil and the third sample, as if they had a common ancestor. There is no connection between them and Quin."

"No connection at all? I find that unusual. Did you verify the reports?"

"We ran the samples several times, and even cross-referenced them with samples we secretly gathered from Ordin and Justis. There is no connection between any of them and young Quin. I have no idea where she came from, Melis, but it doesn't appear to be from Siriaa."

"Are you going to give that information to Gurnil?"

"That's what I wanted to discuss with you and the High President."

CHAPTER 13

"Then let's say there's no connection between Quin and the third sample, and that the other results were inconclusive," Edden Charkisul shook his head at Hadris Jem. "This is disconcerting, to say the least, and if word of this gets out, you know what my opponents are likely to say."

"Or do," Melis agreed. "I'm concerned about the Princess' visit. She's greedy, there's no doubt about that, and had half the credits we paid her spent before she left. If she attempts to go around us and offer Quin's services to anyone willing to pay, it will place the girl in danger."

"Quin is in enough danger as it is, in my estimation," Hadris concurred. "Where she is, she seems little more than a slave."

"It makes me wonder where she came from and how they found her, if she isn't connected to any of them," Melis said.

"This information stays with us," Edden shook his head. "Unless we want her dead."

"Are your enemies that dangerous?" Hadris frowned.

"They're that dangerous," Melis replied. "My team is kept busy, containing threats. So many are spreading rumors that the poison infecting Siriaa is retribution from the gods for supporting the High President."

"Unless their gods are of the mundane and mortal kind, I find no verifiable correlation," Hadris observed.

Dorthil Crasz nodded to a servant, who poured wine into a delicate, handcrafted glass made by the Avii. Dorthil had spent many credits acquiring a full set of the delicate, red-tinted flutes.

"I could have used your help, when I ran for the Presidency against that soft-hearted bastard, Charkisul," Dorthil muttered.

"What's to keep you from taking it away from him?" his visitor asked, sipping the wine and nodding approval.

"I'd certainly need appropriate resources. More credits, too, to pay those I'd need to command."

"What if I can offer all those things to you?"

Dorthil studied his visitor. He appeared to be middle-aged, but Dorthil suspected he might be much older. Centuries older, actually. Dorthil had thought to turn him away when he'd first arrived. The visitor only had to lift a hand and a blast of power was released, rendering Dorthil's bodyguard unconscious.

Dorthil had shown immediate interest, after that.

"You say you're a wizard?" Dorthil asked. "Why would you help me gain the Presidency? What do you want in return?"

Marid of Belancour studied Dorthil thoughtfully, before carefully wording his answer. "I am a wizard—from Yokaru. I know Kondar holds the rights to the volcano fields to the south. I merely wish to mine the sands below the volcano fields. Charkisul will never agree to it. I want your permission as High President to do so, unhindered."

"For how long?"

"Not long. I imagine a few weeks will suffice. The credits will be paid to you shortly after, and we will all have what we want."

"I want proof, first."

"Very well. I can provide spells and weapons that will place you where you wish to be. After that, I only need some time in the volcano fields."

"If you can do as you say, then we have an agreement," Dorthil held out his hand. Marid accepted.

"How did it go?" Morid, Marid's eldest son, asked when Marid folded into his private study.

"Very well. Better than expected. The fool thinks I'm from Yokaru. He has no idea that other worlds exist outside his own. We'll have access to Fyris, never fear. Not only will the collection of the poison bring us the funds we are lacking, it will provide an opportunity to strike back at Glendes Grey and Grey House. Imagine what a bit of that toxin will do if we manage to slip it through to Grey Planet?"

"Are you forgetting that Trikleer is there, Father?"

"I forget nothing. If he wishes to ally himself with those criminals, then he will suffer just the same as they."

Morid didn't respond, although he knew Marid had shoved Trik away—couldn't get rid of him fast enough. Trik hadn't had any say in the matter. Now that Trik, who'd been a cripple all his life until Shadow Grey and Lissa of Le-Ath Veronis adopted him, was an able-bodied, First-Level Wizard, Marid was angry that he hadn't returned to the Belancours with his fully developed talents.

"Do you have buyers already, Father?" Morid asked instead.

"I do, and once they see what I have to offer, they'll pay whatever we ask."

"I have no rights. I'm a half-blood, remember?" I shook my head at Dena's outrage. She'd spent half an hour, pouring out her dissatisfaction at the recent turn of events.

We'd settled inside my suite after Gurnil left us to attend a meeting with Ordin and Justis. I knew the meeting concerned me, but there was little any of them could do to change my circumstances.

"The rights for some should be rights for all. We shouldn't be able to pick and choose who is deserving," Dena fumed. "If Elabeth were alive, she'd hear your case," she added.

"Elabeth is dead. I've been reminded of that often enough, and usually with a blow from a wooden spoon to emphasize it," I said. "So many think I'm personally responsible for her death. I was a child and nowhere near when it happened. I find it curious that vengeance is always leveled against the innocent afterward, don't you? As if an entire nation is held responsible for a crime committed by a few, or those in power."

Yes, I'd allowed my frustrations to surface, and that had never happened before. "Never mind," I sighed, waving a hand. "These are not your troubles, and certainly not your fault."

"It makes me ill," Dena muttered. "I hear rumors about the treatment of her maids. Be careful, Quin." She shivered after she spoke, and that reinforced what I already knew—Halthea was dangerous.

"How long before the ships are built?" Omina asked. She nodded to the servant to pour tea for her brother, who'd come to her suite after overseeing shipbuilding for the day.

"Less than two moon-turns. Perhaps six eight-days. Who can say?" Rath shrugged. "I'd worry that Tamblin is sailing to his death, if I had any concern for your husband, sister."

"My concern is that he'll place you, Rodrik and my remaining son in the same danger he places himself," Omina snorted. "I care not if he and Yevil both perish."

"I'd prefer that Yevil perish first. I blame him most for Fyris' dilemma. Tamblin might not have had the courage to slay his brother, had Yevil not raised his hand to accomplish the deed."

"My Queen?" Farin knocked softly on the half-open door of her study.

"Farin?" Omina lifted an eyebrow at her palace physician, who'd walked in, carrying a sheaf of parchment in his hands.

"I asked the servants to clean out Finder's things. We found this beneath her mattress." He offered the sheaf to Omina. "I've already leafed through them."

"What is this?" Omina began to read the top piece, which was a copying of an old section of a history book, with personal notations and questions in the margins.

"Notes. I believe Finder wrote them."

"She couldn't speak," Omina handed the top parchment to Rath, who read it quickly.

"What if she chose not to speak, or, if she couldn't, preferred not to tell anyone that she held this form of communication? See this line here?" Farin moved to Rath's side and pointed out a question written in the margin. "It says, *why are there so many missing pages?* Only someone Finder's age or younger would not know that answer already."

"Anyone Finder's age or younger would not be taught to write this well," Rath pointed out. "This is a scholar's handwriting."

"How do we know it isn't hers?" Farin persisted.

"We don't," Omina sighed. "Look, here is seeming proof that these were hers." She handed the page in question to Rath, who blinked at what he read. *I feel responsible for Erdin's death, but Irdith is equally responsible. I curse my ability to find things,* was written across the top of a page filled with geographical notations.

"We have that story, do we not, from Chen?" Farin demanded.

"I regret sending him to watch things from the kitchen, and ordering him to keep Amlis informed," Omina shook her head. "He came here, seeking peace from Tamblin's irrationality, and I sent him right back into it. Yes, you're right; we do have Finder's story from Chen, who heard it from Wolter. It does us no good, now. The girl is lost to us. She could have told us so much."

"I'm sad that she didn't write more in these papers. We might have learned many things. Instead, it looks like an advanced student's studies."

"If she hadn't done as Yevil demanded, she'd have died then, instead of that little thief," Rath pointed out. "She had no choice in the matter."

"Nevertheless, she's dead. At least Mirisa is gone, too. What a horrible nuisance she was. She cost us so much," Omina said.

"She cost us our lives," Farin muttered.

"What do you imagine the barbarians are like?" Amlis stared through the window. Rain was falling again, only nothing grew from the spring moisture. Trees that should be blossoming in the early months were bare of bud and leaf.

"My Prince, stop troubling yourself. We have two from Warrel to question late tonight. Are you rested enough for this?"

"Yes. Is Garth prepared?"

"He is."

Wolter surveyed the new crop of kitchen boys with a critical eye. He knew why Chen was dead; secretly cursed those responsible, and had a good guess as to whom it might be.

One of his assistants had been promoted to Chen's place already. Perhaps not the best cook in the lot, but the most trustworthy. Wolter was quite careful where he placed his trust, nowadays.

"Don't make me break a spoon on your backs," he announced at the shuffling of feet and mischievous looks from one boy to another. "Because I will."

Wolter hadn't forgotten, either, that it was Timblor's page, Brin, who killed the Prince he'd served faithfully for turns. Nobody was safe, in his opinion. If he left the palace as he longed to do, the King would send someone after him. He was stuck and he knew it.

Irdith was gone, but Wolter wondered almost daily when the King would send a new spy into his kitchen. Perhaps they were there already, and merely recruited after Irdith's death, with the promise of extra coin and a few privileges.

"Get to work," he ordered. "If you don't know how to do something, say so. I won't tolerate poor effort, for any reason." He watched, a severe expression on his face, as three boys scattered to find work to do in the King's kitchen.

Finder, I miss you now, so desperately, he thought. Rumors had come that she was dead and he grieved for her, just as he did for Chen. Finder had done any job asked of her, without a second thought or a frown for him or Chen. She'd only ever frowned at Irdith, and Wolter suspected that she knew, just as he did, what Irdith really was.

"It doesn't matter," he breathed softly and went to baste the roast. "We're all dead. We just haven't realized it, yet."

It was Garth's idea, and Amlis hoped it worked. This was no traditional questioning. They'd set up a game of cubes. Code words had been arranged, and it would appear as if the men from Warrel were talking of their families.

"We don't need another murder," Amlis breathed as he and Rodrik walked across the courtyard toward the stables. Rodrik had his men stationed in shadows and corners along the way, fearing for the Prince's safety. Both men wore blades beneath long coats, prepared for any attack.

Neither spoke of the fact that Finder would know if there were danger about them. They'd been fools to leave her behind in Vhrist.

Weak moonlight gleamed on courtyard stones, still wet from the earlier rain. Random blocks, worn down by centuries of footsteps, held small puddles of water that splashed beneath purposely striding boots. Amlis cared not that his boots were wet—what was that compared to protecting his life and Rodrik's?

Neither spoke—a careless word could get them killed. If not now, then later, where none might see. When had the walk to the stables seemed so long?

In the morning, I was expected in Halthea's suite to wait on her, with her yellow-winged maids. In an attempt to distract myself, I searched for geography books on the tab-vid Berel had given me. Most of those had images combined with the text, along with descriptions of the land itself, crops produced, if any, lists of cities, their populations and current presidents and politicians.

Best of all, there were images of the planet itself, flattened out so you could see all of it at once. Where Fyris should be, only ocean waters were depicted, washing over a dormant field of underwater volcanoes.

I understood what the western spires were, now—the leavings of a volcanic eruption far in the past. According to the map I studied, more sharp spires jutted from that expanse, instead of a continent. No ships crossed the area, as it was safer and easier to get to known destinations by traveling other routes.

I understood that flying ships recorded data for reproduction in books, but none had recorded any part of Fyris. It troubled and puzzled me, since that meant Fyris was hidden, somehow.

I had no idea how that could be accomplished.

Satellite was a word I had never encountered before. I learned that Kondar had sent small mechanical devices high into the air, where they circled Siriaa constantly and enabled communications and images to be sent to other machines throughout Kondar.

How could anyone in Fyris imagine something so complex? While I pondered that conundrum, the warning came. I'd seen Chen's death too late. Would they hear me now? I had to try.

Wolter stood over the kitchen boy, fists on hips as he oversaw the final cleaning of the worktable. The boy had made the attempt twice already, with unsatisfactory results.

Wolter, a voice shouted in his mind. *You and the Prince, in danger! He is in the stables. Run. Now!*

Without knowing why, Wolter yanked a long knife from a nearby block and raced through the kitchen's back door, his long legs carrying him quickly toward the stable.

"My cousin did murder, several times, of other family members," the recruit claimed after tossing the numbered cubes. "Five. Not good." He handed the cubes to his fellow recruit with a shake of his head.

Amlis listened carefully. Whatever was said by the recruits described Yevil's behavior instead of the designated family member. "Others not related were killed while hunting or gaming. The women he killed died after he bedded them."

"More than one had gaping chest wounds when he was done," the second recruit offered as he threw the cubes. "Eight. Terrible."

Amlis and Rodrik knew the numbers cited did not correspond to those on the cubes. They were describing the instances in which they knew of Yevil's killings.

"How old were you when you learned of this?" Amlis asked.

"Nine," one responded.

"Seven," the other answered. "My father said other deaths came before, but I don't have that information."

"My Prince?" Hirill pushed open the door of Garth's stable room.

"Hirill?" Amlis rose from his crouching position at the cube game and quirked an eyebrow at Hirill. He hadn't informed Hirill of the evening's activities, but assumed that Garth must have passed a message along. His guards had allowed Hirill to pass by, unhindered, on his way to the stables.

"This." The knife Hirill drew was long and sharp as he rushed the Prince. Amlis threw up an arm as Rodrik pulled his blade and shouted. Amlis' arm was struck and he cried out.

Hirill's arm went slack and his eyes rolled back before he could shove the blade farther into Amlis' flesh. When he dropped face-first at Amlis' feet, Amlis and Rodrik stared at Wolter and the bloody kitchen knife in his hand.

I'd known Hirill wasn't to be trusted. All along, he'd kept Yevil apprised of Amlis' movements. Yevil cared not that a message was sent to the Avii—he knew there would be no reply.

One traitor was dead, but that would put Yevil on alert. That frightened me. As much danger as the Prince was in before; that had just increased ten-fold.

I realized, too, that Yevil was more than aware of what ailed Fyris. Did he keep that knowledge from the King, or did the King choose not to accept it?

At least Wolter heard my mental shout and acted on it. I'd placed him in more danger as well, but if I hadn't, he'd have died on the flagstone floor of the King's kitchen.

"None of us are safe." Amlis gripped a wine cup in his healthy hand while Garth wrapped the other, wounded arm with clean strips of cloth.

"My Prince, I have sent for Chen's brother to remove the body in secret. I believe the same knife was used to kill Chen," Rodrik poured more wine into Amlis' cup. "The recruits want to serve you. They are waiting outside the door. What shall I tell them?"

"Put them to work as extra guards or manservants, I care not which. Make sure they know not to talk."

"I think they knew that already," Rodrik snorted. "My question is this—how do we send a message to your mother, telling her of this treachery?"

"Something to consider," Amlis nodded. "Where's Wolter?"

"Outside, with the recruits."

"Do any of ours have experience in a kitchen?" Amlis grimaced as Garth wrapped his arm tightly to lessen the bleeding.

"I may have one."

"Then send him in as an assistant. Tell him to carry a knife in his boot. Always. Wolter saved my life. I will repay that, if I can. Tell him he is welcome in my presence anytime."

"I will." Rodrik walked away to deliver messages.

I slept poorly, even knowing that Wolter and Amlis were safe for the moment. Dreading what was ahead for me, I showered, combed my still-short hair as neatly as I could, then made my way toward Halthea's suite and my new assignment.

Halthea waited for me, a stiff wooden rod in her hand when I appeared early for work inside her suite. Without a word, she whacked me several times between my shoulder blades while I cowered in pain.

"That will show you what waits anytime you disobey or fail to do a proper job," Halthea snapped when the beating stopped. "You will address me as Queen Halthea in my presence, but only when we are alone, do you hear?"

"Yes, Queen Halthea."

"Good. I want my closet organized. I want colors separated, with matching shoes beneath, hear? Do it quickly." With that, she fluffed red feathers and stalked out of her suite.

My back stung from the blows as I made my way to her massive closet. The large space was packed, front to back and top to bottom with dresses, tunics, split skirts, shoes, ribbons and anything else a highborn might possess.

The two Yellow Wings gazed at me with mixtures of fear and revulsion. I'd held back from using my talent, as I had no desire to know what they truly thought of me. It might lessen the pain in the long term when they abused me as well, just as so many others had.

Without speaking, I walked into the closet and began my day as Halthea's newest drudge.

"Halthea wanted her," Jurris shrugged, keeping his Red-Winged back pointed toward his half-brother.

Justis stood behind Jurris on Jurris' private balcony while they waited for tea to be served. Jurris chose to watch the waters surrounding Avii Castle instead of turning toward his brother.

"She was better off where she was," Justis pointed out. "Learning from Ordin, so she wouldn't appear a fool to those in Kondar. Surely Halthea can see the sense in that."

"What does it matter what the Kondari think?" Jurris rustled his wings.

"It may matter a great deal, as we ask such a high price for what Quin provides."

"You think they'll stop asking, or run short of those who are ill?"

"No. I worry that the High President may forbid it, if he learns we're mistreating the provider."

"You think that's possible?"

"I've worked my way through their laws concerning citizens' rights, although it was a long and tedious process. Their language is a difficult one, yet Quin speaks it with ease. The High President is responsible for several of those laws regarding fair treatment of Kondari citizens. If he learns you attempted to kill Quin when she first arrived, he may reconsider the relationship between Aviia and Kondar. If you explain Fyris to him, you know where that might lead."

"Then what do you suggest, brother? I've never known you to take an interest in any woman, let alone an unknown half-blood."

"I am merely attempting to protect you, Halthea and an asset," Justis growled. "If Kondar considers us an enemy, it won't matter that we can fly. Their machines fly faster, and can be more deadly than I prefer to consider."

"I feel Halthea will tire quickly of her new acquisition. Leave it for two or three weeks, then I'll make a suggestion to place the girl elsewhere." Jurris turned to frown at Justis. "I hear your words, but Halthea must be cajoled into seeing reason."

Justis wanted to tell Jurris what he thought of cajoling Halthea, but wisely held back his retort.

Only half of Halthea's closet was organized at the end of six hours, which warranted a second beating and a promise of more the next day. It mattered not that it would have taken any other nearly twice as long to accomplish what I had—it only mattered that the work wasn't completed.

The second beating drew blood on my back, but I was unaware of it until Ordin examined my skin when I arrived in his study for my assignment. He scrutinized my back with a tightened mouth and a deep frown furrowing his brow, but didn't say anything against the Red-Winged Princess.

Instead, he washed the bruised and abraded skin, then applied salve to the wound. "Your feathers are longer, and the colors on the tips are more pronounced," he sighed as he leaned back in his chair and wiped his hands on a towel. "I've never seen any of our feathers carry gold, silver and copper bands on the edges. The colors are always consistent throughout."

"Might that be attributed to the cutting?" I asked, turning to face Master Ordin.

"I know not, as I've never seen wings grow after they've been deliberately cut. The Avii would never consider such a thing. Only Fyris would do this kind of evil, after that pretender took the throne."

I longed to tell Ordin what had transpired in Fyris the night before, but held back. It would only be another reason to despise all of them, and that weight was already heavy enough.

"Master Ordin, a message for you." Justis walked in carrying a paper envelope. "This was delivered with the equipment I ordered for the guards."

I understood what Justis wouldn't say in my presence—that someone hadn't wanted this particular message to go through royal hands before it reached Ordin.

"Quin, take this and read it on the terrace," Ordin handed the book to me that I'd been studying with a nod. "Make notes as usual, and I'll address your questions later."

"Yes, Master Ordin." With the briefest of glances in Justis' direction, I held the book to my chest and walked out of Ordin's study.

"I wish we could make paper as fine as this," Ordin muttered as he opened the sealed envelope and withdrew the contents.

"What does it say?" Justis asked.

"It says the puzzle continues to be a puzzle, only a much larger one. Quin isn't connected to anyone in Fyris. Any connection she might have with the Avii is inconclusive." Ordin handed the paper to Justis.

"You had them check?" Justis' brows lifted in surprise.

"I wanted to know. Sit down, I'll explain," Ordin sighed.

"I don't know what to think," Justis huffed. Gurnil had joined him and Ordin at Ordin's request, after Ordin explained Quin's unusual past. "You say the timing is right?"

"As far as we can tell, and no half-blood in my knowledge has ever grown wings."

"They'd be red, wouldn't they?"

"They were cut away so many times by those imbeciles, who knows what color—if any—they might retain? They'll be white, there's no doubt about that, but the bands of copper, silver and gold? I've never seen anything like it." Ordin shook his head as if he couldn't believe it, either.

"Elabeth was beautiful. Quin is lovely as well. Can we say what Lirin might have looked like, had she reached adulthood?" Gurnil asked.

"We have to keep this quiet. If there's any possibility," Justis ruffled his feathers and his eyes clouded with anger. "The bitch has her now. If Halthea learns of this, Quin will die in a matter of hours."

"What can we do, then?" Ordin asked.

"Hope that she lives through the next three weeks," Justis growled.

Dena had raced after Master Gurnil—he'd left a book out on a Library table that belonged in his private study, and she worried that it shouldn't be left out. After placing the book where none would see it unless they searched diligently, she flew toward Master Ordin's terrace, finding Quin deep in a book.

She waved briefly at Quin before going inside, to find Ordin's study door shut. Without meaning to, she caught words she was never meant to hear. She stayed to listen to most of the conversation before retreating and flying back to Gurnil's terrace.

Could it be? She wondered. She recognized the fear in Justis' voice when he'd uttered those words—if Halthea learned what Quin might be, then Quin would die. Dena's heartbeat still hadn't calmed, so she leaned against a Library wall, a hand to her chest, willing her heart to settle into a normal rhythm.

"I can't ever repeat this," Dena whispered. It could be the death of her, too, if word got out. Halthea would kill anyone who knew.

"You know how to make fish stew? Do it and let me taste," Wolter said. He wasn't sure what to think of the man-at-arms that Amlis placed in his kitchen, but Deeds certainly knew how to peel and chop vegetables, and had already helped bake bread for the midday meal.

"I heard Finder worked for you before beginning her service for the Prince," Deeds said quietly as he filleted fish brought in that morning.

"I heard she was dead," Wolter responded.

"She is. Terrible thing, too. Knocked on the head and hauled to the glass castle. They wouldn't let her live, once she was dumped on their shore."

"It's worse than I imagined, then," Wolter shook his head. "We won't speak of this again."

"As you say, Master Cook," Deeds nodded. "Rodrik asks you to house me nearby, in case my help is needed at any time," he added.

"I have a space in a storeroom—Finder used to sleep there. I'll have a new mattress brought in."

"That will be fine, and I thank you."

"Where is Hirill? His absence is annoying," Tamblin paced beside his window. Occasionally he glanced at the floor, marking the place Timblor had bled after the stabbing.

"I know not," Yevil calmly examined his fingernails as he leaned against a nearby wall.

"He would be here," Tamblin began before stopping midsentence. "Never mind. Have there been any messages? I grow weary of watching recruits bumble about with swords. I want to sail from our shores soon. The barbarians will fall before us. We will be better equipped than those savages, even as poorly trained as my troops are, still."

Yevil's eyes narrowed, but he didn't answer. He merely offered the King a nod and stalked toward the door, intending to ask after messages for the King.

The moment the door closed, Tamblin released a breath. A cage was forming around him, and Yevil held the key. Somehow, Hirill was dead. Tamblin suspected Yevil had a hand in it, but had no idea whether Hirill was Yevil's friend or foe when he died.

"I know why Chen died," Amlis said. Rodrik poured wine for Chen's brother, Fen—they'd met at the inn on the outskirts of Lironis to talk. Garth had managed to remove Hirill's body to the inn the night before, with help from Rodrik's men-at-arms.

"I know you hold me responsible," Amlis continued, "and you are right to do so. Understand this, though. We are all in danger. Not just from the one who commands these deaths, but from the poison consuming Fyris. We have the body of the one who killed Chen. I wish we had the body of his master as well, but we can only do so much in the face of greater adversity."

Fen accepted the cup of wine with a curt nod for Rodrik before turning to the Prince. "It pleases me that my brother's killer is dead. It displeases me that his master is not." Fen released a sigh and closed his eyes for a moment.

"It matters not," he breathed, shaking his head. "I know the situation is tenuous, and our lives count for nothing in this cursed land. I will take the body. It will not be found."

"Thank you. Might I interest you in a place at my mother's castle in Vhrist?" Amlis asked.

"Where Chen was? He spoke fondly of his time, there."

"I'm offering you the same, if you'll carry a message to her."

"After this, I wouldn't mind moving away. I've lived in Lironis' shadow far too long."

"Good. Rodrik's men will load the body in your cart while I draft the message," Amlis said.

My morning began just as the previous morning had—with a beating to remind me of my place.

The two Yellow Wings watched in satisfaction—perhaps my punishment mitigated theirs in some way. If that were true, then they would distance themselves and come to despise me the same as Halthea did. I ignored them and went to work on the closet.

Halthea's closet was organized and neat before my six hours were up, but still I was struck between my wings before I left for Ordin's study. Ordin was furious when he rubbed salve on the opened wound from the day before.

"It is the way of things," I shrugged uncomfortably when he was finished.

"Does it not make you angry?" He frowned at me.

"What good does anger serve, when there is nothing you can do to change your circumstances?" I replied.

"She'd get her comeuppance if she wore yellow wings instead of red," Ordin huffed. "Never mind, take your book and read. Your notes from yesterday were very good."

Rain fell outside Avii castle that afternoon, so I chose a quiet spot in the healing rooms to read.

"Let me see your feathers." Justis arrived while I was so immersed in the book I failed to hear his approach. His voice caused me to jump, although long practice kept a squeak of surprise behind closed lips.

He cursed softly at the wounds on my back when I turned for him, and I was surprised at how gentle his fingers were when they brushed short feathers. "They're dragging the floor, Quin," he said, taking his hands away and turning me to face him. "Get Ordin to show you how to use the hinge to fold them up. It would be a shame if they gathered dust on the tips."

He walked away, then, as quickly as he'd arrived.

I found myself practicing the use of my wing hinge the rest of the evening before bed. Like a muscle I'd never known I had, it ached after a while, but at least it worked. Gurnil and Dena were surprised and pleased that it worked so well.

"When your wings are fully grown and extended, you'll practice flapping before you ever attempt to fly," Dena said. "I can't wait to see what they look like. White wings! They're amazing."

"I told him to stay off the road and be wary," Amlis said. "We've played our hand. If that message is intercepted," he didn't finish.

"One traveling alone may not cause a stir. I believe him safer alone than with two of my men."

"I agree, but that doesn't mean he won't be in danger anyway. I gave him enough coin to get to Vhrist, and Mother will offer more for the delivery of the message."

"Then it's time we rode back to the castle."

"Have you ever wanted to ride in the other direction, instead?" Amlis asked.

"More times than I can count, my Prince," Rodrik replied.

"Did you know there were so many books in here?" Deeds asked as he and Wolter surveyed Quin's old sleeping space. Books were stacked about her mattress, which was worn so thin as to be next to nothing.

"Most of them aren't illustrated, and that puzzles me. I can understand that she might find the illustrations interesting, but the others?" Wolter shook his head.

"What's this?" Deeds lifted a book from the top of a stack and pulled out a scrap of parchment. "It has writing on it." He handed the piece to Wolter.

How long ago were these people observed? Was written in a scholar's hand on the scrap.

"What book is that?" Wolter asked. Deeds handed it to the cook.

"It came from near the middle," he offered as Wolter flipped through the pages.

"Look at this—I barely recall seeing this before all these books were confiscated." Wolter showed Deeds images of the barbarians, barely clothed in rough leather or in fur with bits of shell or other primitive adornments hanging about their necks.

"Those are the barbarians from the northern continent," Deeds shrugged. "My mother used to frighten me into obedience by saying they were coming to kidnap me."

"Who wrote this?" Wolter turned the scrap in his fingers.

"Who knows? Did anyone else ever come here, besides Finder?"

"None. This was filled with dust and abandoned before the girl ever moved in. This makes me wonder, though. Those books are old that hold these images, and they're copies of other books older than that. Whoever wrote this," Wolter waved the scrap, "was right to ask that question."

"Perhaps. Shall we leave it for now?" Deeds asked. "I must replace this mattress and find candles. It is dark and stuffy in here."

"What is this?" Rodrik accepted the package Deeds offered.

"A book I found in Finder's old sleeping place. Take a look at the scrap of parchment and the place it marks," he nodded. "I have to get back before anyone notices."

"Take care. It seems even the castle stones have eyes," Rodrik muttered.

"I feel them," Deeds responded and turned to slip into the shadows outside the Prince's suite.

CHAPTER 14

All day, Halthea was attended by two dressmakers, who took the fabrics the Princess had purchased in Kondar to make new clothing for her. I fetched, carried and served her and both dressmakers as they discussed cut and design.

It wearied me, and like the previous days, I was given no midday meal. At least I could ask for food before going to my studies; Ordin understood and approved my hasty trips to the guild kitchen. There, Master Cook Nina made sure I was given a proper meal before I rushed to Master Ordin's study.

Ordin, too, had begun to quiz me on my readings, and I was happy to answer all his questions. I found the physiology of the body, winged and not winged, fascinating. He and I had discussed the way the heart pumped blood through the body only the day before.

"Quin," Halthea's rod fell heavily on my back, "fetch us tea. Immediately."

"Yes, Princess Halthea," I mumbled. I couldn't call her Queen in front of the dressmakers, but she'd demand it later, when we were alone.

"That girl is an abomination," one of the dressmakers announced as I left Halthea's well-appointed receiving room behind.

"It's better if I keep an eye on her," Halthea replied with a laugh. The Brown-Winged dressmakers followed her lead and laughed with her.

I was glad to get away from Halthea that day. She and the dressmakers had discussed something in my absence, and I was too afraid to use my gift to see what it was. My back still hurt from her last blow when I returned with tea; I served it without a word as they gossiped about this guild member or that while they sipped and nibbled.

"Master Ordin will tend to it," I muttered as Nina studied my back. I ate inside her kitchen—a bowl of lentil stew, with potatoes and carrots added.

"I curse these backless blouses around anyone who hits," Nina grumbled. "While Jurris might hear any other case," she shook her head.

"I know where I stand," I said, dumping the spoon in my half-finished bowl. "Thank you for the meal, Master Cook Nina." I carried the bowl to the scrap box, emptied it and loaded it into the dish machine. At least I knew how to do that.

What I didn't know how to do was make a cruel person kinder. I allowed that thought to simmer on my way to Ordin's study. I also used my gift to research Halthea's parents—how permissive had they been to allow her to become what she was? What I found surprised me.

"Quin, what is it?" I stared stupidly at Ordin when I arrived, wondering whether I should ask my question.

"Wh-who," I stuttered, "was Treven?"

"Has someone frightened you with stories of that bastard?" Ordin stood, suddenly angry.

"N-no, I just, I can't explain it." My feathers, grown long enough finally, rustled at my back in agitation.

How could I tell him that Red-Winged Treven had fathered both Halthea and Jurris? Jurris slept with his half-sister without knowing, and thought to make her Queen.

The Avii thought Halthea's parents went through the gate together. Instead, her mother's husband had forced his wife through first, then followed her immediately. He'd discovered that his daughter was not his daughter. In my estimation, Halthea had inherited—in full measure—her real father's penchant for cruelty.

"Treven was a real abomination, if you ever want to hear of an actual example," Ordin muttered as he examined my back. "Nothing has been written, but enough of us know of his cruelty that it doesn't matter. Quin, he's dead. Stop worrying about that, all right?"

"I will, Master Ordin."

Ordin silently tended to my back, then sent me out to the terrace for my reading assignment. Three hours later, I realized how hungry I was when I returned the book and my notes before heading toward the Library and my room. Dena would go with me to the dining hall. Someday, I hoped to fly there instead of walking.

"Hold them up for a few seconds longer, if you can," Dena instructed.

My wings, half-grown feathers and all, were extended all the way on each side. "I wish you could see this," Dena breathed. "They'll be magnificent when they're fully-grown. They're already pretty, with the thin bands of color at the tips."

"Not everybody feels that way," I sighed, letting my wings droop. Holding them up, when that was something I'd never done before, was tiring. "How long can you fly?" I asked, changing the subject. I had no desire to tell Dena that two Brown Wings and a Red-Winged Princess had denigrated what I had earlier in the day.

"I can fly for more than an hour, but I don't fly that much. Justis might fly for six hours or more. Long enough to reach Fyris or Kondar, I know that much. He used to make the trip with Camryn and Elabeth, when Tandelis was still alive. Elabeth always carried the baby with her.

I can carry someone with me, but not far. Someone with more stamina might carry another for a long distance before having to set down."

"Will you work with me every evening, then, to make my wings stronger?"

"Of course I will. You don't have parents to do that for you, so I'll fill in," Dena promised.

"You're the only friend I've ever had, and you turned into the best one I could ask for," I said. She hugged me for that, and it pleased me.

It is such an unusual thing that I can see or feel danger for others, and never for myself. That's how I'd ended up at Avii castle, after all—I'd never seen my kidnapping. Had I known what Halthea and her seamstresses planned during my brief absences the day before, I'd never have gone to sleep in my room.

My door flew open in the early hours before dawn, and seven descended upon me, yanking me from the bed and tossing me onto the floor. They were masked and dressed alike—in black robes so I couldn't see who they were. I screamed when two of my primary feathers were yanked from tender wings.

Gurnil came running. One of the attackers—the tallest, hit the Master Scholar as he burst into the room, knocking him unconscious and into the doorframe. Dena screamed outside the door; she'd witnessed Gurnil's fall. I knew that he needed my help—his head was bleeding.

My attackers turned back to me, ready to yank out the rest of my feathers. It had already come to me, what they planned to do. Treven had designed this torture, after all, and called it *the plucking*. Such attacks were reserved for his enemies and those he found mildly annoying alike.

These never guessed that I knew who each of them were by employing the gift I had. When a third primary feather was ripped away while one of them moved to harm Dena, I screamed mentally for help.

Two came to my aid.

The Orb and an angry Larentii.

I'd crawled to Gurnil's body to heal him. He had a brain injury that could kill him or alter his mental abilities if I didn't.

Dena had been knocked down, but never lost consciousness. The Orb pulsed over my head, after flashing light so bright it had blinded all of us, then blasted power at the attackers, rendering them unconscious.

Daragar fussed with my wings while I tended to Gurnil. The pain I had from having my largest feathers jerked from my skin was soothed quickly while my healing light joined that pulsing from the Orb.

Gurnil blinked up at me after a few moments, and discovered Daragar and me bending over him.

That's when Justis arrived, with Jurris and several black-winged guards right behind. Justis cursed at the state of my bloody wings, three bloodied white primary feathers on the floor and seven masked and hooded bodies scattered across my bedroom.

Striding angrily toward the tallest, who'd harmed Master Gurnil, he pulled the mask away, revealing the Black-Winged guard who'd attempted to kill me when I first arrived.

Other masks were ripped away. I saw the seamstresses—both of them—from the day before. One of Halthea's yellow-winged maids was there. Two more black-winged guards were revealed, then Halthea herself. I heard Jurris' intake of breath, then.

"That one attacked me." Gurnil pointed at the tall, Black-Winged man.

"Master Gurnil would have died had Quin not attended to him," Daragar said. He'd stepped back to allow Justis room to unmask the attackers, and stood against a wall, blue arms crossed and a frown upon his lips.

"What is the meaning of this?" Jurris demanded.

"You won't find out until they wake," Justis snapped. "The Orb rendered them unconscious. You'd think that Ardis would have learned from his first encounter with the Orb."

"You may deal with the Black, Brown and Yellow Wings as you see fit, brother," Jurris nodded to Justis. "I'll handle Halthea."

With that, Jurris stepped toward Halthea's body, followed closely by two of his guards. "Lift her and fly her to my suite," Jurris commanded one of them.

All gasped as Halthea's robe fell back, revealing her wings. They were as yellow as those of her unconscious maid beside her.

"Where is that cursed Orb? I want her back as she was," Jurris shouted. Justis sat nearby as Jurris paced and fumed on his private terrace.

"This has happened twice before, brother, and the new colors were never reversed." Justis found the situation more than acceptable and quite humorous, but he kept that to himself. "The Orb passed judgment. Halthea planned that attack, for no reason that I can see. You know we have laws against it; you helped Camryn design those laws. As for your question, the Orb is still in the Library, hovering over Gurnil and the girl."

"It has never approached me as it did Elabeth and Camryn," Jurris grumbled.

"I have no answer for that," Justis shrugged. "What will you do with Halthea? The others are in the holding cells at ground level. Their cases will be heard by the Council, and unless I miss my guess, the Orb may attend those hearings. Whether they consider the girl at all in this, the fact remains that Gurnil could have died without her intervention."

"I cannot place her in a holding cell," Jurris snapped. "She needs help."

"She no longer has red wings. The Orb passed judgment already," Justis said as calmly as he could. He wanted to shout at his brother, pointing out that Halthea had broken the law.

"Leave me," Jurris waved his hand, dismissing Justis. "Halthea will remain in my suite tonight, and I will decide tomorrow, when the Council is convened."

Without a word, Justis rose and left his brother alone.

"I want to heal these, making their replacements grow, but this must be discussed by the Council," Daragar fingered the wounds on my wings.

Gurnil sat nearby, while Dena offered him a cup of tea. He accepted it gratefully and drank. Blood still spattered his sleeping robe—he hadn't bothered to change after the attack.

"I thank you for coming so swiftly, Master Gurnil," I said. "I'm sorry they attacked you as well."

"You healed my wound. I am more than grateful for that," he nodded to me.

"Gurnil? Are you well?" Ordin swept in, blinking at the artificial light inside the Library where we were. It was still an hour before dawn, after all.

"I am, thanks to Quin," Gurnil lifted his cup of tea. "Want some? Dena has more in the pot."

"I'll take it. Word came to me, but Jurris pulled me away to check Halthea first. There isn't a foundering thing I can do about a shift in wing color. The Orb made judgment against Halthea. She should have known better."

"They should have known better," Gurnil huffed before sipping his tea again. Dena placed a cup in my hands before moving to serve Ordin. "This won't sit well with some on the Council. You know why," his mouth tightened as he jerked his head in Ordin's direction.

"Prejudice is a difficult enemy to defeat," Ordin agreed. "Perhaps it is time to post a guard outside the Library entrance, my friend."

Ordin sent Gurnil, Dena and me to bed before he left, saying he'd send someone if we were required at the Council meeting. Daragar disappeared once he repaired my bedroom door and I shut it behind me. Leaning my back against the thick wood, I heaved a trembling sigh.

It was more than possible that the Avii would be divided over the night's events, and I wasn't looking forward to it. My lot wouldn't have mattered much, had Gurnil not been injured and Halthea not been changed by the Orb.

Gurnil and Ordin had danced around the truth and not asked me any questions. I couldn't tell them that I'd sent a mental call for help, bringing the Larentii and the Orb to my aid. Letting my wings down, I held the left one in my hand and studied the holes where primary feathers should be.

Somehow, those feathers had disappeared, and I had no idea who'd taken them. My wings draggling behind me, I walked toward my bed, climbed in and pulled up the covers, shivering beneath them while the weight of Siriaa settled on my shoulders.

"Master Ordin and Master Gurnil were called to the Council meeting," Dena said as she set the tray of food on the table beside my bed. "It's almost dinner hour, so I asked for something from Nina's kitchen."

"Have you eaten?" I asked, studying her. She looked pale to me, and her usually sunny smile had fled.

"At midday. I'll go during the regular mealtime and get something."

"Would they have taken all my feathers?" I mumbled, lifting a lid to find a bowl of brown beans, still warm from the pot.

"That's what happened before, when," Dena shrugged.

"I know about Treven," I replied, sliding off the bed. "Let's take this to the terrace. We can talk there, if you want."

"Nothing is written about him—not that most of us can get to, anyway," Dena said, following me as I carried the tray of food toward the terrace doors. "How did you find out?"

"By accident," I said. In a way that was true—I'd gone looking into Halthea's parentage, never expecting to find Jurris' father there. Even Halthea was unaware of who her real father was. Only Halthea's mother and Treven had known, until Halthea's foster-father learned of it during an argument with his wife.

"What do you think will happen in the Council meeting?" Dena asked when I settled on a bench on the terrace. The day was quite fine, still, in direct contrast with the darkness of my turbulent thoughts.

"They will argue," I shrugged and lifted the bowl of beans. "What they cannot refute is the fact that Gurnil was attacked and could have died. Ardis may receive a worse sentence than the others."

"What about Halthea?" Dena's question was whispered, as if she were afraid of being overheard.

"This is what I think," I said. "Jurris will argue that she has already been punished enough. I imagine that she will remain inside his suite, where she was taken last night. The others will be punished in truth, with Ardis' being the worst for striking Master Gurnil."

"That's not fair. She probably ordered Ardis to help her. The others, too." Dena's wings rustled in the late afternoon air, emphasizing her outrage against the Princess. "She can't retain her title—she doesn't have red wings, now. The Orb saw to that."

"Jurris will have the final say," I mumbled around a mouthful of beans.

"There are no more Red-Winged females," Dena observed. "What will happen to us?"

"I don't know," I said and pulled my wings tight against my back.

"It's as if everyone in the castle is afraid to make any noise," Amlis said. "How is Deeds doing in the kitchen?"

"I hear he and Wolter are getting along very well," Rodrik replied.

"Good. I wonder, still, how Wolter knew to come to our aid," Amlis mused.

"Perhaps someone saw or heard something and reported it. You know how gossip goes."

"Yes, but gossip has diminished to an occasional trickle, rather than the raging flood it used to be."

"The times are ultimately more dangerous, my Prince."

"That is true," Amlis agreed. "Shall we take ourselves for a walk near the kitchens? I hear there might be bread and honey available if we ask."

"I'll get my blade," Rodrik replied.

The small opening in the rocks was barely wide enough to fit his body inside. Regardless, Fen hid there, hoping the armed men who searched for him would walk past.

Afraid to breathe, he huddled there, hoping to blend into the surrounding stones well enough that none might see. He'd carried Amlis' message for a day's ride before burying the thing. He knew well enough what it said, and it could cost him his life if the enemy found it on him.

If he made it to Vhrist, he could recite what was written well enough. He hoped Omina would accept his word, instead of handwritten proof. Boots crunched nearby, causing Fen to shrink farther into his makeshift cave.

"This was Finder's sleeping quarters?" Amlis looked about him while Wolter and Deeds poured wine. They'd settled inside Finder's old storeroom, packed as it was with dusty crates, books, broken furniture and things none had thought to call for in turns.

"On a mattress so thin it may as well have been the floor," Deeds passed out cups of wine.

"My fault," Wolter muttered. "I never thought to look into it. Always assumed she took care of things herself."

"Doesn't matter now," Rodrik gulped his wine. "The dead have no cares."

"That doesn't mean we can't care for the dead," Wolter muttered. "Because we do."

"Wolter, I have a question," Amlis said.

"I already know what it is, and I can't explain it any better than you."

"Quin? Quin?" Dena's voice betrayed her panic. I'd been lost for a few moments, misdirecting those who thought to attack Chen's brother.

No, I'd never met him, but knew he was in danger, nonetheless. The seven who thought to kill him had begun to search elsewhere by the time I was done with them. Breathing a sigh, I turned to Dena, who was frightened out of her wits.

"I'm all right. I was lost in thought and memory for a moment," I said, placing an unsteady hand on her arm. "I'll finish my meal here. Why don't you go to dinner? Surely it's time and you must be hungry."

"I am," she said.

"Then go. I'll be fine, here."

"If you're sure."

"I am." I wasn't, and might never be again after the events of the previous night, but I didn't want Dena to worry about me. I had enough worry for the both of us. Fyris was disintegrating, and High President Charkisul's safety looked to become a problem very soon. His opponents were plotting; I couldn't say how I knew that, I just did.

Dena flew away from the terrace, and I watched her bank with the winds rising about the castle, wishing I could do the same. What surprised me was that Ordin, Gurnil and Justis arrived shortly after Dena left. Ordin folded his wings and sat beside me on the bench while the other two stood nearby.

"We have some good news," Gurnil began. "Other news as well, some of it not nearly as good."

"What is that, Master Gurnil?" I asked, setting down my cup. It was nearly empty anyway, and my thirst was gone.

"Ardis will walk through the gate for his attack on Master Gurnil. The others will serve in the glassmaker's furnaces for six turns—two turns for each feather they pulled."

"Halthea will stay inside Jurris' quarters and wait on him as a Yellow Wing," Justis grumbled. He felt, just as I did, that her sentence was far too light. She'd cost Ardis his life.

"Then I wish to petition for Ardis' life," I said, standing.

"Quin, you have no standing here," Ordin said. "I wish it were otherwise, but that's the way things are. We are fortunate that the others were sentenced as they were for their misdeeds."

"Halthea should be the one walking through that gate," I snapped. "Or shoved through, just as her father was." Yes, it was a moment of misjudgment, but I couldn't recall the words, once I'd said them.

"What do you mean, just as her father was? He and her mother went through together."

"Treven was her father," I said. "Her foster father learned from her mother that he was not Halthea's father. He pushed her through first, then followed after. Treven was already dead, as you know."

"How in the name of Liron do you know that?" Justis exploded.

"I can't explain it. I just know it's true," I muttered, sitting down again and crossing arms over my chest defensively.

"That would explain much," Ordin muttered dryly.

"There's a way to find out," Gurnil offered. "I have feathers from both—Halthea and Treven."

"Are you suggesting?" Justis turned to Gurnil. "Never mind, I see that you are. Do it. I wish to know the results. Quin," he turned to me. "I have been ordered by my brother to watch over you carefully. Therefore, you will report to my quarters tomorrow, and take over the cleaning duties performed by the Yellow Wings every day. You may attend your studies after four hours of work, and run errands for me when I ask."

"Yes, Commander Justis." I inclined my head respectfully to him. My life was about to change. Again.

Fen didn't come out of his hiding place until after sundown. From then on, he would travel by night and hide by day until he reached Vhrist and the Queen. Things were more complicated than he ever imagined possible.

"There are books in my mother's library that describe such a thing, but it was never used to warn. Mother says Tandelis received the mind-messages from Elabeth whenever a visit was planned. He couldn't return a message, except by the usual means." Amlis shuffled books inside a leather bag he'd brought from Vhrist.

The bag was usually hidden in a special slot behind his heavy bed, and he and Rodrik had to work together to shove the huge frame aside in order to retrieve it.

"Why would a message come to Wolter instead of you?" Rodrik asked.

"I don't know. Damn. I don't have anything here that might explain it." Amlis shoved thin books and papers inside the bag with an agitated sigh. "It doesn't matter—Wolter arrived in time before Hirill could kill me. He says the voicc warned him that he and I were in danger, and sent him to the stables to help."

"While you and the cook weren't connected before, you are now," Rodrik's voice and expression were wry.

"That's not true. Wolter handed Finder to me on the day I went looking for her. I can't believe how covered in soot and filth she was."

"Finder is dead, need I remind you? That is the only connection you and Wolter had, until now."

"I'm glad Deeds offered to show Wolter how to handle a sword. We need as many allies as we can muster."

"It is time to make our way to Vhrist, my King." Yevil's smile was as false as his heart when he dipped his head in Tamblin's presence. "It will be wise to get our troops prepared for the voyage by making sorties on the warships already built."

"Worried that they won't have their sea legs?" Tamblin quirked an eyebrow at Yevil. "No matter." He waved a hand, dismissing any reply Yevil might make. "You're right—we can't just load them onto a ship and expect everything to go well immediately. Alert the commanders. I'll give the message to the Crown Prince myself."

"As you say," Yevil bowed and left the King's chambers.

"Do you have any questions?"

It was obvious that being Commander of the Avii troops, as well as the King's brother, afforded some luxury. Justis had a wide window in his bedroom, in addition to a private terrace, a receiving area and a personal library outside his sitting room.

"Not about cleaning or straightening," I said.

"What do you have questions about?" One of Justis' black eyebrows rose, but there was a faint twinkle in his eyes, telling me it was all right to ask about other things.

"What keeps Fyris hidden?" I asked.

"Of all the questions waiting to be asked, you offer me that one?" Justis turned away to stare through the window. The sill was low, offering an uninterrupted view of the sea beyond the castle. Somewhere across those waters and past the curve of Siriaa, lay Fyris.

I held my breath, hoping he wasn't angry. Instead, his wings drooped as his shoulders sagged. "You may as well know," he said. "It's a spell. Elabeth told me once that a powerful wizard was responsible. I can't imagine anyone holding that much power, but Fyris remains hidden. Elabeth wasn't tolerant of lies, so perhaps it is the truth."

"The spell was placed on the land itself?"

"No." Justis turned back to me, then. "It is said that the Prince of Fyris' ring holds that power within it. Another thing I find difficult to accept—how could a spell such as that be held in something so small? Elabeth said as long as the ring stayed within Fyris' boundaries, the spell would work. If the ring is taken away, Fyris will be revealed."

Justis' answer chilled me and I shivered.

"What's wrong?" he asked.

"Are you familiar with the old tales from Fyris?" I asked. "The ones that say to be wise in making wishes?"

"Because they might come to pass and make you regret the wishing?" Justis nodded.

"Yes. Exactly." At that moment, I wanted to walk to Justis' terrace, sit on the grass that covered it and consider what Yevil truly intended to do.

CHAPTER 15

Halthea examined her wings in Jurris' wide mirror before hurling her hairbrush at the offending glass and shattering it. Shards of glass fell and crashed upon the wood floor of Jurris' dressing room. What did it matter that it was broken—the glassmakers would have another to replace it the moment Jurris asked.

He'd sent her maids away, too, and that infuriated her. She'd had red wings and was entitled to her maids. That filthy Orb and that aberration of a girl had robbed her of her birthright.

Nobody would call her Queen, now. Not with yellow wings.

"What in Liron's name is going on?" Jurris arrived and surveyed the mess Halthea made. "Clean that up. Immediately," he snapped.

"I'm not your servant," Halthea shouted.

"You have yellow wings. You're everyone's servant, now," Jurris hissed. "I've done everything I could to keep you from the gate. Clean that up and stay quiet. I have a meeting with the Guild Masters to attend."

"Pig!" Halthea shouted at Jurris' retreating back.

Many of the books on Justis' shelves hadn't been touched in a while, and the Yellow Wings who'd cleaned before my arrival hadn't touched them, either. I was dusting them when Justis walked in later to change clothes. He had a Guild Masters' meeting to attend with the King.

"Nasty work?" he queried as he walked past on the way to his closet.

"No. I don't consider dusting books nasty work. It allows me to consider what I'd like to read later."

"I can't believe you'd want to read any of it."

"I can't believe anyone wouldn't."

"You're a strange girl."

"That is nothing new," I replied, pulling down a thick book and wiping dust off the top before tending to the front and back cover. "People in Fyris thought I was mute because I never spoke."

"Why wouldn't you speak?"

"I don't think I could, until I was nine. After that, it was better if I didn't speak. Everybody thought I was mute and stupid. They said things around me that they wouldn't say, otherwise."

"And talking suddenly might get you killed."

"Exactly."

"How bad is it there?" he asked.

"As bad as you can imagine it is, it's worse. Timblor is dead, at the hands of his page. Tamblin is little more than Yevil's puppet. Yevil has attempted to kill Amlis at least three times; Hirill was spying for both sides and is now dead. Is there anything else you'd like to know?" I replaced the book and lifted down another.

Justis blinked dark eyes at me for a moment before muttering a soft curse. "Why should we worry about their deaths?" he added. "They're doing a fine job of killing themselves."

"That doesn't include the people and animals dying of the poison," I said. "Babies are dying. Animals are dying. People are sick from the wasting disease," I shrugged and rustled my feathers. "Kondar wonders where the poison is coming from. Fyris' shield keeps them from learning the answer."

"Kondar knows of the poison?" Justis' eyes widened in surprise.

"Yes. It is spreading far beyond Fyris' shores. When I stood upon the grass while we were in Kondar, I could feel it. The ground groaned at the sickness of it."

"I curse the day that fool killed Elabeth," Justis snapped and strode out of his suite.

"He's no fool," I whispered after Justis. "He's an intelligent evil."

⁂

"Kondar knows of the poison?" Gurnil frowned at Justis. "I thought the shield held it back."

"Somehow, it is escaping Fyris and bleeding into Kondar. Likely through seawater," Justis grumbled. "Elabeth would have held it at bay, just as she always did, had that fool not murdered her and the others."

"The First Ordinance forbids us from revealing Fyris," Ordin tossed up his hand in a helpless gesture.

"It also commands us to hold the poison at bay, but only one Red Wing held that ability. It was always the Queen, who passed it to her heir. Elabeth only had Halthea as an option for the longest time, and for obvious reasons, refused to confer the talent."

"She never thought to die as she did—in her prime," Gurnil huffed. "She waited to see Lirin's red wings I'm sure, before designating her as the heir."

"They couldn't be any other color; Camryn was the Queen's only mate," Justis observed. "Red Wings beget Red Wings."

"There was no question about Lirin's heritage or impending wing color," Gurnil sighed. "Until now."

⁂

"The data was collected by fishing vessels equipped to gather information," Edden Charkisul's Chief of Sciences reported. "You recall that we authorized the equipment and the expense months ago. We finally have results from all the vessels. It's frightening, as well as inexplicable."

"What do you mean, inexplicable?" Edden frowned.

"While the equipment indicates that the poison is seeping from the ocean floor in these areas," the scientist tapped several points along a three-dimensional map, "the drones we've sent down find nothing. The poison is carried in the seawater itself, and is more concentrated along these lines," he drew a track along the map, halfway between Kondar and the southern ice cap.

"How can that be? If it isn't coming from the seabed, then where is it originating?"

"You know there's only volcanic rock from a long-dead volcano field here," the scientist drew a circle on the hovering map. "We've sent drones burrowing through the sand to take samples of the volcanic rock, but there's nothing there, either, except the residue that's infecting other sites just the same. We don't send ships there, because the jagged outcroppings beneath the waters can damage the hulls."

"I'm well aware of the topography of our planet," Edden rubbed his forehead. "This is untenable, and only lends credence to those claiming it's a blight from the gods. We have to find the source, then see if we can contain it."

"We'll get back to work, but I and my staff are at a loss as to where to begin."

"I appreciate your efforts. Keep me informed," Edden mumbled.

"I will."

"Quin?" The voice woke me after I'd fallen asleep. In my hazy mind, it sounded like Berel Charkisul's voice.

"What?" I mumbled, attempting to wake. I seldom slept so heavily, but I'd been more than weary when I'd gone to bed.

"It's me. Berel."

When my eyes opened enough to see, I found the tab-vid he'd given me glowing beneath my pillow. Until that moment, I had no idea it could be used as a communication device. I was also puzzled that it worked inside Avii castle, but shoved that thought aside.

"Berel?" I tapped the screen of the tab-vid after pulling the device into my hands.

"Good. I was worried I wouldn't reach you," Berel sighed. "I have a question."

"What's that?"

"Do you know anything about the poison?"

Berel's directness numbed my brain for a moment. "I don't know very much," I replied when I could get my mind—and my mouth—to work again. "I know it exists, but I have no idea what it is or how it got here."

"That's pretty much what we know, too," he grumbled. I could see his troubled frown in the tab-vid's screen. "It seems to be increasing, but nobody can find the source of it. It's making people sick. I know how that feels—to be so sick."

"I know," I said, shaking my head at him and praying he wouldn't ask if I knew the source of the poison.

"Are any Avii sick, yet? Father says there is evidence that many fishermen have fallen ill because the poison is in the fish they net in the ocean."

"I haven't noticed any Avii who are ill, and I think they'd be brought to me if they were," I said.

"Do you think it's safer where you are?" he asked.

"I don't know. It may be that the Avii aren't as susceptible to the poison, but eventually, even they might fall ill."

"Why is it showing up now?" Berel mumbled distractedly. I didn't answer, hoping he hadn't meant it as a direct question to me. As it was, I didn't hold all the facts, and only knew the former Avii Queen had somehow held the poison at bay in the past.

"This is impossible." Amlis surveyed the troops assembled outside the castle. "Half of them have no uniforms, and even less training. They can't even stand in a straight line for inspection." He and Rodrik, both mounted, watched as Tamblin's officers shouted at the newly recruited soldiers. Uneven lines stretched across the courtyard, and few knew how to stand properly.

"While your father's goals were ambitious, there were not enough experienced soldiers to train what he recruited."

"Recruited is the wrong word," Amlis snorted. "He drafted. All the principalities knew they'd be taxed heavier and the royal arm would be held against their necks if they failed to cooperate. Warrel wouldn't have cooperated if they'd had a choice."

"At least your two new men-at-arms are already trained well enough."

"Is there any way to bring Deeds and Wolter with us?"

"Deeds, yes. Wolter might be a bit of a problem," Rodrik shrugged. "Does your father intend to consume camp rations on the road, or trust the inns to serve proper food?"

"A good question. Let's find out," Amlis' smile was grim.

"How is this possible?" Firth Quel, Edden Charkisul's Chief of Sciences, asked.

"If we hadn't gone back to reexamine these samples, we wouldn't have found it," Firth's assistant sighed. "While it appeared to be nuclear waste at first, we dug deeper and found the organism."

"And you're saying the organism produces waste more toxic than nuclear waste? That's impossible," Firth shook his head in disbelief. "Kondar only flirted with nuclear power until it was deemed unsafe and all the experiments were shut down. We knew we didn't produce enough waste to cause this contamination, and now we find this."

"It's only a single organism," the assistant cautioned. "We'll have to search for more. This could be an aberration, as we don't have more samples to verify our findings."

"You say this one is dead? Is there any way to discover how much of the waste it might produce and how quickly?"

"It died shortly after we collected it, so I can't say for sure. I fear it may reproduce much like a virus, and who knows what it feeds upon?" Firth's assistant said. "Our only sample is dead and we have little else to go on."

⁂

"We leave for Vhrist tomorrow. Is that enough time to prepare?" Amlis asked. He, Rodrik, Wolter and Deeds had gathered in their chosen meeting place—in Finder's old sleeping quarters, which Deeds has claimed for his own. "I hope you don't mind that I've chosen you as my personal servant. It's what Father would allow."

"I feel safer with you," Wolter sighed. "I don't trust many, here. At least I can prepare meals for you and your personal guard."

"That will be much appreciated," Amlis replied. "How are the blade lessons coming along?"

"He's doing well—for a cook," Deeds grinned.

⁂

Berel studied the time-lapse vids carefully, noting every movement outside Avii castle. He'd studied the inside bowl initially, but no activity could be seen there, other than Avii flying back and forth while animals grazed and groves and fields were tended.

He'd turned to the perimeter of the castle, then, watching the thin strips of sand surrounding it. There'd been no word or records of Quin until recent months, but there had been two instances when the Avii had requested assistance from Kondari physicians.

If Quin could heal his sickness, she could heal anything. He'd also learned, from listening in on Melis Norwal and his father's conversations, that Quin had no DNA connection to the Avii. That meant she'd come from somewhere else, and it wasn't difficult to see that she hadn't flown there—her wings were barely forming when she arrived in Kondar's capital the first time.

He'd set his comp to the designated time periods, when he imagined Quin had arrived at Avii castle, then asked it to account for any anomalies in activity there.

Berel had chosen a late hour, when his father and servants thought him asleep, to test his theories. He was ready to give up, however—two hours had passed with nothing of note occurring. Then his small comp beeped; it had found something. Berel stared at the images, his mouth open in surprise.

Halthea sneered at the two Yellow Wings who'd been her servants. They desired to treat her as less then they? She'd show them. She'd show that foolish half-blood, too, but it required careful planning. Perhaps she'd fly to Kondar afterward, and convince them to take her in. They were fascinated by the Avii, and would leap at the chance to accept her.

For now, she'd pull sheets from beds and make them up if she were forced. If Jurris thought to give her clothes and jewelry away to Wimla and Vorina, she'd show them, too.

I didn't mind cleaning Justis' quarters, and he seldom asked me to run errands for him. In the afternoons, I studied with Master Ordin, had dinner with Dena and talked, or, if Gurnil sat with us, we'd discuss books. Dena turned to reading at night, just to keep up with us.

She also kept her promise to work with me, and my wings grew longer and stronger every day. After four weeks of cleaning Justis' quarters, all my feathers were grown and Ordin said my wings were almost long enough to attempt flight.

"You're not as heavy as some of the others, so it will be little more than a tall child's weight to carry. Suitable enough to get you started," he smiled at me. "Dena is doing a fine job of strengthening them."

"Dena is a wonderful friend," I said.

"You haven't had that, have you? A friend the same age?"

"No, Master Ordin." I didn't say that I was coming to think of Berel as the same—a friend. He and I chatted now and then through the tab-vid, and he always smiled at me when we talked.

"I'm quite pleased with your paper," he tapped a finger on the sheaf of paper on his desk. "I read it, and am amazed at the translation you did from the Kondari language. I could only get through parts of it, and relied much on their illustrations and photographs. I now have full knowledge of wet-lung disease. Gurnil is in the process of setting it for print, and it will become a book in his Library."

"I enjoyed doing it," I said. "I look forward to the next one."

"I've never seen anyone this thirsty for information," Ordin chuckled. "I'll assign a paper on the liver next week."

"I'll begin my preparations tonight, then," I said.

"I saw Halthea this morning, dumping an armful of sheets into a bin at the laundry," Ordin said, changing the subject. "I don't believe any of us are safe while she's running loose through the castle. I thought Jurris would keep her confined to his quarters, but he sent her away. Likely tired of her whining," Ordin grimaced.

"Ordin, we have to watch our backs, then," I said with a nod. "I'm used to this sort of intrigue, and saw too many nobles dead from knife wounds. I hope there's a way to keep weapons away from her."

"Jurris doesn't think she's a threat. He believes her to be like all other Yellow Wings, now—something benign and beneath notice—except for her haranguing."

I wanted to call Jurris a fool, but held back. Perhaps this was akin to what Wolter and I thought of Irdith; we both knew she was dangerous, but both held our tongues lest the danger visit us. Ordin thought Jurris a fool, just as I did, but it would benefit neither of us if we voiced our opinions aloud.

"May I go, now?" I said. "I want to pull a few weeds growing on Justis' terrace before dinner."

"You may go. I don't believe Justis has ever had anyone take care of him so well."

"Then he's never had a proper servant," I said. "In Fyris, I'd be beaten for not doing a proper job."

The small basket I'd borrowed from Ordin was filled with young weeds thinking to sprout in the spring weather. The grass was barely showing green on Justis' terrace, and the weeds would only claim moisture and root space if they weren't pulled.

"Taking care of my lawn as well?" Justis had flown in moments earlier and landed nearby, watching me work for a few moments before saying anything.

"It needed to be done." I was on my knees, pulling the last of the weeds when he spoke, so I leaned back and gazed up at him, blinking in the late afternoon light.

"Your knees are dirty, young Quin. Run to your suite, take a bath and I will join you and Gurnil at dinner tonight."

"Is it all right if Dena is there?"

"Of course." A small smile lifted a corner of his mouth, while dark eyes glittered from the sun's setting far to the west. I noticed that the breeze played with his feathers and his hair, ruffling both gently and making him appear younger than he was.

"I'll go now," I said, rising and stretching my back to get the kinks out.

"Good. Tell Gurnil I'll meet you in the Guild Masters' dining hall in an hour."

"I will." I hurried away before Justis could change his mind. Dena would be overjoyed that Commander Justis had chosen to have dinner with us.

"This came for you," Justis handed an envelope to Master Gurnil as he took a seat at our table.

"Thank you," Gurnil nodded at Justis. "Would you like to join me in my study for an after-dinner drink?"

"I'll join you as well," Ordin said, taking the last chair at our table. Dena's eyes widened when Ordin took the chair next to hers, while Justis chose the one across from her.

An after-dinner meeting meant the information contained in the envelope was important and of interest to all three. Holding back from using my talent in an attempt to solve the mystery of the envelope, I turned my attention to dinner. "Dena and I can get your plates," I said, scooting my chair back.

"Ask for extra meat and gravy for me," Justis said. "I've been drilling the Black Wings, today."

"I will," I said. Dena stood with me and we went to gather plates for Justis and the others.

"I wish they'd drill on my off-days, so I could watch," Dena said as we walked toward the kitchen to get plates.

"Ask Master Gurnil to change your days," I shrugged. "I don't think he'll mind."

"I'll ask to change one, then, Commander Justis always does drills with all the Black Wings midweek."

"Did you always work in the kitchens before?" I asked.

"Yes, and the younger ones were never allowed to choose off-days. They were always assigned."

"I don't see why Master Gurnil would object, then," I said. "As long as the work is done."

"If you hadn't come, I'd still be in the kitchens," Dena said. "I need five plates," she informed the yellow-winged server when we arrived at the counter. "Commander Justis wants extra meat and gravy—he has worked hard, today."

"We always accommodate Commander Justis," the Yellow Wing—a perky girl barely older than I, dimpled at Dena's request. "I see he's with Master Ordin and Master Gurnil. Do they need extra as well?"

"They didn't say," I said.

"So, one vegetable plate, three regular meals and one with extra meat and gravy," she said, beginning to dip food onto plates.

Dena and I each carried a tray to our table—she had three plates while I carried two. Once the meals were sorted out and the trays given to a yellow-winged boy to carry back to the kitchen, she and I sat to eat.

"Have you attempted to fly?" Master Cook Nina pulled up a chair to join us. Her question, oddly enough, was aimed at me.

"Not yet," I said.

"Nina?" Justis lifted an eyebrow at her.

"All right, my granddaughter has a cough," she sighed.

"And you want Quin and me to take a look?" It was Ordin's turn to lift an eyebrow.

"Yes, if you wouldn't mind."

"Do babies often get sick?" I asked. I hadn't heard that they did—not among the Avii, anyway. In Fyris, few lived, nowadays.

"Not often, but it happens at times," Ordin replied. "Nina, have you eaten?"

"Not yet; I had the day off, to help take care of the baby. I came to find you and Quin, because it seems to be getting worse."

"Eat, then, and we'll go as soon as we're finished," Ordin said.

"I'll get your plate, if you'll tell me what you want," I said.

"Just the usual," Nina sighed.

Just as Ordin said, the moment we finished eating and returned our plates to the kitchen, we followed Nina out of the dining hall.

"Quin, I'll carry you, as it's quicker to fly," Gurnil offered.

"I'll take her," Justis said. "Lead the way."

That was the first time I'd been carried by any Avii, and it was by Justis. Almost afraid to breathe as he lifted off a nearby common terrace and extended his wings with a mighty whoosh, I watched in fascination as his wings lifted and dipped, his primary feathers spread and communicating with the wind.

Gurnil, Ordin and Dena flew ahead of us, while we followed close behind. I was held tightly against Justis' chest, my wings pressed against him as he carried me. Closing my eyes for just a moment, I savored where I was and allowed the dream, slight as it was, to form before bringing myself back to reality.

"Master Ordin, the baby has the wasting disease in its lungs," I whispered after he and I examined the infant.

"That is what I thought as well," Ordin agreed softly, "although it would normally require Kondari technology to determine that for certain. I've never seen this," he added. "Can you heal it?"

"Yes," I nodded. "Are you going to tell Master Nina? It could cause a panic."

"I'll hold off for now," he said. "So she won't worry."

"The baby will be fine after I heal him," I shrugged. "No need to make things worse. At least not yet."

"I agree."

With that, Ordin and I returned to the crib where the baby slept, his breathing labored and punctuated with a frequent cough. Ordin lifted the child and placed him in my arms. "No need to worry," I crooned to him before the light enveloped me.

"If anything ever happens to me, get Quin," Justis said, accepting a glass of wine from Master Gurnil. He, Ordin and Gurnil were gathered in Gurnil's study after seeing Quin and Dena to their suites.

"I'd like two guards posted outside the Library, instead of one," Gurnil responded.

"I'll see to it," Justis said. "If babies are falling ill, here," his feathers rustled, "then the poison truly is seeping beyond Fyris."

"This is frightening, and I'd like to discuss it with the physicians of Kondar, but there's the First Ordinance to consider."

"Our hands are tied," Gurnil agreed. "No matter what. It makes me wonder if this was in the plan—for us to die if the one who could neutralize the poison every sixteen turns were killed."

"I think I'll call in our oldest, just to make sure they're not in jeopardy. That's who the poison will kill first—our most vulnerable. That means we have to be vigilant and check our youngest and oldest." Ordin shook his head. "I'd like to keep this from the other healers for now, so it'll involve Quin and me."

"I can do without a daily cleaning if that will make a difference in time," Justis offered.

"I'll remember that," Ordin said. "Gurnil, what does the message say?"

Gurnil lifted the envelope with a sigh. "We'll see if Quin is correct," he said and slipped a finger beneath the flap.

The DNA presented from both samples has revealed that the oldest sample is the parent, while the newer sample is the child, the pertinent paragraph revealed. Gurnil read it twice, at Justis' request.

That night, as I practiced flapping my wings while Dena watched, I lifted myself off the floor. I wept when my feet touched the flagstones again. I was going to fly. Soon.

"Berel?" Edden Charkisul acknowledged his son, who walked into his study while he worked late, studying proposed legislation.

"Father?" Berel said, "I have something to show you." Berel sounded unsure of himself, and Edden wondered if Berel worried whether he might be in trouble.

"What is that?" Edden set aside his own tab-vid and held out a hand to accept the one Berel extended.

"Research. I know I wasn't supposed to overhear what you and Commander Melis said, but I did. It sent me in this direction, and the tab-vid shows what I found."

"Bring a chair and sit with me," Edden said, tapping his son's tab-vid to enlarge the images. Berel reached for one of his father's guest chairs and pulled it toward the desk.

"Mother," Amlis embraced Omina. His father had wisely stayed away from the Queen, choosing to take quarters in a seldom-used wing of Vhrist's castle, in order to be closer to the troops.

"Where is Yevil?" Omina whispered softly in Amlis' ear.

"Never far from Father," Amlis whispered back. "I think he's frightened, Mother. Father, not Yevil." He pulled away and offered her a false smile.

"I hear the troops barely know how to hold a sword," Omina said, taking a seat waving for Amlis to do the same. "I thank you for your gift, too."

Amlis knew she meant Fen, and breathed a relieved sigh. He'd worried that Fen might be killed along the road. "Did it arrive in good condition?" he asked.

Omina snorted. "It looked as if it had been dropped in mud and briars," she replied. "It was sound enough, beneath all the dirt and scratches, however. I am sorry to hear about Chen."

"We are all sorry, Mother."

"When does your father plan to set sail?"

"He thinks a week of sailing with the troops will get them used to the sea, then he plans to leave Fyris for the barbarian shores."

"Will you and Rodrik travel with him?"

"That is his desire," Amlis said.

"My desire is otherwise."

"As is mine."

"I sent him to bed, after thanking him for bringing this to my attention," Edden set the tab-vid before Melis.

"What does it show?" Melis asked as Edden took a seat nearby. "Is the information time-stamped and protected?"

"All of it," Edden nodded. "He'd already done it, but I made copies, placed them in my personal archive under my code and then brought this straight to you. Nothing has been altered. I do suggest enlarging the images, however, so you can see that it's Quin, although she seems covered in filth. Make note of the sailing vessel as well. I haven't seen anything like that in my lifetime. It resembles those we made when we first began our sea explorations, centuries ago."

"Look at the sailor's garb," Melis breathed. He watched as four people slipped onto a small boat from the main vessel, which hadn't been visible on the water until it appeared suddenly on a clear, sunny afternoon.

Not far away, waves washed upon the thin, sandy strip surrounding the thick glass of Avii castle.

"You can barely make out Quin's hair color, she's so covered in filth, and do you see, there?" Edden pointed. "She's dressed, with no evidence of wings. They'd have been pushing against her blouse if she'd had much at the time."

"There's no question that's her," Melis said. "But who is that with her? Have their images been run through the recognizer?"

"Twice, with no results. No chip implants in any of them, or on the vessel, and every registered vessel has a location chip embedded somewhere, in case it gets lost or stolen."

"So they're leaving Quin at the castle, then," Melis said as he watched Quin and one of the unknown sailors disappear inside a narrow doorway.

"Looks that way. I want to question Gurnil about this, but worry it might be a mistake."

"As do I. See, the sailor is leaving, without Quin," Melis pointed out. "He's getting into the boat, and the other two are rowing him toward the ship."

"Keep watching. You'll see the point where the vessel disappears again, just as it appeared in the beginning."

"Might I suggest doing another search, Edden?"

"For what?"

"We have satellite images that go back decades. Shall we do a search for similar appearances and disappearances, all from the same coordinates?"

"How far back do you suggest we look?" Edden sounded interested.

"Let's do twenty turns first, and see what that yields," Melis said. "And go farther back than that, if we feel it's warranted. Now that we have coordinates and can program the comp on what to look for, it'll be easier—and faster."

"Do it," Edden said, rapping his knuckles on Melis' desk in a decisive gesture. "Bring the results to me as soon as you have them."

"Berel, we found a baby, sick with the wasting disease in its lungs," I said when he called. I was concerned that others among the Avii were already ill, or would become so quickly.

"Did you heal it?"

"Yes. She's fine, now," I said. "I'm worried about the others, now."

"Me, too. Father worries about the people here, and if the Avii fall ill, what will we do?"

"I don't know," I mumbled, shaking my head at Berel's image. "As far as I know, I'm the only one who can make someone well if your medicine and physicians can't."

"What about Princess Halthea?" Berel asked. "I worry that she'll sell your services to the highest bidders, so only the wealthy might survive the poison."

"That has been handled, up to a point," I said distractedly. How could I tell Berel that the Orb appeared to save me and make Halthea a Yellow Wing at the same time? Likely, none in Kondar knew of the Orb's existence, let alone that it held enough power to make changes such as it had.

"When did you begin healing?" Berel asked. My breath stopped.

"Nobody knew I could, for a long time. My first healings were done for animals," I replied truthfully.

"You can heal animals?"

"Yes. They like me," I said, rustling my feathers. "They are as deserving of a healing as anyone else."

"What if someone came to you that didn't deserve to be healed?"

"I don't heal anyone of their advanced age to keep them from death," I said. "That would be wrong. If I were asked to heal someone with evil intentions, I would do my best not to do so. They are undeserving."

"Can you tell—when they're evil?" he asked.

"I can, but I beg you to keep that secret," I said. "It could kill us both."

CHAPTER 16

"I feel guilty that we're tapping my son's tab-vid," Edden muttered, tossing the chip recording to Melis. "She gave him information in confidence, yet here we are, looking to exploit it. I wish we could come out and ask the girl who those sailors were and where they came from, but we can't. Not without alerting the Avii King and his Black-Winged brother."

"I'd like to present our findings to Firth—it may be that the unidentified DNA sample given to him by Gurnil is connected to those sailors."

"True, but there's still no race connection to Quin, so how might they have come upon her? This mystery deepens by the day," Edden rubbed his forehead. "Never mind that—give this information to Firth and see what he and his assistant can make of it. What have you found in your other research?"

"Three separate occurrences so far, when a seemingly ancient ship appears near the original coordinates, one or two are left at Avii castle and the ship sails away, disappearing as it always does, along the same general latitude."

"That doesn't deviate with the tides?" Edden asked.

"No. It is just as baffling to me as it is to you."

"Did you examine the sample?" Marid asked.

"I'm glad you placed a spell-shield around it. There's enough radioactivity from only a few of those organisms to make any mortal ill."

"Imagine what many of those can do—against your enemies," Marid smiled.

Marid's guest had arrived late at night, and Marid kept the lights low in the Belancour receiving area—to mask how things appeared worn and run-down. For years, few had sought out the Belancour clan, and seldom paid what Marid had once commanded for spellwork.

He cursed Grey House, blaming them for his troubles. This though, he nodded at the sphere, which his guest held carefully in both hands—this could garner enough to pay for anything he might want.

"I expect the organism will die easily enough, once I have what I want?" his guest asked.

"As easily as I can form a spell," Marid chuckled.

"Then I'll buy. When can you deliver?"

"Soon. Very soon," Marid said.

"I will not leave him behind to usurp my place," Tamblin thundered. Omina didn't cower—she'd learned long ago to never show weakness to her husband. Yes, she'd seen Tandelis and the Avii royals die in Tandelis' throne room, and that included two babes and all men-at-arms. She'd been unaware of the plot, so there'd been no time to warn them. She was surprised, actually, that Tamblin left her alive when others died about her. Now, Tamblin worried that his son might take his place.

Fool.

"Then what's to stop anyone else from doing the same?" she snapped at him. "You have few nobles scheduled to sail with you. Which of those left behind will take your throne and rally the people of Fyris behind them?"

Tamblin went pale at Omina's words. "I will not leave the boy behind," he growled. "Get yourself to Lironis to protect my place. If you think any of those weak, sniveling pretenders are strong enough to withstand me when I return, then you are a greater fool than I imagined."

"As you wish it." Omina snapped her skirts as she whirled and strode from Tamblin's makeshift study.

"Boy!" Tamblin shouted for a page, who came running.

"My King?" the boy bowed low after sliding to a stop on the flagstone floor.

"Find Master Yevil for me. Do it quickly."

"Yes, my King." The boy departed as quickly as he'd arrived.

Ordin and I checked an older man and his two wives—he'd asked all the healers whether they had any older ones sick for any reason. All of these were ill. The man had fading brown wings, while both his wives had yellow.

All were ill from the poison—they loved fish pulled from the waters north of Avii castle, and had sickened from the subsequent exposure. I offered Ordin a slight nod to let him know they suffered from poison sickness. He'd asked me to make them comfortable—nothing more. It was easy to comply with his request, as it coincided with my own decision. "If they want a quicker death," Ordin told me earlier, "the gate is always available."

I made them comfortable as requested, leaving them feeling better than they had in weeks. As Gurnil and I walked out of their quarters, I received the premonition. No, I didn't want to send mindspeech to the ones who could help, but there wasn't anything else I could do.

Amlis, I shouted mentally, stopping beside a glass wall and placing my hand upon it to hold myself upright. *Rodrik! The Queen is in peril. Run.*

Amlis barely noticed the wall being blown away as he leapt to protect his mother. Yevil held a strange object in his hand and barely missed killing Omina with it when Amlis rushed to her aid.

"Stand where you are," Yevil hissed when Rodrik raised his blade.

"Get away, you filth," Rath appeared in the doorway and shouted at Yevil. His blade, like his son's, was drawn and pointed at Yevil.

"Stand back, Father; he can kill you with that abomination," Rodrik snapped.

"Yes, I can, can't I?" Yevil laughed. "Back away. I have orders from the King."

"You are filth and an evil," Omina said, straightening her dress and staring Yevil down. "Whomever Tamblin asks you to kill, you take pleasure in toying with beforehand. Get it over with, then," she shouted. "I've hated you and that thing I married for a very long time."

"You think to take all of us down?" Omina's captain of the guard arrived with several guards at his back. He studied the room with a practiced eye before turning to Yevil. "Because as fast as you can move," he said, "I'll warrant there are those in this room who'll move faster."

Yevil lifted his hands in surrender. Rodrik jerked the weapon from him and stuffed it in the waistband of his trousers before nodding to the guards to tie Yevil's hands behind his back.

"I'll be out as soon as word gets to the King," Yevil shouted over his shoulder at Omina. "How much longer do you think to survive?"

"Quin?" Ordin offered water and apple juice as I blinked my eyes open.

I found myself inside his private study, with Dena and Master Gurnil nearby. "You fainted, I think," Ordin said as I accepted the apple juice and drank it first.

"I blacked out," I agreed, sipping water after emptying the juice glass.

"Do you feel ill?" Ordin asked, taking my wrist in his hand and checking my pulse.

"No. Tired, perhaps, but that's it." I couldn't tell him that Omina had almost died at Yevil's hand, or that the King had ordered her death.

"Then you should lie down for a while, and have a quiet dinner in your suite, with Dena, here," he said. "I'll check you in the morning. I believe Justis will allow a sick day or two, if needed."

"Thank you. A rest sounds good."

I went over the events in Fyris after lying down. Somehow, I'd managed to make Yevil's aim go awry, but failed to understand how I'd done it. Yes, Yevil was in Omina's dungeon for attempting to murder the Queen, but as he'd said, the King had ordered him to do it.

Never had I wished so much ill upon anyone as I wished upon Yevil and Tamblin at that moment. Both had so many lives to account for, and would ultimately kill all of Fyris if a way wasn't found to save its inhabitants.

"The King is leaving Yevil where he is for the moment," Rodrik said, carefully placing Yevil's weapon on the desk inside Omina's study. "Amlis and I still fear for your safety, Lady Queen."

"He has no care for me or the only son he has left," Omina huffed. "Yevil has poisoned any emotion left in the man."

"Yet he still listens to that abomination, even knowing that he was behind Timblor's death," Amlis snapped. "There is no logic to any of this."

"Perhaps we should consider an envoy to the glass castle," Farin strode in, a concerned expression on his face. "I hear from your guard captain that Tamblin has ordered Yevil released in two days, to supervise the troops on a practice run. It is a training exercise for the troops, as well as a test for the new ships."

"Any other man would be dead already, for attempting to murder the Queen," Rodrik muttered.

"Then I suggest we hide that weapon, or send it to the glass castle with an envoy," Farin said.

"I am dead already, if Tamblin thinks to allow Yevil to walk freely from my dungeon," Omina countered. "Find a boat and I will go."

"Omina, you cannot count on the edict to protect you. Not after their King and Queen were murdered," Farin observed. "If you go, you will not go alone."

"Mother, I will go with you," Amlis offered.

"Neither of you will make this journey without protection. Wolter, Deeds and I will go. Tamblin and Yevil want all of us dead; therefore, we will ask for mercy from the glass castle," Rodrik declared.

"Then take Fen and me as well. We'll die, here, without the Queen's protection," Farin insisted.

Orik, captain of the Sea Hawk, jerked his head up as Amlis and Rodrik stepped inside the inn near the waterfront. The inn wasn't the best one; it was poorly constructed, needed repairs and smelled of beer, piss and food. Orik had been drinking most of the day, and had just started to eat the bowl of stew the barmaid left before him when the Crown Prince arrived.

This is it, Orik thought, as the Prince's appearance cleared his mind swiftly. *He knows I left Finder at the glass castle and now I'm as dead as she is.*

"Captain Orik," Amlis sat across from him while Rodrik remained standing.

"Prince Amlis," Orik nodded his head in an attempt at respect.

"I need your boat. And your silence," Amlis leaned in to whisper while dropping a bag of coins on the table between them.

Orik blinked at Amlis in half-drunken shock.

"I'll stay," Rath shook his head at Omina. "He told you to travel to Lironis. Let everyone believe that's your goal. I'll have my men hold him off as long as possible after he finds Amlis missing as well."

"Rath, he'll kill you," Omina sighed.

"He means to kill both of us—you know that. He's just waiting for the best opportunity. His mind was always weak; it's worse, now."

"And Yevil spills poison daily into that ever-growing emptiness," Omina huffed. "I don't want you to stay. Your death will come the moment he learns I've sailed away."

"We'll die anyway," Rath muttered. "Now or later—what does it matter? If not at Tamblin or Yevil's hand, then by the poison beneath our feet. I'll buy time for you, Amlis and my son. I suggest you leave quickly, however, and travel light."

"What about my father?" Beatris' eyes filled with tears as she blinked at Rodrik.

"My love, we must leave many behind, or our intentions will become common knowledge. My father is staying behind—at his choice. He means to buy us time to get safely away."

"What if we're turned away, or worse?" Beatris angrily wiped tears from her cheeks.

"Omina says we'll sail for Lironis if they won't speak to us or allow us in. I know none have sailed to Lironis for a very long time and the port is crumbling," Rodrik held up a hand to stop his wife's argument. "We'll take our chances there. If Tamblin wants to attack us in

Liron's city, we'll see how many of those left behind wish to support him against the Queen."

"How can the King think to make sailors so quickly from those who've only walked solid ground all their lives?" Beatris turned away. "He conscripted my cousins, Rod. They'll die on the sea—they barely know how to swim."

"Beatris, my love, it is as Wolter says," he pulled her into an embrace. "We're all dead. We just haven't realized it, yet."

"I went to Lironis at the Queen's request sixteen turns ago," Wolter said. "I worked here, in her kitchen, before that. That's why I know how to prepare fish and shellfish."

Wolter stirred the fish stew after tossing in a few herbs and seasonings. "Taste." He held a spoonful of soup toward Deeds, who lifted an eyebrow before tasting.

"Good," Deeds mumbled with a nod. "Very good."

"Is all prepared?" Wolter asked softly.

"Everything is in place," Deeds replied.

"If another ship appears, do we have time to reach Avii castle when it arrives?" Edden asked. He, Melis and Firth had gathered inside Edden's office after a long day of meetings, where many things had been discussed and very little decided.

Most of the discussion involved the tainted fish pulled from the waters surrounding Kondar, and how much that taint could affect the people. Many council members had business concerns involved, and any moratorium placed on the fishing industry would destroy those businesses.

Others argued that the poison would adversely affect the population, and Kondar wasn't prepared for the increase in needed health care if the poisoned seafood were sold for consumption.

"We have to find the source, and I can only guess that this has something to do with it," Edden sighed. "Do we have time to get an airship there?"

"We can have something ready to go from one of our island bases," Melis pointed out. "Here, perhaps?" He pointed to a large atoll between the western edge of Kondar and the eastern side of Avii castle. "We only have to alert the commander, once we notify him of our intended target."

"My question is this," Firth began, "what do we do, once we get there, and how do we explain our actions to the Avii king and his brother?"

"Master Gurnil," I said, "What will happen if some from Fyris decide to leave Fyris?"

He and Ordin chose to have a quiet dinner with Dena and me inside the Library. Dena had cleared off a Library table and set out a cloth to protect the surface so we could eat and talk.

"That could cause problems, I think," Gurnil replied thoughtfully. We'd eaten in silence at first; we were all hungry, although I felt better after sleeping for several hours after I'd fainted.

"What kind of problems?" Dena asked.

"I believe it involves the spell used to hide Fyris," Ordin explained. "The worst would likely happen if Tandelis' ring traveled past the boundary. There has been discussion in the past, with speculation that the spell would be neutralized if that happened. Fyris would be exposed as a result."

"Why is it so important that Fyris remain hidden?" I asked.

"I can't really say—all I know is that it involves Liron and the First Ordinance," Gurnil said. "Perhaps it was to keep the poison at bay as well, but we know now that it has traveled past the boundary to infect the waters around us."

"The fish are poisoned. Kondar eats fish, too," I pointed out. "They know this, I think."

"We can't tell everyone to stop eating fish—it will cause panic when they realize it could make them so ill," Gurnil said.

"Perhaps they ought to panic," I replied. "The ones who are mature and healthy may have no cause to worry immediately, but in Fyris, there are few children and the old are dying faster. Will that not happen everywhere, if the poison isn't contained?"

"It will," Ordin agreed.

"Is there information written on the First Ordinance?" I ventured to ask.

"There is, but it is locked inside Jurris' study. He alone says when it may be read by any other. There are sections, too, in the text, written in a language none can read. We have no idea what it says."

"Master Gurnil, I think I can read it," I said, trembling at the thought. I'd never seen written words I couldn't decipher.

"Quin, Jurris is in a foul mood of late. Give this some time, and I will ask at a better moment," Gurnil held up a hand. "I wish to see that text deciphered more than anyone, but dealing with the King is often a delicate matter."

"Of course." I understood Gurnil's words—up to a point. Jurris cared not that his people were in danger, just as those from Fyris were.

"I heard that Halthea was forced to move out of Jurris' quarters and into the Yellow Wing dormitory, where the unmated Yellow Wings who work inside the royal suites stay," Dena said.

I turned and blinked at her—it seemed that much had happened while I slept the afternoon away.

"I heard Jurris tired of her breaking everything within reach," Ordin murmured. "I also heard from the glassmakers that they've replaced his large mirror four times."

"Then I pity the Yellow Wings around her," I said. "She will make them miserable."

"I hope she doesn't think to get her red feathers back," Dena said. "The Orb itself made that decision. Yellow Wings had nothing to do with it."

I knew from the tone of her voice she resented that Halthea had yellow wings. Dena felt it tainted every Yellow Wing in Aviia, to have Halthea as a member.

"I hope things smooth out," I said. "Don't fret about it, friend," I reached out to pat her hand. "Since she's with the unmated Yellow Wings," I turned back to Gurnil, "Does that mean?"

"I believe he's working on voiding their relationship," Gurnil said. "And as he's King, the only permission he needs to do that is his own."

"Jurris, you don't need my permission to put her away. I would have done it sooner," Justis said, once Jurris' rant reached a conclusion. Justis leaned against a wall in his brother's study, watching while Jurris paced and grumbled about Halthea.

Wisely, Justis hadn't pointed out that Halthea's behavior was no different from what it had always been—the only difference was that she no longer had red wings. That, as it turns out, had been Jurris' sole interest in Halthea.

Justis noted, too, that his brother's study and quarters looked much better, now that Halthea was no longer there to badger the yellow-winged servants. Books and papers were stacked neatly, writing instruments were set in neat rows and everything was clean of dust.

The window had been washed as well, leaving Justis a clear view of clouds floating in the early evening sky outside the castle. "You think I'm doing the right thing? What if her wings turn red again?"

"They won't. When have you ever seen the Orb reverse its decisions?" Justis shrugged and pulled away from the wall.

"True," Jurris shook his head as he considered Justis' words. "There's no chance, is there?"

"None."

"What will we do? We have no Red-Winged females, now."

"Get one with your other wives. Either or both could produce a Red Wing daughter, you know. Surely Ordin has explained genetics to you."

"He has, but it's so complicated," Jurris muttered, raking fingers through his hair. "You think we ought to try? Will you send Wimla and Vorina to me? We should have dinner, I think, and I'll make my proposal to them. Both are on birth control, for the obvious reason. Now that there are no Red Wing princesses," Jurris shrugged.

"A sound decision," Justis agreed. "I'll send for them immediately. When will you notify Halthea?"

"Tomorrow. That will be soon enough, I think."

Halthea folded another sheet; she didn't care that it was crooked. It should feel blessed to be folded by her. Yellow Wings worked with her in the laundry room, pulling sheets and towels from large dryers and dumping them onto tables for folding.

Halthea was assigned to fold, since she had no experience and even less desire to know anything about the washers or dryers.

"I just overheard something," a Yellow Wing rushed in. "The King is sending for his other two wives."

Halthea jerked her head around as the gossip started. Did they think she wasn't there? Perhaps time was shorter than she thought, if Jurris was already considering Wimla and Vorina as mothers for his children. Plans would be made over dinner, and a weapon would be found.

"The word is out that she's leaving in the morning for Lironis," Tamblin's spy reported to the King.

"Good. Arrange an accident along the way. Halfway to Lironis should suffice."

"I'll see to it." The spy nodded and turned to go.

"Don't be gentle about it," Tamblin said.

"As you will it, my King."

Two trunks stood beside the door of Omina's suite—packed by her oldest maid. They were a ruse, to fool any who thought she might leave before her planned trip in the morning. It would be difficult—but not impossible—to slip away in the night.

Amlis and Rodrik had already left the castle—they'd gone drinking at an inn near the harbor and made sure the servants all knew. Wolter and Deeds had gone with them, as extra bodyguards.

Omina had to be more devious in her departure; Farin planned to go out to tend a sick child, with a servant to carry his bag and a man-at-arms for protection. Omina intended to be the servant, while Fen would serve as the man-at-arms.

Omina had never dressed beneath her station before, and knew it had to appear real to any who saw her, smelly clothing and all. With a sigh, she studied the maid's dress spread across her bed before reaching for the laces of her gown.

"You're just a man at arms. You can't even swim," Amlis slurred his words as he pointed his tankard of mead toward Wolter. "I'll bet anyone twenty royals that you can't do it."

"I can dive off a ship's prow—and swim back to the docks," Wolter declared, sounding just as drunk.

"Hmmph." Amlis drank from his cup, spilling more than he swallowed.

"I'll take that bet." Orik walked up to their table and dropped a small bag of coins at Amlis' elbow. "My ship is in the harbor. Shall we see your talents, master guard?"

Orik waggled his eyebrows at Wolter, who snickered drunkenly. "I get half your take when you win," he informed Orik.

"Fair enough," Orik agreed. "I enjoy watching a land walker get his comeuppance, though. The sea is nothing to tease, man. It'll take you faster than a maid's wink if you're not careful."

"Then I'll buy two rounds for every man here," Amlis announced, "and when we get back to announce the winner, I'll buy another round."

A cheer rose from those who'd chosen that particular inn for their nightly drinking as Amlis tossed a bag of coins to the owner. He, Wolter, Deeds, Rodrik and Orik walked out the door.

"That was a good idea—to buy them drinks so they wouldn't follow," Rodrik murmured as they made their way down a steep street toward the Sea Hawk. Orik's ship was docked on the southern end of Vhrist's harbor, where it was easier to slip in and out.

"I didn't want an audience just as we're escaping," Amlis remarked. "By the time we're well away, they can chase all they want. I'll warrant no pursuers will wish to follow where we're going."

"I'd take that bet," Orik agreed grimly. "When will your lady mother arrive?"

Fen wore the Queen's livery, a borrowed sword at his side. A sharp knife was in his right boot—ready if he needed it. He looked up as they left the castle behind; the moon was barely a sliver hovering overhead. Few clouds marred the sky, and those hung low and to the west.

"Master Healer?" A palace guard stopped them.

"It is I," Farin spoke. "I was summoned to attend a sick child at Noble Rolst's."

"His child is sick?"

"That's what I was told, so of course I must go—the Queen demanded it."

"Of course. You are wise to take these with you," the guard nodded at Fen and Omina, whose head and face were covered by a hooded cape. "It is dangerous to walk about in these times without a guard."

"The Queen said that as well," Farin agreed. "I must go, now."

"If you need more guards," the guard offered.

"No, I think we will be fine," Farin held the man off. "I hope to return in a few hours."

"I'll watch for you, then," the guard offered.

"My thanks."

"What is taking so long?" Amlis fretted as he paced the deck and watched the docks for his mother and Farin.

"Stop fretting. It won't get them here any faster," Rodrik dropped an arm on Amlis' shoulder. "Orik is only sailing with four, and they wish to leave Fyris as well. One of them is a woman, with a child."

"What?" Amlis turned to stare at Rodrik.

"He says she's his tailor, and she worries that her child will sicken again."

"Her child was sick?"

"He didn't explain it fully, so I suggest we ask later. Shall Deeds and I go looking for the Queen? Even I am worried, now."

As stern as she was, Omina wanted to weep when the docks appeared in the distance. She hadn't walked so far in a very long time and her feet ached from the bruising cobblestones beneath her feet.

Two things happened at that moment—Fen drew his blade and Farin grabbed her arm.

Run! The voice in her head commanded. She ran as six brutes appeared between buildings, their knives drawn and murder and thievery glittering in their eyes.

Rodrik heard the Queen's scream and ran faster. Yes, the voice had come a second time to him, and he knew to obey its command. Fen was wounded but still fighting when he and Deeds arrived, their blades drawn. Was it too late?

The Queen was down.

"Six men, lying in the street," Farin panted as Rodrik carried Omina aboard the Sea Hawk.

"They're all dead," Deeds growled as he followed Rodrik. "Farin, get yourself together—the Queen needs your help."

Amlis forced himself to move. When he'd seen Rodrik carrying his mother across the dock toward the gangway, he feared the worst. He'd heard her labored breathing as Rodrik carried her past, however, and understood that she still lived.

"What does she need?" Wolter asked.

"Get clean water. Whiskey if you have it," Farin fought for breath to speak. "I have the rest in my bag." He handed the bag to Wolter—he'd had to carry it after Omina was stabbed by one of those foul bandits.

"Right away." Wolter ran across the deck toward the galley.

Amlis shuddered at the amount of blood soaking into his mother's clothing. "Don't let her die," he whispered to Farin as Farin dumped half a bottle of whiskey over the wound.

"It won't be from blood loss," Farin muttered, blowing out a troubled sigh. "It'll be from infection, if we can't stop it."

Omina's face was quite pale as she lay on the narrow bed inside Orik's quarters. The wound was in her side; Farin was thankful the knife had missed the bowel and other organs. If infection set in, though, her death would be a slow and painful one.

Pulling a wad of folded, clean cloth from his bag, Farin shoved it against the knife wound to stanch the flow of blood.

"Have any of you ever sailed to the glass castle before?" Orik asked. "We left harbor half an hour ago."

"No. None of us have," Rodrik replied.

"In two hours, we'll go through the strait."

"What's that?"

"Some wizardry or devilry, you decide," Orik breathed. "It shortens the trip between us, somehow. Otherwise, we'd be traveling at least three days, if my star calculations are right."

"They're likely correct," Omina's voice was weak as she opened her eyes. "I know about the strait, Captain."

Deeds and Sofi studied Fen's shoulder wound while Yissy looked on in curiosity. "Not much blood, and that's not good," Deeds mumbled, washing the thin, bloody line with a whiskey-soaked cloth.

"That girl could help him. She helped me," Yissy's voice was high and firm.

"Yissy, hush," Sofi muttered. "That girl is gone."

"What girl?" Fen asked. After all, if someone could heal him, he wanted to know about it. He was a dead man if an infection came. The smell of the bandits who'd attacked them almost guaranteed that their blades weren't clean.

"She's dead," Sofi sighed. "They called her Finder, as if that were a proper name for anyone with such ability."

"How did she die?" Fen knew of Finder—through Chen. As for holding any sort of power, that had never been mentioned.

"Taken to the glass castle," Sofi said. "I can't say more than that, I'm afraid. She was a half-blood, if I understand things correctly."

"You're right—she's dead," Fen lay back on the bed they'd given him. "They don't let anything like that live."

Things were about to go strange in a short amount of time, and I was in a quandary as to what to do about it. Some things I couldn't control—or at least I felt as if I couldn't.

Other things, well, I hoped I'd be allowed to control those as needed. The first thing I needed to do, however, was go straight to Gurnil and explain what I knew to him. Instead, he came to me, the Orb hovering over his head as if it were guiding him to my side.

CHAPTER 17

"Stop asking questions and come with us," Ordin snapped.

"How do you expect me to explain this to Jurris?" Justis frowned as he gathered clothing from his wardrobe. He'd been in bed when Ordin arrived, and Ordin had a difficult time convincing the Commander to get up.

"The Orb spoke to Gurnil, then to me," Ordin said. "I've never heard of it speaking to anyone except the Queen before. It told both of us to go with Quin to the Receiver's Crevice—there's a boat coming."

"An envoy?" Justis grabbed pants and almost leapt into them.

"So it appears. None have come for more than twenty turns—since Tandelis sailed the last time."

"What do you suggest I do if the murderers are on board?"

"Quin says it isn't them," Ordin said. "She says Omina, her youngest son and a few others are coming, because the ones who murdered Camryn and Elabeth want them dead, too. That isn't what needs our attention first, however," Ordin added, then explained what else the Orb had said.

"Filth," Justis muttered as he shoved feet into sandals and nodded to Ordin. "Lead the way, Healer. Let's get this over with. My brother will have to do his duty, according to the First Ordinance and according to Avii law. He's never done it before. Let's hope the Orb stays with us, tonight, to explain that to him."

Halthea slipped around the corner; Wimla and Vorina slept in a combined suite designated for them, on the level below Justis'. It wasn't difficult in the past for him to fly down to their terrace, as it was directly below his.

Halthea had kept him from his other wives on many occasions, never allowing him to forget that together they would make a Red-Winged heir. He was looking to make an heir with one or the other, now—whoever could produce a Red-Winged child first.

Cursing softly, she walked from grass to tile, heading toward the glass doors that would allow her into the combined suite. No guards stood there—Halthea had seen to that. She'd poisoned the drinks she'd offered them earlier.

Both lay dead beside the doors.

Too bad, one of the Black Wings was quite handsome. Halthea reached for the door handle. It turned easily.

"I see it," Gurnil said softly. He, Dena and I stood in what I'd learned was the Receiving Crevice. The boat, its white sails aloft, floated in the distance.

"Master Gurnil," I said, blinking as the vision came, "Halthea is on Vorina and Wimla's terrace."

"Commander Justis will see to it," Gurnil replied. "At least I hope he will."

"The airchopper is on the way, High President," Melis said, following the glowing spot on the screen.

"Why now—at night?" Edden shook his head. "All the others came during daylight. Will ours arrive in time?"

"They are on an intercept course," Melis replied. "Our troops should arrive just as they do."

"You will do this, or your wife and child will die." Dorthil offered Jhak a cruel smile.

Jhak had been abducted on his way to guard the High President's home for the night. "You have them?" He was terrified, suddenly.

"I do—they'll be released, once the High President and his son are delivered to me."

"What will you do with them—the High President and Berel?" Jhak's voice trembled. He cared for both and he enjoyed his job. This would destroy everything he'd built so carefully, along with taking his life if any discovered what he'd done.

"That's not your concern," Dorthil laughed. "Don't worry, the moment my associates have both in their charge, you and your family will be free to go."

Jhak laughed bitterly. There'd be no place for him to go afterward—he'd be a traitor, according to the laws of Kondar.

Ordin hushed both women—he'd herded them into Vorina's closet and told them to remain silent. Wimla shook with fear—her life had never been threatened before. It came as no surprise, however, that Halthea was behind the threat. Justis waited in the receiving area for Halthea to make her way into Vorina's suite—it was closest to the terrace doors.

Jurris swallowed the last of his wine and set the glass down before straightening his collar and checking his image in the mirror. He'd decided to visit Vorina and spend the night in her bed.

Moon-turns had passed since he'd done that; Halthea wasn't at his side, filling his ears with promises that were never delivered, and he was free to do as he wanted. With a second glance at the mirror, he walked out of his suite and past the guards standing at his terrace door. Both fell in behind him; they'd follow wherever he went.

Halthea crept through the darkness, feeling her way through the suite with one hand, holding the long knife she'd stolen from the kitchen in the other. It served them right, to die in their sleep. She smiled at the thought.

"Remain calm, my King," one of Jurris' guards hissed as he stared at the bodies of two dead guards.

"My wives are inside," Jurris' whisper was urgent. "I am trained well enough to help."

"Then let us proceed with caution," the guard said softly. All three walked through the open terrace door and into blackness.

Berel woke—there was an unfamiliar noise outside his bedroom.

"Jhak?" he called out. Jhak headed his father's night guards, but generally they protected the perimeter of the house. They only came inside if his father invited them. Berel knew Jhak well—he'd visited several times when Berel was hospitalized.

"Time to get up, Berel," Jhak walked inside. "We have to go."

"Why?" Berel pushed the covers back and sat up, blinking sleepily at the guard.

"Because I made a mistake, and you and your father are about to pay for it."

"You've started a coup, haven't you?" Berel woke in a hurry.

"Under duress. If I don't follow through, they'll kill my wife and baby."

"What about my father? He isn't here," Berel said. He was angry—and frightened.

"Others have been sent to his office. They'll keep him alive—for now."

"Getting rid of the High President and offering as many prayers to the gods as you think to offer will not relieve Kondar of this spreading poison," Firth snapped. He'd been kidnapped and herded unwillingly into Edden's office, finding the High President and Melis inside, watching a screen. Melis turned off the screen immediately, once he realized it was a takeover. Ten military officers—high-ranking ones, actually, had arrived to seal the coup for the one bent on taking over the High President's office.

"What do you intend to tell the people?" Edden demanded. "They elected me, not Dorthil Crasz."

"Who's in charge here, you or us?" A general waved a weapon in Edden's direction. "We have your son. If you want him to live, then I suggest you do as I say."

Everything was unraveling at once.

Jurris unknowingly walked toward Halthea.

The airchopper making its way toward us had just received new orders.

Omina would die if she didn't receive aid soon—her wound festered already.

All of them could die if the airchopper's commander obeyed his new orders.

The balance in Kondar was gone. The balance that was Siriaa was about to crumble. It terrified me.

Do not fire your weapons, I sent mindspeech to the pilot and his crew.

As weak as the moonlight was, Jurris could only make out vague shapes in the darkness. His guards had spread out to cover more ground, leaving Jurris in the center. The King didn't have to ask who would attack his wives—he knew who it was.

"Halthea, we are here," he called out. "Stop this and I will let you live."

He never suspected how vicious she could be, or that she'd attack him first. It was as if a wild animal clawed at him, drawing blood. First from his shoulder, then his chest. The lights blinked on suddenly and he was blinded as he fell.

He heard Justis snap Halthea's neck as darkness came.

Fire rained from the sky as Amlis and Rodrik carried Omina to the deck. Projectiles struck the railings about them, splintering the wood and flinging sharp slivers toward exposed skin and eyes. They ducked as the airship dipped closer and continued its assault.

Farin and two sailors were already dead; the physician's body, sprawled across the far side of the deck, was almost cut in half by the dangerous weapons aimed at the ship. Deeds and Wolter had already shoved Sofi and Yissy overboard to save their lives, before following them quickly into the water surrounding the boat. Amlis and Rodrik intended to follow their lead.

Hoping that the water would save them from the burning boat as well as the danger from overhead, Amlis and Rodrik leapt overboard, the Queen between them. Omina screamed as she fell, before the cold seawater closed over her head.

Orik, who'd gone after Fen, pulled the wounded man with him, as more projectiles rained upon the Sea Hawk's deck. Boards creaked and groaned beneath Orik's feet, then collapsed behind him as he struggled to move faster. The ship exploded from below, launching him and Fen into the sea.

"We have to help them," I shouted.

Gurnil and Dena were too frightened at first to render aid—the flying craft continued to fire at the ship and we all ducked when the ship exploded with a mighty boom, flinging burning wood and shredded sail into the air. Reflections of the fire as the ship burned lit the waters before us, and the airship's noise deafened us as it flew closer.

"They're still alive," I shouted over the noise. "They're in the water."

Fly, the Orb shouted into my numbed brain.

I flew. Perhaps it was instinct—perhaps it was the hours of practice with Dena. Regardless, I flew perfectly—unerringly, casting the wonder of my flight aside and focusing on the task at hand. I had to rescue those I could before they drowned or died in the airchopper attack. I had no idea whether I could gather all of them before either of those things happened.

What I do know is this—something protected all of us from the weapons that night, as I flew low over the sea. Gurnil, mastering his fear, followed close behind and then Dena after him. Desperately, we hooked elbows with one and then another victim, all of whom were flailing in dark, choppy waters.

Gurnil and Dena held Omina between them first, hauling her toward the narrow strip of sand and the safety of the crevice beyond.

We flew several rescue missions, terror causing our hearts to pound as projectiles continued to rain into the ocean about us. The three of us worked under the most difficult circumstances that night, to save those who'd escaped the ship.

I wondered, too, at what had caused the ship to explode. The projectiles fired at us held nothing to cause such a conflagration. Using my talent, I searched for a reason as I pulled Sofi and Yissy from dark, freezing waters.

Yevil's weapon. That caused the explosion. At least it was destroyed and I hoped there were no others like it. Shaking aside that fear, I dropped my live cargo onto the sand surrounding the castle and went out again.

⁂

Once we had all safely inside the crevice, I learned something new—the weapons firing against the glass castle had no effect. I feared the glass would crack and chip before crashing down. It didn't.

It stood, impenetrable against what Kondar's new regime had sent against it.

That was the least of my worries at the moment.

"Master Gurnil, please take them to the Library," I begged. Amlis, lifted to his feet by a shocked and open-mouthed Rodrik, stared and blinked at me.

"Finder?" his voice quavered.

"I have to go," I said.

In some way that I didn't understand as yet, the Orb transported me to Vorina and Wimla's shared quarters. I heard the Kondari weapons continuing to fire outside the castle as I knelt at Jurris' side.

The King was dying.

Wet and shivering from my ordeal outside the castle, I reached out a hand to help and began to glow.

⁂

EPILOGUE

"Liron is dead. We know that," Marid snapped. "Why not profit from what he asked us to conceal? He didn't pay nearly enough in the beginning, you know."

Morid shook his head at his father's words. "What if we can't contain it?" he asked. "You didn't provide spells for that; you merely hid a small continent. Others contained the poisoned organism."

"Not our problem. I have buyers waiting. After they pay when we deliver, we'll disappear. I've grown tired of living on Shaaliveer—haven't you?"

The End

ABOUT THE AUTHOR:

Connie Suttle lives in Oklahoma with her patient, long-suffering husband and three cats. For information on forthcoming titles, please visit Connie's website at www.subtledemon.com, her blog at subtledemon.blogspot.com or find her on Facebook—Connie Suttle Author. She is also on twitter: @subtledemon.

8121215R00146

Printed in Great Britain
by Amazon.co.uk, Ltd.,
Marston Gate.